KU-168-712

THE CASE OF THE FOOL

Tarot reader Dolly Greene, returning from a happy holiday in St Lucia with her hot new police sergeant boyfriend, arrives home to find a surly Russian girl waiting for a reading. Marina is young and beautiful but oddly charmless; and her cards reveal nothing but conflict, misery — and death . . . Dolly also finds that during her two-week absence, squatters have taken over No. 7, and a mysterious Brazilian woman has moved into No. 3. She'd prefer to forget about the Russian beauty's malign reading — but like ripples radiating from a stone tossed into Barnes Pond, Marina's cards come back to disturb Dolly and all those around her, and Death will surely leave his calling card for someone on Tinderbox Lane . . .

SPECIAL MESSAGE TO READERS

THE ULVERSCROFT FOUNDATION
(registered UK charity number 264873)
was established in 1972 to provide funds for
research, diagnosis and treatment of eye diseases.
Examples of major projects funded by
the Ulverscroft Foundation are:-

- The Children's Eye Unit at Moorfields Eye Hospital, London
- The Ulverscroft Children's Eye Unit at Great Ormond Street Hospital for Sick Children
- Funding research into eye diseases and treatment at the Department of Ophthalmology, University of Leicester
- The Ulverscroft Vision Research Group, Institute of Child Health
- Twin operating theatres at the Western Ophthalmic Hospital, London
- The Chair of Ophthalmology at the Royal Australian College of Ophthalmologists

You can help further the work of the Foundation
by making a donation or leaving a legacy.
Every contribution is gratefully received. If you
would like to help support the Foundation or
require further information, please contact:

THE ULVERSCROFT FOUNDATION
The Green, Bradgate Road, Anstey
Leicester LE7 7FU, England
Tel: (0116) 236 4325

website: www.foundation.ulverscroft.com

THE CASE OF THE FOOL

E. V. HARTE

LARGE
PRINT

First published in Great Britain 2018
by
Constable
an imprint of Little, Brown Book Group

First Isis Edition
published 2019
by arrangement with
Little, Brown Book Group

The moral right of the author has been asserted

Copyright © 2018 by Daisy Waugh
All rights reserved

All characters and events in this publication, other than
those clearly in the public domain, are fictitious and
any resemblance to real persons, living or dead,
is purely coincidental.

A catalogue record for this book is available
from the British Library.

ISBN 978–1–78541–704–7 (hb)
ISBN 978–1–78541–710–8 (pb)

Published by
F. A. Thorpe (Publishing)
Anstey, Leicestershire

Set by Words & Graphics Ltd.
Anstey, Leicestershire
Printed and bound in Great Britain by
T. J. International Ltd., Padstow, Cornwall

This book is printed on acid-free paper

For my Roman friends, whose kindness, generosity and good spirits made the writing of this novel such a pleasure.

CHAPTER
ONE

Tinderbox Lane, London

Dolly Greene was feeling pretty damn jaunty. Unusually so, she suspected, for a woman in the late summer of life, dumped and divorced some years since, with few career prospects and an abiding shortage of cash. She bit her cheeks, as she considered this happy outcome, to stop herself from smirking. But to no avail. By the time she drew up outside Number Two Tinderbox Lane the smirk had turned into a grin so wide and so damn jaunty she was actually in danger of dribbling. Partly it was from the pleasure, pure and simple, of being reunited with her daughter, Pippa, who was sitting on the doorstep, smoking a rollie, waiting to welcome her home.

Mostly, though, it was thanks to the new love interest in her life, and the accompanying most excellent sex (still so fresh in her mind). It had been a magical holiday.

Pippa watched her mother's approach, tatty, overstuffed suitcase dragging sloppily behind her, and wondered if, in twenty-two years, she'd ever seen her looking so cheerful. Things had obviously gone well, then, with the new police sergeant boyfriend. She thought better of remarking on it, and instead cut straight to the other news: less important, perhaps, but more urgent. There was a Russian girl waiting for a Tarot reading in Dolly's consultation room.

"In my what?" Dolly chortled. Pippa generally referred to all of Dolly's clients as "crackpots", and to her consultation room as —

"Your broom cupboard, then. I was trying to sound professional. All the windows are open, so she can probably hear us. And she's Russian. And I charged her £50. So, you know . . ." Pippa shrugged. She glanced at her mother, who was frowning slightly over the inflated price. But Pippa was always telling her mother she should put up her prices. And the Russian girl had been flashing a thick bundle of cash, which, Pippa felt, was crying out to be spent.

"She's in there now?" Dolly eyed the house. She would have liked to unpack, have a bath, catch up with her daughter — but the girl had already paid (£10 more than Dolly normally charged) and she was waiting. "I don't suppose she wants to come back in an hour or two?"

"I don't think so, Mum."

"When did she make the appointment?"

"She didn't. She just turned up about half an hour ago. Waving her money around. I tried to tell her you weren't here, but she's very stubborn." Pippa leaned forward. "She's Russian, Mum: very *jumpy*."

"Is that normal for Russians?"

Pippa wasn't sure. "I'm just saying, be prepared. She's rude. Plus I don't think she speaks much English." Pippa looked behind her mother, up the lane. "Where's Raff? Don't tell me you dumped him?"

"Goodness, no, Pippa. We had a *wonderful* time . . ." The words hung there, or so it seemed to Dolly, loaded with all the sex they'd had. Embarrassing. "Anyway . . ."

Pippa smirked. "I'm very happy for you. Anyway, I got some Prosecco to welcome you home — so hurry up and get rid of her. I missed you!"

"You did?" Dolly's warm grin returned, and this time it was only for Pippa. "I thought you might be pleased to have the place to yourself for once!"

The Russian girl was sitting at Dolly's small card table, wrapped in a giant puffa jacket, which, in that tiny room, appeared to have taken over most of the space. She looked pale and surly somewhere deep inside it. Also, on closer examination, beautiful. Of course. Amazing cheekbones. Luminous skin. No make-up. Massive, deadpan eyes.

"Hello, sweetheart," said Dolly, head poking round the cupboard door. She always called the punters "Sweetheart" if she distrusted them on sight. The word just seemed to pop out, as if informing her of the fact, and to compensate in advance for any consequent, inadvertent, unkindness. "Give me a couple of minutes, will you? I'll be as quick as I can."

"I am waiting here already half an hour," the Russian girl said in husky Russian monotone.

"Yes, well." (My goodness, *very* jumpy.) "You'll have to wait a few minutes more. I'll be with you as soon as I can."

The Russian girl said nothing, so Dolly closed the door again and headed to the kitchen. Clearly, she was going to need some coffee (at least) before she dealt with this one.

Dolly had been reading the Tarot for friends for many years; but for her customers, from the downstairs cupboard at Number Two Tinderbox Lane, only since her divorce eight or nine years ago. She was good at it, too: intuitive, kind, and occasionally, genuinely psychic. But she wasn't a good businesswoman, and in truth, she never had quite as many clients as she would have wanted. Too often, her intuition, combined with her curiosity (some might call it nosiness), led her onto long and pot-holed investigative detours, unlikely to generate income, impress "social media commentators" or increase what Pippa, in her modern way, insisted on calling the tinderboxtarot.com "client base".

Whatever. The kettle boiled. Perhaps this surly Russian girl would have a lot of surly Russian friends, and they'd all come flocking to her for readings. At £50 a pop. Maybe.

Dolly reached for the nearest Tarot pack: she was never far from her cards at home in Tinderbox Lane. This was the pack she used to read for herself: the pack she conferred with, privately, three or four times every day. The pack without whose companionship and advice she might have felt quite at sea. She pulled herself a card to guide her through the Jumpy Russian reading ahead, turned it over — and felt a prickle of discomfort.

She had pulled the Fool.

The card shows a young man and a barking dog standing together on a sharp cliff edge, setting out on an unknown journey. The Fool looks carefree and joyful as he steps blithely forward. But the dog's attitude is less clear.

The Fool card can represent many things — optimism and innocence; fresh starts and new adventures . . . but every card has a dark side. And a Fool who steps forward too blithely will stumble right over the cliff top.

It was a warning. She felt certain of that. But for whom, Dolly or the Russian?

She abandoned the coffee, faster than she should have done, perhaps, and returned to the broom cupboard to find out.

Number Two Tinderbox Lane was light and bright, with bookshelves covering most of the walls. It was pretty and welcoming, if a little worn around the edges. But it was by no means a large house. In fact it barely qualified as a house at all. Apart from the aforementioned broom cupboard, which opened from the kitchen end and out onto the back garden, there was actually only one small room on the ground floor: it had enough space for a breakfast bar, a TV, a tiny sofa and an armchair, but not enough for a table.

Upstairs there was just one bathroom and one bedroom, which she and Pippa shared, and would continue to share until Pippa, who was currently coming to the end of a Masters degree, could find a job that paid well enough for her to afford to leave home. Dolly would have used another room for consultations if only she had one, but the broom cupboard was all she had. It was the only space available.

"Right then!" she said brightly, squeezing past the puffa coat, sitting herself down, feeling a pleasant sense of harmony settle around her just as it always did in this small room. She'd not had time to light any incense this afternoon, but after so many years the sweet smells of mugwort and frankincense were never far away; and no matter what time of day, the light that seeped through the little window above the back door was, somehow, always soft and welcoming. The room may have been small, but Dolly loved it. "Sorry about the delay, sweetheart," she said. "My name is Dolly. As you know. Lovely to meet you. Tell me, what's your name?"

A pause. The girl gazed at Dolly as if considering whether to answer.

Ferret. The word popped into Dolly's head. *She looks like a ferret with those wide cheekbones and those watchful black eyes.* It wasn't helpful.

"My name is Marina."

"Ah-ha!" Dolly chortled. "Goodness, Marina! Are you all right, sweetheart? You sound like you want to murder me!"

"Of course not."

"Of course you're not all right, or of course you don't want to murder me?"

"Of course. I am not all right, or why I'm coming here? Of course I not want murder you. I want read my cards."

Dolly took a breath. *Be kind,* she told herself. *Be patient. Cultural differences. Language barriers . . . The girl didn't mean to be as rude as she sounded.* "Well, sweetheart, why don't you tell me how I can help you, and we can get started."

"I want read my cards."

"Yes, I had worked that out." Dolly smiled. Marina didn't. "But people usually like to say a little, first."

"Why?"

"Well — for example — have you had your cards read before?"

"Yes."

"*And . . .?*"

"My grandmother read when I am child. But she is dead and anyway I live here in UK and I must find out something very important. Very important."

"Okay . . . Well, we can —"

"I want to know if my boyfriend he will marry me."

"Ah!" Dolly sat back. *That old chestnut.* "Okay. Well. Let's have a look, shall we? Let's see what the cards have to say."

"I don't think he want to marry me. But sometimes I think he want so much to kill me."

"Oh! Goodness, Marina. Well . . . that's quite a big difference, isn't it?"

"So he want kill me. Or he want marry me? Which?"

Dolly slid the Tarot pack across the table. "Have a quick shuffle, sweetheart. Let's ask the cards."

"I think he want kill me," Marina said, shuffling Dolly's precious cards with a brutal efficiency that made Dolly want to take them back again. "He want this because I know many thing. He say think better if I am dead."

Dolly wanted her to stop talking: too much information distorted the reading. On the other hand — it begged the question: "Why on earth would you want to marry him if you think he wants to kill you?"

Marina looked up from the shuffling, her foxy eyes deadpan yet watchful. "Well that is why I'm coming here," she replied, as if it was obvious. "Of course, if he don't want kill me, I am very happy marry this man. I know many thing about he and he know many thing about me . . . you understand? So."

Dolly asked Marina to pull ten cards from the pack, and the two women fell silent as Dolly laid them out on the table. A long pause. Perhaps it was because of the suncream she could smell still lingering on her clothes; perhaps because she had rushed too quickly into the reading after pulling the Fool. Or perhaps it was because nothing the girl said so far seemed to make any sense — but, for once, the cards said nothing to Dolly. Not at first.

There was Justice reversed, at the centre of the spread, and the Seven of Swords across it — suggesting exploitation and deceit — and the Death card just ahead of it . . . and then the Moon, reversed, and the Seven and the Three of Cups, both reversed — hinting of debauchery, drug addiction, a possible *ménage a trois* . . . A Six of Pentacles suggesting dependency —

8

exploitation and dependency — the Tower, and at the end of it all, the Five of Swords. Her client was involved in a fight with no rules, and no winners . . . except, perhaps . . . Dolly placed a card on top of the Five of Swords, and turned up the Devil.

"*Well now* . . ." Dolly said, playing for time.

"What does it say?"

"Give me a moment, sweetheart . . ."

"He want marry me?"

"Give me a moment. I need to see . . . I have to tell you, Marina . . . there isn't an awful lot to suggest *marriage* here . . ."

"So do he want marry me?"

"Well, as I say —"

"He do or he do not?"

"Give me a moment . . ."

Not only was there nothing to suggest marriage in Marina's cards — there was nothing to suggest any love, affection, warmth or gentleness of any kind. Not anywhere on the table. It was quite exceptional. Desolate.

In a reading, Dolly was always compelled to tell the truth — of course she was. But not all of it. And only (this was an important rule) in a way that might be helpful. She said: "The question you might want to ask yourself, looking at these cards, Marina, isn't so much whether you *will* marry this man, as *whether you should*. Are you sure you want to marry him, sweetie?"

"Yes."

"But you don't love him."

Marina shrugged. "Maybe."

"I think you hate him."

"I love him. I hate him. What difference?"

"Well, you're right, of course . . . They can often get a little muddled."

"He take care of me. I take care of he."

"Does he? Do you?"

The girl only shrugged.

Drowning, thought Dolly. The word popped into her head.

A silence fell while she tried to reconcile this. The wretched girl was drowning. But in what?

"He make me as a prisoner," Marina said.

Dolly didn't reply. She turned over another card. The Hyrophant: two supplicants crouched before a throne. The girl wasn't lying, then. Or not entirely. The Devil and Hyrophant . . . What was that peculiar syndrome — there was a name for it, the relationship between captive and captor, and love and hate. Munchausen? Stockhausen? Stockholm. Stockholm syndrome . . .

Marina leaned over the table. "Because I am *Russian*. Without some papers, because he steal them from me."

"He stole your papers?"

"Of course he steal my papers!"

"Well —"

"He think he is holding me here forever. But I can find another way. It's not a problem. I always find a way." The defiance in the girl's voice made Dolly look up from the cards. Marina was staring at a corner of the room — somewhere above Dolly's head — and the gesture struck Dolly as so helpless, so angry, she

10

wanted to pause the reading and give this pathetic, angry girl a hug.

But Marina hadn't come to her for sympathy and cuddles.

Dolly's gaze returned to the cards on the table. She frowned. *How very confusing . . .* What was happening? Their meaning seemed to be shifting and sliding before her eyes. *This is what two weeks in the sunshine did for you. Two weeks of sex and sun and happiness.* She took her time. Forgot about the beady fox eyes opposite waiting impatiently for their answer, forgot the smell of suncream, forgot about everything but the cards, and slowly, surely, a picture began to emerge . . .

. . . of Marina unhappy, to put it mildly. A living, breathing knot of malign energies and negative forces: of love and hate. With the girl's foxy eyes and her disagreeable manner set aside, and only the cards to guide her, Dolly could see that Marina was as much victim as perpetrator. As much perpetrator as victim . . . She was snarled in the middle of thick, dark fog, and she was too blind to see out.

"Tell me about these stolen papers," Dolly said. "You mean your passport and so on, I presume? I take it you're not legal here in the UK?"

The girl shrugged. "I have not my papers. Not money, not nothing."

"You think he destroyed your papers?"

"I say him — give me papers and I go home. I leave you in peace!"

"All right . . ." Dolly's eyes stayed on the cards. "Well then — and what did he say to that?"

"Of course. He don't give me papers. He want me stay."

"But you could report him if he's stolen your papers, and you want to go home. The authorities would help you. So why don't you do that?"

"Of course I mustn't go." Marina cracked a lifeless smile and leaned across the table. "I must stay, because of love."

"Love?" muttered Dolly. "Are you sure?"

She turned over another card, laid it on the Three of Cups — it was the Three of Swords. Someone was suffering. Was it Marina? Again, Dolly set aside the girl's cold manner. People hid their feelings in any number of fashions. "One of you," Dolly said, "is going to get badly hutt."

"I think we can be happy."

Dolly ignored this. The girl wasn't bright. She wasn't bright at all . . . Dolly turned over another card: the Two of Swords. It showed a figure, blindfolded, two large swords held across her heart: wilfully closed and blinded. Dolly saw Death and the Devil. She saw debauchery and darkness, stupidity, stubbornness, hatred and sorrow . . . and gave an involuntary shiver.

"What?" the girl said angrily. "Why you are body shaking like this? It's not cold. You are wanting frighten me! But why? I am not easy frighten."

Dolly shook her head. Lying on the table between them there were so many warnings it was hard for her to know where to begin . . . She was incapable of fobbing people off — clients or otherwise. (It was another reason why her business didn't flourish. And

12

perhaps, also, another reason why she was divorced.) She would not — could not — send Marina on her way with the words that Marina had come to hear, not if she didn't believe them herself.

"I'm not trying to frighten you," Dolly said. "Don't be silly. But I do have to say that I don't think you will marry this chap. At least I hope you don't. You won't be happy with him." If Marina spoke, Dolly didn't hear it. She paused for a long time before continuing at last: "In fact, Marina, I don't believe you will be happy or safe until you're well away from him."

A beat.

Marina shook her head impatiently. "But does he want marry me?"

Dolly glanced up from the table, exasperated. "But *why*? Why would you *want* to marry him?"

"Because if I leave, he get all the flat."

"What flat?"

"This is not his flat. This is my flat. *I* was the friend with the old lady, not him. He is always sleeping all the time. *I* spend my nights talking with her, making her happy. When she pee in the sheet, *I* lift her from bed, and carry her to toilet."

"On your own? You must be very strong."

Marina paused. "Why you say this?"

Dolly shrugged. She didn't know. "Never mind. Carry on."

"She is small like child. Very thin. Very small. I help her. Not him! So now he own this flat. Because he steal my documents. *He* haves *my* flat. So he have to marry me! You understand now?" Marina glared at Dolly and then, dismissively, at the cards on the table between them. "Why I tell you all this? Why not the cards? Why I have explain?"

Again, Dolly ignored her. "So . . . you befriended an old woman, did you? Is that right? A lonely old woman . . . And she left you her property?"

"No! She left this for me, but she not left this for me because she is very stupid old woman! She think I must being an English woman for her stupid flat. And of course, he tell her this. He think — then she leave the flat for him, then I marry him. And he think I wait, wait, wait every day for he marry me. Or he think I just leave. But I will leave never without my money. You understand me?"

"I think so," Dolly said. "The flat is in your boyfriend's name, is it? Because the old lady didn't want to leave it to a foreigner."

"Yes!"

"But you *are* a foreigner . . ."

"Of course! She is stupid old woman . . . Nice lady, yes," she added unexpectedly, as if surprising herself. She paused. "But she say, I marry him, it make me English woman."

"And she wanted you to marry him?"

The girl rolled her eyes impatiently. "Of course she want! She think he is . . . *bees knees*. He swear we marry. And then —" Marina ran an untroubled index finger across her slim throat, denoting, Dolly gathered, the old woman's death. "And then everything change. Of course."

14

"You say 'of course'," muttered Dolly, "an awful lot, sweetheart. But it's quite a peculiar situation, isn't it?"

Marina shrugged.

A long silence. Dolly stared at the cards. And felt a little sick. "He killed her, did he?"

Marina's face relaxed as if there might be a little trust between them at last. As if perhaps Dolly might not be so completely useless after all. "Maybe, yes. But this not important now."

"Excuse me?" said Dolly. "I think it *is* . . ."

"I think next he wake up and he kill me. Or I kill him. Maybe I kill him first."

"Oh, I wouldn't do that," Dolly muttered. She looked up at the girl. "Tell me," she asked her suddenly, though why, she didn't know, "how did you find me down here at the bottom of Tinderbox Lane? Did somebody recommend me?"

"Of course," Marina said, black eyes sliding away. "Everybody know you in this place."

It wasn't true.

Nothing the girl said was true.

Dolly nodded slowly and felt the cold creeping down her spine.

Their half-hour reading crawled by. If Pippa hadn't been sitting in the room next door, Dolly might have offered the girl a refund and brought the thing to an early end. But somehow, with Pippa watching, she couldn't quite bring herself to do anything so unbusinesslike. And so they ploughed on. But it felt to Dolly like a pointless consultation, leaving Marina angry and unsatisfied, and leaving Dolly in need of a drink. Finally, with barely hidden relief, she collected up the cards and sent Marina on her way.

"I'm not sure I've been any help to you, Marina," she said. "I don't think you really wanted to hear what the cards were saying . . . I'm sorry. So — I'm just going to wish you the very best of luck." It sounded as feeble as Dolly felt.

Marina raised a fine, cold eyebrow. She zipped up her enormous puffa jacket and said to Dolly: "Perhaps I invite you my wedding party."

"That's very nice, sweetheart," Dolly said. "Let's hope it never comes to that."

With one last Russian shrug, Marina breezed away, her little feet moving like a dancer, and the spring flowers on Tinderbox Lane wilting ever so slightly in her wake. Dolly saw this. Or felt it. In any case, it was going to take a while to shake this reading off.

Thank God, she thought, for Pippa — and the Prosecco.

CHAPTER
TWO

Tinderbox Lane lay tucked in the depths of a no-man's land, somewhere between the expensive, family-friendly suburban paradise that was Barnes, south west London and the expensive, family-friendly suburban lesser-paradise beyond. The area didn't have a name, and despite estate agents' best efforts, the City bankers hadn't yet fully colonised. This was due to the usual factors: a preponderance of ugly ex-council houses in the nearby area, a nasty, busy road, a noisy bus station and bad parking. There were dribs and drabs of new money seeping in, however, and it wouldn't be long before the fat cats discovered it en masse. Because hidden away, amidst the usual factors, there was, around Dolly's lane, a little oasis: a network of small streets, many of them too slim even to allow cars. And Dolly Greene, who had bought her tiny house in the divorce settlement, considered herself extremely lucky to be living there.

Tinderbox Lane was a cul-de-sac; more accessible than some of the little streets nearby. It stood, in fact, slightly separate from the others, coming directly off the noisy road and ending in a wasteland of sycamore and holly, an invisible mesh fence — and the back of the bus station. People could walk past Tinderbox Lane for years without even seeing it. No cars could get down it, and by some magical oversight the council had yet to insist on installing streetlights. And so, for the time being at least, for the small group of neighbours who called it home, the lane offered a welcome sense of being forgotten.

It was pretty, too. High bushes grew along one side (obscuring any usual-factor sounds and views) and on the other side, in a short, neat row, were just seven small nineteenth-century worker cottages.

Number Seven was closest to the road. It had been empty for years, and nobody seemed to know who owned it.

Numbers Six, Five and Four were occupied by the recently separated Rosie Buck and her two young children, India and Nadya. The three houses had been knocked together not long ago, to make a "luxury family home"; Rosie's then husband, Fraser, seeing it as an investment opportunity, had snapped it up (and christened it "Windy Ridge"). For business reasons, or perhaps, even, because deep down he knew he wouldn't always be around, he had placed the property, unmortgaged, into his wife's name. And for this Rosie Buck thanked her lucky stars, because he had since vanished pretty much off the face of the earth. Last spotted boarding a flight to Panama, he hadn't been seen or heard of for six months.

Beyond Windy Ridge stood Number Three. Number Three Tinderbox Lane had only recently been vacated by Dolly's neighbour, Maurice Bousquet, who had died suddenly late last autumn. The house had been empty for several months, but when Dolly left for her holiday two weeks ago (thanks, in fact, to his small bequest) a mysterious Brazilian woman called Lucky was just beginning the process of moving in. Dolly had yet to meet her.

Finally, at Number One, furthest from the noisy road, and on Pippa and Dolly's other side, there lived a nondescript man in his mid- to late thirties, named Terry. He had a beard, and a job in IT which allowed him to work from home, many pairs of jeans and trainers, and a face that needed to feel the sun. He didn't have many friends — or none that visited — and he tended to keep himself to himself. Dolly thought he was surly and didn't like him. Pippa thought he was pathetic. Rosie, who'd never spoken to him, insisted he was "rather sweet". So far as anyone knew, Lucky Crystal at Number Three had yet to voice her opinion.

It wouldn't have taken Sherlock Holmes to work out that Dolly and Pippa were mother and daughter. They shared many features: the same red-brown hair, the same hazel-brown eyes and freckles, the same wide mouths and small, straight noses. They shared the same laugh and even, in their own ways, though it might irritate both to hear it, a similar low-cost, urban-hippie way of dressing. Pippa wore her hair long, loose and messy. Dolly wore hers a little shorter, but also messy, and generally pulled up in a crocodile clip. Pippa, who had inherited her father's slim, long-limbed physique, dressed in leather jacket and combats every day. Dolly, several inches shorter than her daughter and significantly more curvaceous, wore knee-length skirts and big jumpers — because combats would never have suited her. In their own ways, and in similar ways, both women were attractive — probably more attractive than either realised.

As it happened, Pippa's powers of attraction were not, currently, at the top of her concerns. She was more worried about her low earning-power (and slow-starting career). Her Masters degree was due to finish in the summer, and despite having been applying for jobs pretty much solidly since Christmas, she had yet to be called in for a single interview.

That same afternoon, after having sent the Russian girl on her way, the two women were sitting out on the front doorstep, enjoying the last few rays of a weak, spring sun, when lumbering up the lane towards them came Pippa's old professor, Derek West.

"Oh shit! Mum," whispered Pippa, "I forgot to tell you . . ."

Professor West, aka "Professor Filthy" (so named by Pippa), had developed a harmless, though annoying, passion for Pippa the previous academic year, and in his attempts to befriend her had come to Dolly for a Tarot reading, at which point he had instantly transferred his affections. Pippa had thought this was funny. Dolly, less so. In any case, he was divorced and lonely and well meaning, and really not very filthy at all — and one way or another he appeared to have inveigled his way into their lives. "I forgot to tell you, Mum, Professor Filthy moved into Windy Ridge."

"*He what?*"

"Rosie Buck's run out of money. As we know. Due to Mr Frosty having buggered off to Panama —"

"Shhh!"

"Mr Frosty-Fuck. I beg your pardon."

Dolly snorted with laughter. "He's called —"

"And Mrs Frosty's far too posh to get a job like a normal person — so she's got a lodger instead. And I think Filthy thought . . . actually God knows what he thought, Mum. But in any case, you're off the hook. He's been hanging around Rosie Frosty-Buck like an overgrown puppy ever since you left." The professor was looming close now, waving at them with his long, chaotic arms. The afternoon sun was gleaming off his moon specs, and it looked very much as if he'd forgotten to do up his flies. *Never mind.* Both women were trying not to laugh.

"Welcome home, Dolly!" he yelled, with so much exuberance it would have taken a heart much harder than Dolly's not to have warmed.

"Thank you, Derek." Dolly smiled at him. "Pippa tells me you're our new neighbour!"

"Indeedie-Dolly, so I am!" He drew up in front of them. His jeans waistband was too close to his nipples, and his lank, floppy hair needed washing, and his specs were too small for his big face. Really, everything about him looked gangly and wrong. "What do you think about *that?*" he grinned. "I am now a fully fledged member of that most exclusive of clubs: The Tinderbox Lane Residential Community! Such that it is. Expect to see me popping in and out of your lovely house all the time! And vice versa, of course! You're both welcome at Windy *any time*."

"That's a lovely invitation," Dolly said.

"It's what communities like these are all about. Isn't it? Popping in for drinks . . . borrowing bowls of sugar. All that stuff. People tend to forget the importance of these things . . . Well . . ." He saluted. "Here I stand. One neighbour: at your service!"

"That's wonderful news," Dolly said faintly.

"So, how was the great holiday, Dolly? Did you and Chief Inspector Plod have an absolutely marvellous time? I bet you did!" The professor tucked his thumbs under his armpits, and dipped into a PC Plod plié: "'Ullo, 'ullo, 'ullo!" he said. "Did he take his truncheon?" The professor gave a gutsy laugh.

Dolly said, "I've told you before, Derek, Raff is not an inspector, and certainly not a chief inspector. He's a sergeant."

"Oh, yes." Filthy straightened up.

"And it's a bit of a tired joke, you know — about Raff being a policeman. It's not really funny. And anyway not all policemen . . ." Dolly paused. She felt silly, but she'd started so she finished: "Not all policemen have truncheons, Derek."

He winked. "Gotcha, Dolly. Only joking. Didn't mean to offend."

"I know you didn't," she smiled. "Forget it. How are you finding life on the lane?"

"Ah!" the professor perked up. "I'm glad you ask that, because I've been sent down here by my new landlady. By which, of course, I mean the stupendous

Mrs B. She wants you both to come to dinner tonight over at Windy."

"At 'Windy'?" repeated Pippa.

"Are you free? Rosie's been cooking up a storm!"

"Oh, Derek, that's such a lovely thought," said Dolly. "But I must admit I'm rather exhausted . . ."

"Oops. Should've clarified. 'Q' was rhetorical. Only one 'A' applies! I'm not going back to Rosie with a negative. No way."

Pippa laughed. "But you might have to!"

He looked sternly at his former student. "Listen here, young Pippa. Rosie's been under a lot of pressure lately. As you know. She needs her friends around her. So — I'm asking you, girls, to step up. Do the neighbourly thing. She's been cooking like a lunatic since nine o'clock this morning."

"Oh goodness. Well . . ." Dolly felt guilty at once. Poor Rosie. "Perhaps we could just pop in for a drink?"

The professor shook his head. "The invite is very much for *dinner* . . . if you don't mind. And by the way, Dolly, we've invited the sergeant."

"I'll have to check with him."

"No need. I already pinged him a text, Dolly. *Mea culpa*. He's on his way!"

"But I haven't . . ." Dolly paused. There was actually no reason she couldn't have dinner with them tonight. None at all. And, really, it was very sweet of them to invite her. "Well, Derek . . . Thank you very much. How lovely. I would love to come. Pippa? Are you busy?"

"Actually I'm pretty sure I've got a shift at the pub," Pippa said.

"On the night your mum just got back from holiday?" cried the professor. "I doubt that very much!" He was right. As it happened. "Don't be a stuffy bunny! Plus . . ." He winked at her. "As you know, Pippa, we have one or two things to discuss, do we not? As residents of said Tinderbox Lane Residential Community. Have you mentioned it yet?"

Pippa looked uncomfortable. "Mentioned what?"

Dolly ears pricked up. "What? What haven't you mentioned, Pipp? What's happened? What am I missing out on?"

Professor Filthy tapped his big nose. "We shall discuss it all tonight! Eight o'clock, yes? Excellent. I shall see you both shortly."

CHAPTER
THREE

Rosie was, indeed, cooking up a storm. In her open-plan kitchen with state-of-the-art saucepans etc., she bustled from one worktop to the other, between seafood grillplant, rotisserie forno and legume-spiraliser, adding sprinkles of things to other things, and stirring. Rosie loved to cook.

"Golly, Rosie — are you feeding the five thousand?" asked the professor.

"Oh dear," muttered Rosie, "have I overdone it? I'm hopeless at quantities."

Rosie had long forgotten how to economise. That was part of the problem. Add to that her myriad insecurities — exacerbated by ten years with a bullying husband who had made it a habit to remind her that nothing she did was ever good enough — and she always ended up cooking too much of everything. Tonight there were four different spiralised legumes to choose from, some grillplanted salmon for the non-meat eaters, some over-rotisserised boeuf "for the men", and a kelp and tofu risotto for the vegans, just in case. There were no vegans coming to dinner. Rosie hadn't bothered to check. Nor any non-meat eaters, come to that.

She'd also made a raspberry, pomegranate and mango Pavlova, and a toffee-caramel and passion-fruit fondant. There were some out-of-season strawberries, which tasted of diluted orange squash; and some blueberries, which tasted of cellophane.

"Well — I should think we'll be eating this stuff for a month. But I'm not complaining. It looks scrumptious!" declared the professor, rubbing his hands together. And he meant it. He'd been living off Pot Noodles since his wife left him, four desolate years ago. And now . . . his eye wandered from the blue candles and spring-theme flower decorations on the dining table to the feast being prepared on the breakfast bar, and — really — he could not believe his luck. *What a find was Rosie Buck!* "I think," he said to her, "I'm falling in love."

Rosie blushed. She blushed a lot. "Don't be silly," she said. But it was a nice thing to hear, after all the awful things that had happened lately. Really. Very lovely. The professor had only moved into the spare room ten days ago and already she was getting quite used to having him around. More than used to it, truth be told. He cheered the place up. Even the kids didn't appear to object to him much. (Although it was possible, of course, given how rarely they looked up from their iPads, that neither had yet noticed he'd moved in.)

Raff Williams had warned them he was running late, so Dolly, Pippa, the professor and Rosie were already sitting at the table when he arrived. The doorbell rang, and Dolly leapt up to welcome him.

"Here he is," she said, leading him back into the kitchen, a wide smile on her face. "Better late than never!"

He looked as sunkissed and happy as her mother, Pippa thought. And quite handsome, actually, with the tan . . . He had a broad, kind face which seemed always on the point of breaking into a smile, and shiny, humorous blue eyes and thick hair — albeit, mostly grey . . . and he was taller than she remembered. Was it completely gross to fancy your mother's boyfriend?

Decidedly, yes (she decided). In any case, sunkissed and tall he may be, he was still a policeman. Nobody of her political disposition could possibly fancy a policeman. Plus he was old. Which placed him very much at the overlap of the Venn diagram, between boring and appalling. So that was that.

Except she liked him, really. How could she not, when he made her mother so happy?

"Ahh — the fine sergeant is gracing us with his presence!" cried the professor, standing up and opening his long arms wide. "'Ullo, 'ull —" He was already mid-Policeman-Plod-plié when he remembered how badly the joke had gone down last time. He glanced at Dolly, and straightened up. "Come on in, Raff, my old chap. Come on in!"

Rosie dabbed her mouth with a blue napkin and tripped across the vast expanse of slate-look fibreglass flooring (£475 a square metre, as the elusive Mr Fraser

27

Buck used to remind people) to give the late arrival a peck on the cheek.

"Raff, you look gorgeous!" she said. "And that's even out of your clothes! I mean . . ." She blushed. "Uniform. Not out of your *clothes*, clothes. Crikey! What am I saying? You look gorgeous *not* in your uniform. Because you know what people say about men in uniform —"

"Word to the wise, Rosie," interjected the professor loudly: "When located in crater, hole, ditch or similar self-made terrestrial hollow . . ." (Perhaps he should rent a uniform one weekend, when Rosie's kids were away? It might be a laugh. She might like that) ". . . better to lay down the spade and *stop digging!*"

But Raff only laughed. The effect of his uniform *on the ladies* (as Derek might put it), lay somewhere in the overlap of the Venn diagram between Perk of the Job and Unendurably Stale Joke. It was something he had long ago learned to take with a pinch of salt. "I'm flattered, Rosie!" he said. "Thanks for having me round." He glanced at the table. "And what a feast!"

"No, but I wasn't meaning to flatter. I only meant . . ." Rosie could feel sweat breaking out behind her ears, and it was going to make her hair frizzy. She did her best to rescue the situation. "You look ever so well, Raff. And so does Dolly. You both look like you've had a super holiday."

"We certainly did," said Raff.

Dolly had been away from Tinderbox Lane for a fortnight: an unusually eventful fortnight, so far as she could tell, and there was a great deal to catch up on.

"Derek, we've got the full complement now. Shall we . . .?"

But Derek, who had refused to start until Raff had joined them, wanted to discuss the wine first; and then, when Raff said he preferred beer, the merits of old-fashioned home brews.

". . . but anyway . . ." said Dolly.

"All righty . . . ITEM NUMBER ONE," the professor began at last. "ITEM NUMBER ONE on the Tinderbox Lane Post-Holiday News Agenda —"

"Get on with it, Derek." Rosie nudged him gently. "Never mind 'items'. Dolly wants to know what's been going on, and I don't blame her."

"ITEM NUMBER ONE," he said again, "is, of course, our new Brazilian friend and neighbour, now resident at Number Three; the gorgeous Mademoiselle Lucky Crystal. Henceforth to be known as —"

Rosie said: "No, Derek. She's not gorgeous. Actually, don't say that. It's disrespectful. Just because of — you know . . . She's actually very normal. A very normal, lovely person, I expect. And anyway — remember she told you, didn't she, we're not supposed to call her Lucky Crystal any more. She doesn't like it."

Raff said (sounding disappointed): "But it's her name! What are we supposed to call her?"

"Well . . ." Rosie hesitated. "It's — Brazilian, isn't it? Obviously. And a lot more normal than 'Lucky'. What's she called, Derek? Can you remember? Only we mustn't forget, because otherwise she'll think we think she's a stripper."

"She *is* a stripper!" Pippa and Raff exclaimed simultaneously.

"Yes, well I'm not sure if she *is* a stripper any more. Now she's got Maurice's money. I think she's a poet. She was muttering about writing poems, didn't you say so, Derek? But they're probably in Brazilian. Anyway — we mustn't call her 'Lucky' any more. We have to call her . . . oh, Derek, what the heck is her name? Can you remember?"

"If you'd allowed me continue the moment previous, Mrs B, I could have told you: her actual name is Isabelle Ferrari. No relation, sadly. Very common surname, apparently, in Brazil. Yes, she may be a wealthy lady, thanks to the generosity of our late lamented neighbour, Mr Bousquet. But it's got nothing to do with racing cars!" He honked with laughter. "She's called Isabelle Ferrari and she has a *very* interesting background. Not your average stripper background, by any means."

"Oh really?" interrupted Pippa. "What's the 'average' stripper background then?"

"Give him a break, Pipps," Dolly sighed.

"Why? I'm just *asking*. It's a perfectly reasonable question. What's the 'average' stripper background —"

"She's a bit of a handful, your young Pippa, isn't she?" observed the professor, to Dolly.

"Let's just hear the story, shall we?" Raff said, feeling an argument brewing. "Judge for ourselves how average her background isn't or is."

"But how will we know?" persisted Pippa. "Is any of us an expert on 'average stripper' biogs? I don't think so."

"Well, *Sergeant* . . . it turns out the lovely Isabelle is a somewhat unlucky lady."

Raff chuckled. "Hardly. She's just inherited a fortune."

He had a point. Things had certainly gone well for her lately. Dolly and Pippa's former neighbour Maurice Bousquet had lived like a pauper, recycling teabags and refusing to pay his license fee, until the day he was found dead. But it now turned out he'd been a rich man. Quite how rich, they could currently only guess at because his estate — a maze of secrets and hidden trusts — was still being untangled. In any case, he had left a winning scratch card to Dolly and Raff, worth £10,000. Hence the Caribbean holiday. And so far as anyone knew he had left everything else not to his jailbird son, nor to his teenage grandson, but to one (very) Lucky Crystal, aka Isabelle Ferrari, aka Thursday-night's pole dancer down at the Lamb Tavern.

"She inherited a fortune — agreed — but it was only the other day, wasn't it? The poor lady came to the UK with nothing. I don't know how aware you are of Brazil's recent history . . .? I must admit, I sneaked a quick Google after we had our natter, and it's actually been pretty nasty there for some time. Long before the Olympics and whatnot. A very nasty regime *prior to that*, so to speak. Political assassinations — you name it. That sort of thing . . ." The professor paused. He realised he couldn't quite remember what sort of thing. Population: 200.4 million. International dialling code: +56. (He was always good with numbers.) Other than that . . . lots of *coup d'etats*, probably. Nasty generals . . . or nice generals? Too many generals. "The fact is," he continued, "poor old Isabelle had a husband who was a journalist . . . A very courageous journalist. Not like the sort of dross you get in the UK. Fighting the brave fight, he was, with the sword of truth, and so on. And on April 23 1986 at 12.30p.m., *he simply disappeared*."

Dolly glanced at Pippa. "Probably not your usual stripper biography then, eh, Pipp?"

"Well I wouldn't know, would I?" replied Pippa, irritably.

Dolly chuckled and turned back to the professor. "Did Isabelle ever find out what happened to him?"

"Who?"

"The husband!"

"Ah, well —"

"He's probably knocking back scrumptious rum cocktails in Puerto Rico with *my* husband," interrupted Rosie bitterly. And then blushed. "Sorry. That was awful. *Sorry*. I don't know where that came from. Poor lady. Imagine having a hero for a husband . . . It must be . . ." She could only give a wistful sigh. (Her husband, by contrast, as everyone round the table knew, was wanted for questioning over the death of a local prostitute: hence his disappearance.) The professor put a hand on hers. There was something very natural about it. Dolly wondered if they were already sleeping together. If not, they ought to be. They were a perfect match.

"Isabelle left Brazil eighteen months later. A broken lady, really. Absolutely heartbroken, as you can imagine. She arrived in the UK with a suitcase. That was it."

"Did she look for him, though?" Pippa asked.

"Who?"

"The *husband*."

"Ah, well." The professor shook his head. An expert on the subject, after a thirty-second natter on Isabelle's doorstep, and a five-minute chat on the lane two days later. "Of course. She *looked* . . . but in the end there's only so much looking one can do, isn't there? She decided she simply had to get out of Brazil. Get somewhere safe. Start again, so to speak."

"But what about the husband?" Pippa persisted. "What happened to him?"

"Almost certainly tortured," said Derek, solemnly. "Probably to death. Isabelle never saw him again. No children, thankfully. Okay? So that's Isabelle, currently residing at Number Three. She tends to keep herself to herself, but I am sure we will all get to know her well enough in due course. She seems like a very delightful lady. Speaks immaculate English, by the way. Except for the weeniest little accent, you wouldn't even know. I suspect she comes from a very good family. Originally. We can only wonder how it all went so wrong. Which brings us rather neatly, if I may say so, to ITEM NUMBER 2 . . ."

"No it doesn't!" said Dolly. "Not yet! We've only just started on Item Number 1! Tell me, what's she like? Is she nice — Rosie? Pippa? Have you spoken to her yet?"

"Not as such," said Rosie. "But she's got ever such a nice smile."

"What about you, Pipps?"

"I've seen her walking around. She looks a bit crazy."

"Crazy?"

Pippa thought about it. "Well, like she's on the look-out for bullshit. You know what I mean? Just so she can make it clear to everyone that she won't be taking it . . ."

Dolly and Raff laughed. The professor wasn't listening. Rosie tutted (there were kids in the house).

Only Derek had actually spoken to Isabelle Ferrari then, and from him, there was no more information forthcoming. He was keen to move on to the more important ITEM NUMBER TWO: *the new residents at Number Seven*.

"What?" cried Dolly. "Has someone bought it at last? Pippa! Why didn't you tell me?"

Rosie was about to speak but again the professor put his hand on hers and she fell silent. Pippa reached for her tobacco pouch. She had always been a leftie. She'd found herself growing increasingly more so as her Masters degree drew to an end, and the impossible realities of leading a solvent or independent life in her own home city loomed closer . . . She didn't want to be around for this conversation. No matter what line her mother took on the subject, it was likely to be less radical than her own. And then they would be bound to fight. And she'd missed her mother. She didn't want to ruin their post-holiday honeymoon.

"I'm going out for a smoke," she said, "I'll leave you to break the news, Professor."

"Will do." He winked. "Actually I was wondering, Pippa, if the very ravishing Russian girl I saw moping round outside your house this afternoon had anything to do with any of them? Did she say?"

"No — I don't think so," Pippa replied, slightly taken aback. "Why?"

"Oh you know. Same sort of age. Same sort of hang-dog, pointless type of look about her."

"But how did you know she was Russian?" Pippa asked.

"Ah! Потому как, young lady," he answered gleefully, "Я мог бы просто сказать!"

Pippa stared at him. "You speak Russian?"

"Not just a pretty face, eh?" He glanced at Rosie to see how she'd taken it, but she was distracted — one of the children was shouting for her from the media room. "As it happens I studied a little bit of Russian at uni. Tell me, Raff — I always wondered. No offence. Do police officers such as yourself tend to go to uni? Generally speaking? Or are you, let's say, a man who was educated more at the University of Life?"

Nothing the professor did or said was ever meant unkindly. Raff knew this. He reminded himself of it, now. But even so . . . "I didn't go to university, no," he answered carefully. "Nowadays it's a bit different, of course . . ." He would have liked to tell Professor West about his son who had just completed a PhD at Kings College, London in an aspect of astrophysics wholly incomprehensible to ordinary mortals, having graduated from Cambridge with a First Class degree. He would have liked to do that, but he didn't. He was too elegant, or too shy; or both. Instead he fell silent.

"Hmmm. That's very interesting," said Derek. "I hope you don't mind my asking?"

"Of course not."

"But . . . would you have *liked* to have gone to university?"

"Oh for heaven's sake!" snapped Dolly, saving Raff from a reply. "What about ITEM NUMBER TWO? *Who has moved into Number Seven?*"

CHAPTER
FOUR

Inside Number Seven, silence reigned. Its three new inhabitants, wrapped in thick coats due to the lack of heating, were each engaged in occupations related to their survival. Two were on laptops, researching their civil rights and/or recycled household furniture. One was putting together a barricade for the front door. Squatting is a serious business — a full-time business, more to the point, requiring stamina and guile, practical intelligence, courage, subterfuge, anonymity — and a solid understanding of the law.

This particular crew was small — unusually so, for London — but between them, the three youngsters — or "Unknown Persons" in legal terms — believed they had the necessary skills to survive. In any case, after two or three years moving from one squat to another with a commune of twenty quarrelsome others, it was a relief to be in a place that couldn't fit any more. Added to which, they were making a point.

To squat in an empty commercial premises was one thing. To squat in a private residence had lately been made a criminal offence; and with so many commercial properties empty in the city, residential spots were generally deemed more trouble than they were worth.

So went the argument of the faint-hearted. Geordie, Gigi and Trek, Oxford University graduates and dedicated anarchists all three, were anything but. In fact ITEM NUMBER TWO on the Tinderbox Lane Residential Community agenda were very happy with their new premises. Having already fixed themselves up with electricity and wi-fi, they had no current intention of moving on. And so, while on one side of the wall, over their elaborate but tasteless banquet, Professor Filthy and friends were discussing how best to get rid of them, on the other, the three anarchists were discussing how best to stay. They agreed that a localised charm offensive would likely be a sensible first step.

"Love thy neighbours," muttered the one called Trek, a meaty lad with a heavy-jawed, unhandsome face. He'd been First Eleven Captain at his public school. But that was a lifetime ago. Right now, he was at the back of the room, boring holes into some handy metal bars he'd rescued from a Luxury Housing site just behind Barnes High Street. "Love thy neighbours, and thy neighbours shall delay calling in bailiffs . . . We need to gauge hostility levels. See what we're up against."

"Likely to be fairly high," replied Geordie. "This is not Walthamstow, my friends. This is Nirvana. We're in Posh Land here . . . Which, of course, is one of the reasons we want to stay put . . ." Geordie, true to character, was hogging the only comfortable spot in the house. He was lying on his back, laptop balanced on his lean stomach, long legs sprawled across a leatherette sofa that he and Trek had pulled off a skip this morning. He laughed with lazy relish, and the laptop rocked. "By the way, have either of you spotted the couple next door yet? They are *classic*. Fucking *classic Daily Mail-reading* bastards. I don't know if they're aware of us yet, but if they are, they must be *apoplectic*."

Trek looked up from his metal bar. "I think I spotted the wife. She looks like a startled rabbit. With botox . . ." He thought about it. "Well, a startled rabbit with no fur on its face. And lots of botox . . . Do you think you could win her over, Geordie?"

"She might just hop away. The way startled rabbits are prone to. Could be one for you, Gigi. You can talk about carrots or something . . . What about the bloke? The tall guy. Has anyone spoken to him?"

"Not me," said Trek.

"Well — maybe you should. Try something about cars."

"I don't know anything about cars."

"Doesn't matter," replied Geordie. "As long as you sound confident."

"There's one of our age at the end of the street. She looks all right," said the girl, Gigi, who was lying on her belly beside an empty fireplace (scouring recycle websites for a free immersion shower). "We might be able to get somewhere with her." Gigi, pixie-like as the name suggests, with vast brown eyes and a pointy, clever chin, spoke in the dulcet tones of a girl accustomed to men leaning in to hear her. She was, in her limber, pixie-grubby way, more or less irresistible; an earth goddess, wonderfully at ease with her own sexuality . . . Geordie and Trek had both enjoyed the honour of knowing her in the biblical sense — and that was cool. Everyone was cool with that. Especially Gigi and Geordie.

Her primary relationship was with Trek, however. Which was lucky for Trek, because he was basically in love with her. And it worked well for Geordie, too, who didn't go in for primary relationships. Who simply did not believe, so he said, in the "construct of monogamy". He just loved sex. Or, as he put it: "the intense reciprocity ignited by a living two". Sometimes, in fact, by "a living three". And once, by "a living seven" — but he hadn't enjoyed that. Too many fluids. Not enough reciprocity. Whatever.

Geordie had a way with words, and an extraordinary way with women. To Trek's eternal jealousy — and bewilderment — women simply wanted to have sex with him. In all his life, Geordie had never once made an offer of intense reciprocity and been rejected. Partly, this was because he was a consummate planner. He never did anything, never made a move, without calculating the angles in advance; and partly, of course, because success breeds success, and life — as any anarchist would tell you — is mightily unfair. Geordie always got the girl. (Lately, in fact, his 100% hit ratio had been getting him down. It didn't change his behaviour, not at all: but these days, when he woke beside yet another Geordie-yielding body — and he generally had at least two of them on the go — he found he felt a little desolate. There was a hidden corner of his heart that longed to find a woman who could make him work for the adulation.)

"I'll do the young one then," said Geordie.

"Of course you will," replied Trek, irritably.

"Well I won't, if you don't want me to," he snapped. "It was your idea we had to befriend these cretinous —"

"I didn't say they were cretins," replied Trek.

"I think it was implied."

"Far from it. The problem with you, Geordie," said Trek, "you think you're the only non-'cretin' in the fucking universe. For the record, I think you're the biggest cretin of us all."

Gigi sighed. "Boys, boys . . ."

And for a second, they all fell silent again.

Geordie, on his leatherette sofa, released an ostentatious sigh. "Right then," he said. "I'll take that as a plan, shall I? You two, tackle the non-cretins next door. I'll make friends with the girl of our age at the end of the road . . . I think that leaves the angry-looking woman with the fucking amazing body at Number Three. What do we know about her?"

Gigi said: "She's Spanish, I think. Or South American."

". . . and then there's Scary Tarot Lady . . ."

Gigi looked up. "Who?"

"Hilariously, we have a professional Tarot reader on the street."

"No! You're joking. Which house? Is she scary?"

Geordie shrugged. "Only if you believe in that crap . . ."

"Well," answered Gigi, seriously, "I don't completely doubt it, no. Do you?"

"*. . . Doubt thou the stars are fire. Doubt that the sun doth move . . .*" murmured Trek from the metalwork corner. He'd read English at university.

Geordie ignored them both. "Scary Tarot Lady lives at Number Two, I think. She looked like she was returning from some sort of holiday this afternoon."

"*. . . Doubt truth to be a liar,*" said Trek, who'd started so would finish.

"And I think she's the mother of my one . . ."

"*. . . But never doubt I love.*"

"Google it, Gigi — there's a website. Tinderboxtarot.com. I use the word 'website' loosely, mind . . . A truly shitty little website — it's rather sweet . . . Then there are two young kids belonging to the *Daily Mail* couple next door, but I don't think we need to pay much attention to them. They're not much use to us."

"Oh yes they are," Gigi said. "Seriously. Always got to be super-nice to the kids."

"And finally," Geordie continued, "I'm fairly certain the only other person living on this street is the beardie dude at the far end. He may yet prove to be our greatest hurdle — or our greatest friend. Or neither. But in any case — until we can actually trace who owns this beautiful new home of ours, I think the name of the game . . ." he stood and stretched his elegant limbs "*. . .* has to be Operation Ingratiate."

"Codename Tinkerbell," muttered Trek. Which was droll enough, for someone in the middle of sawing a metal grate. But the three of them were so fed up with each other, it didn't occur to anyone to laugh.

Geordie sniffed his armpit, exposed from the stretch. "I need a wash." There was no shower at Number Seven Tinderbox Lane. Nor any hot water, yet. "I think I'll head over to Killer Kale's. Use his bathroom. See you guys later."

Nobody bothered to reply. He patted his jacket for tobacco and headed out onto the lane — where, as chance would have it, he discovered Pippa still on her cigarette break, sitting on the doorstep outside Windy Ridge, staring at the moon. It was a beautiful moon.

"*Doubt thou the stars are fire. Doubt that the sun doth move*," murmured Geordie, "*Doubt truth to be a liar* . . . Beautiful moon, isn't it?" he said.

And that was the beginning of that.

CHAPTER
FIVE

Inside Windy Ridge, meanwhile, Dolly's welcome-home dinner had taken an argumentative turn. Sergeant Raff Williams, Professor Derek West and Mrs Rosie Buck were united in their determination to oust the squatters from Tinderbox Lane, no matter what. Nor was Dolly exactly delighted to hear of their presence on her street — but (she argued), the house had been empty for so long . . . and considering the homelessness in London, and the number of uninhabited houses, and the ridiculous price of London property and so on, it struck her as mean-spirited and narrow-minded at least not to entertain the idea of giving the squatters a chance.

"They might be lovely people," she said, somewhat half-heartedly.

Derek groaned and rolled his eyes. Raff shook his head. Rosie tutted sorrowfully. And Pippa, whom Dolly felt might have supported her, was having the longest cigarette break known to humankind. Dolly was on her own. "Well, but they *might* be lovely!" she said. "And they might be desperate and homeless and in any case, frankly, what's it to us? It's not our property they're squatting in. And if they're friendly people, it might be rather nice, perhaps, to have some younger blood on the lane." She didn't really believe it. But, on the other hand, she didn't much appreciate the kneejerk hostility of her middle-aged companions, either. "I'm just saying," she said — she addressed herself mostly to Raff, whose business it wasn't but whose opinion she cared about most — "let's give them a chance!"

"I don't think so," said Rosie. She stood up, exuding disappointment, offence — *hurt* — at having gone to the trouble of cooking for someone who turned out to have such a stupid and dangerous point of view: "It's all right for you, Dolly. You haven't got kids."

"I have," said Dolly. "In fact — I'm wondering where she's got to."

"I mean, *young* kids. Impressionable kids."

"I'm with Rosie on this one," said Derek — as if that was news. "It's all very well, this bleeding-heart liberal whatnot. It has its place, yes, it surely does. But not on Tinderbox Lane. Not when there are kids involved."

"And not in this day and age," added Rosie.

"Agreed." Derek nodded. He reached a long arm across the table, spoon in hand, and scooped another gobful of toffee-caramel fondant from the dish. "So. Dolly," he continued, "with apologies — the question is, what to do next. Raff — you're a man of the law. What do you suggest?"

Raff glanced at Dolly. He cared far more about keeping in her good books than he did about any squatters moving into Number Seven. Even so, he thought she was wrong about giving them a chance. In his professional experience — which (to be fair) was not small — squatters only ever brought trouble with them, and he wanted to protect her from that.

"Depends if the squat's been designated residential," he said. "Let's assume it has . . . In which case, it shouldn't be too difficult. They're breaking the law, and they can be evicted fairly quickly. But you can't begin any kind of proceedings against them until the owner of the property files a notice of eviction. So. First of all — who owns the property?

Derek, Rosie and Dolly looked from one to the other.

"It shouldn't be too hard to find out," Raff said.

"Well — but I know that my husband, Fraser, was trying to get to the bottom of that before . . . before everything. He wanted to buy it and sort of expand. As if this kitchen wasn't already big enough . . ." Rosie paused. A look of tremendous sadness fleeted across her face. She swallowed. "Anyway I don't think he got very far. He said he was hitting a few roadblocks."

"All well and good," said Derek. "But given the way things have turned out — and I don't mean to be rude — but, I mean, can we actually believe a single thing that hubby of yours ever said? I would moot, not."

Rosie blushed. Dolly thought she might be about to cry. "Maybe, Rosie," she said quickly, "you can have a look through what papers he left behind. If he left any. It might give us a lead — don't you think? And I suppose," Dolly conceded, mostly because she hated to see Rosie looking so wretched, "it might be helpful to know who owns the place — just in case things turn nasty. Though I'm sure they won't."

"Excellent," said the professor. "Solid advice from Dolly and from the sergeant, if I may say. First things first, then. I suggest we Organise to Formalise. As they say in the army."

"Do they really?" muttered Dolly.

"We need to discuss all this with the other residents. Do we know what they think? Are they even aware of the situation? We simply don't know. I suggest we reconvene — here, at Windy Ridge, due its capacious kitchen area. Are you happy with that, Mrs Buck?"

"Ooh, absolutely," said Rosie.

"— within the next few days. As soon as our Brazilian friend and — what's the young fellow called at the end of the street? — as soon as they can be enticed — or possibly dragged — to the table."

"I don't think I can face spending an evening with Terry," Dolly said. "He's a very depressing man."

"*Nonsense!*" said Derek. "All in a good cause!"

Dolly didn't reply. The professor's noisy, nasal tone was beginning to grate. Soon she wouldn't be able to stop herself from being rude. She pulled a face at Raff, who'd been longing to leave for some time, and abruptly they both stood up.

The professor saw them out, issuing orders and fine-tuning plans as he followed them across the bleached white floorboards of Rosie's hall, right up to the moment he finally closed the front door behind them.

The silence had never seemed so beautiful.

"*Ahhh!*" sighed Dolly, breathing in the cool air. The night was fine and moonlit still. And Pippa was nowhere to be seen. Dolly tutted. "Pippa must have just gone on home. I don't blame her — a bit rude though."

"Shall we check?" said Raff. It wasn't a ruse to get himself invited back to Dolly's place — or not entirely. After so many years as a police officer, confronted every day by the worst of human stupidity and cruelty, the fact of a young woman slipping out for a cigarette and disappearing into the night left open too many horrible possibilities. "Or maybe you should call her?"

Dolly checked her mobile. There was a message from Pippa. It had obviously been tapped out in some haste.

Sorry to abandon u Mum. Prof Filthy driving me nut. Wll send thanx Mrs frosty-duck in morngn. Gone to pub w friend. See i later xxx

"*Really*," she laughed, showing it to Raff. "Who brought that girl up?"

"And who's Mrs Frosty-Duck . . .?"

"Mr and Mrs Fraser Buck . . . Mr and Mrs — actually it's Frosty-Fuck. Pippa has a filthy mouth . . . Anyway, it's because when the horrible Fraser was around poor Rosie always looked so sort of pristine and like butter wouldn't melt . . ."

Raff chuckled. It made his handsome, broad shoulders shake.

"She's a bit of handful, your young Pippa," he said. It was a surprisingly good impression of their host. Dolly burst out laughing. "But she's not, you know. She's wonderful."

They stood quietly for a moment, in the lovely moonlight, wondering what to do next. The situation was awkward and, considering their age, slightly

48

absurd. Dolly would have liked to invite Raff back to Tinderbox Lane for the night — but how could she, when she and Pippa shared the same bed? Since her divorce there had, of course, been a small handful of relationships: generally short and unsatisfactory — certainly none that threatened the equilibrium of her relationship with her daughter. And none, to be brutal, with a man whose home was a twenty-year-old caravan in a corner of Barnes Common. (And whose pet, kept in a large reptile cage in a false bottom beneath the caravan bed, was a beloved 70 lb python.)

But now, here was Raff and here was she, standing on the moonlit lane, neither knowing quite what to suggest or where to go ... Somehow she and Pippa were going to have to find a way around this situation which didn't — as Pippa might say — completely gross them out.

"We could go back to my pope-mobile, if you like," said Raff. "It's not exactly the Ritz, but ..." Since his own divorce, many years ago now, Raff Williams had never quite got around to buying himself a house. He had lived for his work, and for those alternate weekends with his clever son; and in the beginning his son had thought the motorhome on Barnes Common (with added python appeal) was a great novelty. There had been very little incentive to upgrade it. Since then, of course, Raff had always been meaning to find himself a flat somewhere, or a little house ... but then the years had rolled by, and London property prices had rocketed ... Until this moment, right now, in the moonlight, his lack of bricks and mortar had never bothered him. "I'm sorry," he said. "It's not ideal, is it?"

"*Don't be silly.*"

"Really? It's not too uncomfortable?"

"Noooo! Of course not," she said. And corrected herself. "Well, it's quite cramped, isn't it? With the snake and all . . . But we can manage." She wondered if maybe one day he would consider perhaps upgrading to — anything, really, would be an improvement on the van. But it was too early in their relationship to suggest such a thing.

In the meantime, here they stood. Too old for this silliness. Dolly giggled. "We're like a couple of teenagers," she said. "What shall we do, then? Do you want to come back for a quick drink? And then, I don't know, maybe —"

A violent *clang* echoed from somewhere inside Number Seven, making Dolly and Raff spin round in alarm. It was only Trek, working on his barricade, hammering bits of metal, but they weren't to know that.

"*Raff!*" whispered Dolly, staring at the little cottage. "They've got *lights* on! They've got *electricity* in there!" Her good-natured liberalism wavered. It was all very well not objecting to the idea of squatters, even squatters moving into your own precious street. But this was something she hadn't considered. "I hope I'm not bloody well paying for that!"

CHAPTER
SIX

Marina gazed out from the back window of the Number 209 bus. It was two o'clock in the afternoon, and she had just finished a six-hour cleaning shift at a bed and breakfast in Hammersmith. She worked a lot: she had the cleaning job Monday to Saturday and a second job four nights a week, checking coats at a members club in Mayfair. She also kept house for her lazy boyfriend (waited on him hand and foot), and attended a course to improve her English twice a week.

And that was fine. One step at a time. One day after the next. She had no choice but to keep on going. And on going. And on.

It didn't stop her from dreaming, though. And as she looked out through the dirty bus window onto grey skies and roadworks and anoraks and puddles, she imagined herself basking under a canopy of Californian flowers, under a blue Californian sky — dressed in a fluffy white wedding dress and diamante tiara, glowing under the loving gaze of her man —

Who was scrubbed and tuxedoed and upright and looking . . . quite different from the one she'd left snoring in her bed this morning. These days, she hardly saw her boyfriend standing up, anyway. The idea of his wearing a tuxedo was preposterous. It didn't stop her from dreaming.

And one day it would happen. One day, he would lift his lazy arse off that sofa and pull a small, square box out of his back pocket, and get onto one knee, and change into a tuxedo, and drop the ring into a glass of Champagne, and she would have a wedding planner, and a string quartet and a red Ferrari, and a canopy of Californian flowers, and a mother and father in co-ordinating wedding gear, wiping their eyes, looking on . . .

Marina's parents were long dead. Nothing about them had ever co-ordinated. And the bus was arriving at her stop. She rang the bell, pulled the big puffa hood over her head and prepared for the rainy trudge home. The flat where she and her boyfriend lived was in a long, quiet street just behind Barnes High Street, equidistant from the beautiful, desirable Barnes Pond at one end and the beautiful, desirable River Thames at the other. It was on the upper floor of a two-storey line of Victorian terraced houses, purpose built as maisonettes: so the property had its own front door, and its own stairway. All of which, as Marina knew well, added value. The place would have been worth at least £750,000.

It wasn't large, however, and beneath her and her boyfriend's accumulated mess, it was still decorated in the dead old lady's 1950s furnishings. Marina didn't like it much. Nevertheless, it was home. And it was valuable. And she knew exactly how valuable, because she went online to compare it with the sale prices of similar properties in the area at least twice a week. It was a constant source of encouragement.

Marina thought of Russia, and her old parents, and of the small apartment she used to call home. The loneliness whistled on. She didn't notice it, because it never stopped. She had an impression — or the impression of an impression, perhaps — of a previous life when the man she lived with could sometimes drown the noise out: a life when he and she plotted and planned, and the rest of the world seemed like nothing more than a bountiful, unreal fuzz of free stuff, waiting to be taken. This impression — what others might call a "happy memory" or even "friendship", wasn't anything she thought about or hankered after. It was, simply, part of the current greyness. Part of the woman she had become, and part of her connection to the only person, other than her mother and grandmother, she had ever lived with. The two of them had been through some big experiences together. But Marina never looked back. She only held on. And plotted and planned. And survived. She was stubborn, and lonely, and necessarily sly, and not very bright — and above all, a long, long way from home.

As she trudged doggedly onward, Marina remembered they were low on teabags, and so took a lengthy detour to the least expensive corner shop to stock up on more. But the shop had sold out of their cheapest brand. She left without buying anything, and trudged on, tea-less, through the rain.

This was only today, after all. Tomorrow was bound to be different.

She was still young. She was still lovely. And who knew? Maybe tonight he would be waiting for her with that ring he had promised, and some beautiful, sweet-smelling blue flowers in a vase, and a freshly run bubble-bath . . .

Marina delved into the bush beside the front door and pulled out a rusty chisel. She and her boyfriend didn't own a key to the flat — her boyfriend had lost the only one they ever possessed many moons ago, and to replace it would have involved buying and installing a whole new lock: an unnecessary expense in Marina's eyes, and an unnecessary bother in the eyes of her boyfriend. Instead they had a system, very neat, involving the chisel and a specific nudge and twist to the top lock. Not everyone could master it, but nifty little Marina could do it without thinking, without looking: she could turn the lock, open the door and return the chisel to its hiding place while simultaneously checking her Instagram.

As it turned out, the bath was already occupied when she let herself in. Not by her lazy boyfriend, who was lying on his back in a similar position but different spot to the one she had left him in, almost eight hours earlier. At some point, clearly, he had shifted himself from bedroom to sitting room. Also, judging by the dirty cup and plate on the coffee table beside him, he must have made himself tea and toast.

Marina scooped up the dirty crockery on her way to hanging up her coat.

"Hello, love," he said. "All right?" He was busy with his hands, rolling a joint, and he didn't look up.

54

She passed the closed bathroom door en route to dumping the cup and plate in the kitchen, smelled soap and heard the splashing of water. "Who is that in there?" she asked.

He didn't reply at once. He was smoking.

"Why is someone in bathroom?" she asked him again.

". . . what's that, love?"

"Who is in bathroom?"

"Oh." He waved a lazy, tobacco-gnarled hand, exhaled a gust of cannabis. "Pal of mine. Got no water at his place . . . Is there a cup of tea going? Actually he's been in there ages — I'd forgotten about him. He'd probably like a cup, too."

Marina turned around, back towards the kitchen, and as she did so the bathroom door opened and out stepped Geordie. God-like, frankly, in that sordid flat. He was a handsome lad at the worst of times. But this was quite an entrance. His dark, damp hair was swept back, and the steam from his hot bath swirled majestically behind him, presenting that well-honed torso (life is unfair), and lean hips to really quite dramatic advantage. Trumpets should have been playing. He looked like Caesar, Marina thought. She missed a beat. Personal pleasure — sexual or aesthetic — was a low priority in her day-to-day life, and it took her a moment to recognise it. She looked him up and down, and up and down again, and gave him an astonished, and dazzling smile.

"My God," said Geordie, seeing that beautiful smile. "I think I hear trumpets playing . . . You must be Marina?"

The smile vanished, replaced at once with the usual surly suspicion.

"Who are you?" she said.

"I'm Geordie. Just moved into a place round the corner . . . Unfortunately we don't have any water — so I was borrowing yours. I was going to come last night when you were working but . . . as luck would have it —" he grinned at her "— I came today. And beheld an angel. Hope you don't mind? Kaylin said it was okay."

The angel didn't blink. She said: "Hot water cost money."

"That's right," he replied, stung by his lack of effect. "Which is why we don't have any. It's called 'sharing' . . . Not something you Russians tend to embrace much any more."

The corridor that opened onto the bathroom and kitchen was not large, and each was blocking the other's path onward. If either was ever to progress, one of them would have to budge. It was Geordie who relented — of course. With wry, post-feminist irony (lost on Marina) he flattened himself against the wall, steam rising from that muscular chest: "*Ladies first,*" he said. She brushed past him into the kitchen — to be confronted, as ever, with idle Kaylin's midday detritus: a blackened frying pan with congealed half-rasher of bacon; a dehydrated splodge of baked beans on the floor, and beside it, lying on its side, an empty ketchup bottle. Kaylin was not a young man: closer to fifty than thirty, no longer the blond-haired pretty boy of his youth, but a scrawny and jaded-looking man: there was little very pretty left of him. From the way he lived, and dressed, and talked — and from the people he called his "pals", it was clear that his self-image had lagged some distance behind the reality — and showed no signs of ever catching up.

Geordie's voice, slightly mocking, came from behind her. "Did I hear Kaylin mentioning a cup of tea?"

She took them both some tea. Then she cleared up the kitchen: she washed the frying pan, wiped the beans off the floor. Finally she made herself some toast, and took it with her into the bedroom. She had another job starting in five hours and she needed to get some sleep.

To say that Kaylin did nothing at all, all day, every day — would be an exaggeration. Everybody has to do something in life, and sometimes the act of safeguarding one's own idleness can be more demanding than doing anything else. This was not quite Kaylin's situation, but he had dedicated a lifetime of wily effort to his own inactivity, and by and large, he managed it well . . . Best of all, he liked to be lying on the sofa in his free flat behind Barnes High Street, a joint in one hand, and some succulent part of Marina's young body in the other . . . (For such an idle man, he had a remarkably strong sex drive.) And in truth, despite Marina's two jobs and language classes, he did spend quite an impressive proportion of his time doing just that.

Even so, he didn't do *nothing*. Of course not. Everybody needs to make a bit of cash every now and then — and Kaylin liked to supplement what income came his way with a little small-time dealing, preferably from the comfort of his own sofa. It was really nothing much — a bit of weed; a bit of low-grade, heavily cut coke, when he could get his hands on it; some ketamine; some roofies . . . He kept them, and the cash they generated, in a largish metal safe box — bought from Ryman's one day in the foggy past — tucked away under the floorboards in the sitting room, under the rug, under the sofa, which was Kaylin's favourite spot. Since he was generally lying on the sofa above it, there didn't seem to be much point in keeping it locked. But there was a key — of course. Somewhere around.

Marina was lying quietly on the bed watching *Beverly Hills 90210* on her back-of-lorry iPhone. She heard Kaylin shouting for her, and she waited. Sometimes, he would shout a few times and then give up . . . On this occasion, sadly, his voice became increasingly agitated. With a sigh, she paused the show and left the bed to find out what he wanted.

He had moved. His entire body was in a different place. This, in itself, was a mild shock. The rug had been pulled back. He was on his knees, arse in the air, head hovering over the gap in the floorboards. The god-like figure of Geordie — less god-like now — was hovering above him, a look of great concern on his face.

"MARINA! Where the fuck is the fucking . . ." Kaylin's voice was muffled by the floorboards. Anyway, the word he was looking for didn't spring to mind.

Marina, leaning against the doorframe, watched him for a moment and didn't speak.

"MARINA!"

Geordie glanced at her apologetically, embarrassed by the tone of his pal's voice. "Kaylin was going to sell me a bit of weed," he said. "But he thinks the stashbox may be locked."

"Have you fucking locked the box, love? What the fuck did you wanna do that for?" He was really angry — not so much about the box being locked as the added effort its locked-ness necessitated for him to complete his business.

"I have lock it," Marina said. "Too many people coming in this place now." She indicated Geordie. "Your friend, coming here for his bathes . . . And when I working you leave sometimes door open. Anyone can take."

"All right . . ." said Kaylin, his head emerging from between the floorboards. "So where's the fucking key?"

She shrugged. "Of course, it is where it always is."

"What? Well — I mean, seriously, love. Give me a break. Where is it usually then? I can't fucking find it anywhere."

Marina indicated with her chin, since her arms were folded. "The key is there. Under box. Is easy to find."

"I can't fucking see it," Kaylin said, staring at her. So she crossed the room, got onto her knees, delved in the dust between the floorboards and immediately presented him with the key.

He sighed, a huffy schoolboy sigh, leaving her still holding it, and clambered back onto his sofa, exhausted. "Honestly, love," he said, resting his head so that his eyes looked up at the ceiling. "You'll be the death of me. Can you sort him out? He only wants £20-worth anyway. I don't know why I fucking bother."

Marina unlocked the box.

In general, Geordie disapproved of transactions involving money, but sometimes there was no avoiding them. And he was still human, after all. As she lifted the lid, Geordie saw that the box was crammed with cash: notes of different denominations, each bound efficiently together by elastic bands (Marina's work). It was hard to be sure, but he reckoned there must been at least a couple of thousand pounds in there. His eyes bulged of their own accord. Luckily Kaylin was still looking at the ceiling, and Marina was attending to business, so nobody saw it, but Geordie felt it: he felt his heart miss a beat at the sight of all that money, and was ashamed.

"That's a lot of cash," he said casually. "I'm not surprised you keep the box locked, Marina. You should be thanking your beautiful girlfriend for looking after it so well, not yelling at her . . ."

Kaylin sighed, and said, words slurring somewhat, "Piss off, pal."

"I'm serious."

"Just coz you wanna fuck her."

"Just because I . . . what?" Geordie was embarrassed. "Don't be a twat, Killer my mate. I'm just saying — you should show her a bit of respect." He turned to Marina. "My apologies, Marina. I'm sorry your boyfriend is a fucking idiot. I don't know how you put up with him."

Marina didn't look up, and didn't reply, and neither did Kaylin.

Geordie watched her at work, neat little fingers at the little weighing scales. She had lovely hair. Thick, dark hair, cascading down her slim shoulders. How could she stand to live with this man? On second thoughts the answer to that was obvious. Who was he kidding? Killer Kayle owned his own flat (although quite how that came about remained a mystery. And Geordie could joke about it well enough — but it wasn't a question he actually wanted to probe too deeply.) Meanwhile the girl, Marina, was illegal, presumably. She probably reckoned that if she played her cards right, the stupid sod might even marry her one day. Christ, what a world it was. He felt sorry for her.

He really did.

"Did you hear me, Killer?" he said, feeling quite angry suddenly. "You're an idiot. You should apologise to Marina."

There came no answer, only a loud snore. Kaylin was fast asleep.

CHAPTER
SEVEN

They were sitting at the breakfast bar one Saturday morning a week or so after Dolly's return and, normally, it should have been a pleasant moment. But today, they sat in silence: Pippa sullenly checking her phone, Dolly, infuriatingly, trying to guess what it was that was making her daughter so hostile. There had been a hum of distrust between them ever since the dinner at Windy Ridge, and Dolly hated it.

"What's wrong, Pippa?" she asked her yet again.

"Nothing," replied Pippa. Again. "I already told you. I'm fine. Have you got many readings booked this afternoon?"

"I know there's something wrong . . ."

"There's nothing wrong, Mum. Everything's fine."

Dolly gazed at her daughter. "There is," she said at last.

"I saw someone outside Putney Tube station the other day — handing out fliers for Tarot readings . . . Maybe you should do that? I can help you, if you like."

"That would be good," Dolly said. "Next time it's quiet." But she was not to be distracted. "How about I read your cards, Pippa? Just for once. Just for fun."

"No thanks, Mum."

"But the cards can help you."

"I don't want you to read my cards!"

"Pippa, *what's wrong?*"

"Oh, for God's sake! *Nothing* is wrong!" Pippa snatched up her leather jacket, lying in a heap on the only armchair. "I'm going for a walk." And with that, she more or less ran out of the house — in such a hurry that she left her phone behind.

Dolly didn't need Pippa's phone in any case. She had her own way of prying into her daughter's private affairs. As Pippa well knew. She didn't like to do it too often — it was, she felt, no different from reading her daughter's diary (if Pippa kept a diary, which Dolly highly doubted). But needs must. And if Mohammed wouldn't go to the mountain —

Pippa's mobile bleeped.

— then the mountain would come to Mohammed. Dolly ignored the phone, and picked up the Tarot pack instead. The cards would tell her what was up with her daughter, even if Pippa didn't want to play along.

She pulled three cards, and Pippa's mobile bleeped again.

She turned over the cards —

— and only then, and only to confirm what the cards were suggesting, did she turn to Pippa's mobile. It was locked — of course. But there were two messages, the top lines of which were visible; both from someone called Geordie:

Hey — you around?

And

?Che? Just seen you striding past m . . .

Dolly made herself a fresh cup of coffee and waited for Pippa to return. She was back before the kettle boiled — looking grumpy and unhappy, but also a little shamefaced. She apologised. Dolly said:

"I'm sorry too. I was poking my nose in . . . By the way, you left your phone . . ."

Pippa was already bent over it, checking the messages.

Dolly watched her: saw her daughter's face and shoulders relax. She thought, whoever this wretched "Geordie" is, he'd certainly made quite an impression.

"I read your cards, Pippa."

Pippa grinned. A different girl to the one who had stalked out of the house moments earlier. "I knew you would."

"You're not angry?" Dolly asked. "I thought you were going to yell at me."

Instead, Pippa laughed. "And what did they say, Mum? Tall, dark stranger? Something along those lines?"

Dolly didn't smile. "That's right, Pipps . . ."

Pippa's smile faltered. "And he's going to whisk me off on a white charger, right?"

"I wouldn't have said he was planning to do that," said Dolly. "No. No, I wouldn't have said he had any intentions . . . along the knight on white charger lines."

"Yeah — I was joking, Mum."

"Mmm . . . I wasn't."

"No. Of course you weren't."

"Pipps — I know it's none of my business. I *know* you're going to tell me to keep my nose out, and I don't

64

blame you. I'm just saying — I don't think he's a keeper."

"Oh for goodness' sake!"

"That's all. That's all I'm going to say . . . Just — please. Look after yourself."

"Mum, I'm twenty-two years old. I may still live at home, but *I am not a baby*. And you've never met him. And you don't know what you're talking about. And for the record I'm not actually *looking* for a 'keeper' as you put it, I'm looking for a bit of fun. And I've found it. All right? So, please. Mind your own business — and leave me to make my own mistakes."

"Of course! Of course I will. And I'm sorry . . . But what do you expect me to do? I can't say nothing, can I? Not when I know. Maybe I shouldn't have read your cards, but I did, and now — Who is this 'Geordie' man anyway? How can he have seen you striding past in the last few seconds —" Dolly stopped, realisation dawning. "Oh my, oh, Pippa! *Pippa! Don't tell me . . .*" She laughed — she wasn't certain why. Nerves, mostly. "Don't tell me you're sleeping with one of the squatters! You are *ridiculous!*"

It would have been hard, really, for Dolly to have been any more infuriating. She was aware of it and tried her best to pull back. "I don't mean *ridiculous*, I mean — what do I mean?"

"I don't know, Mum," Pippa snapped. "What do you mean by ridiculous?"

"Oh, I don't *mean* ridiculous . . . I just mean, *why?* What do you want to do that for? Of all the men in this great, big city . . ." She laughed again, more heartfelt this time: "For heaven's sake, Pipps. What are we going to tell Mrs Frosty-Fuck and Professor Filthy?"

Pippa couldn't help laughing.

Dolly said she wanted to meet him. Of course. Pippa said it was out of the question.

"But he only lives a few doors away, Pipps! And if he's —"

"He's *not*. Nothing. He's not *anything*. We're just having fun. All right? You don't get it — it's nothing like it was in your day . . ."

"Oh come on! You're still human, aren't you?"

"Yes! *No.* Everything's different . . . And just because . . ." Pippa didn't want to continue, and actually Dolly didn't want her to, either. Maybe things were different these days. Maybe young women, like her beautiful, precious daughter, really could climb into any number of fun-filled beds without the slightest emotional fallout. And maybe elephants could fly. In the meantime, this young man — Squatter Geordie — Dolly didn't need Tarot cards to tell her, she only needed to look at the light in her daughter's eyes to know that he represented a lot more to Pippa than just "fun".

A silence fell. Finally, with a sigh, Dolly conceded. "Well, if you don't want to introduce us, I understand. Maybe it's a bit awkward. Just take care of yourself, will you? Some people aren't very nice."

"Squatters, you mean?"

"Don't be dim." Dolly didn't bother to defend herself after that, and Pippa left soon afterwards. She hugged her mother before she left, but they didn't quite look at each other.

Dolly said, "Are you back tonight? If not, I might ask Raff over . . ."

And Pippa said: "No — yes. *No.* I don't know. I'll probably stay at Nicole's. I haven't seen her for ages . . . So — whatever. Invite Raff — or don't. I mean. Whatever you want, Mum. I won't be back tonight."

Mother and daughter heaved sighs of relief as the front door closed between them. This was not how it used to be. Dolly felt like crying.

CHAPTER
EIGHT

She bumped into the professor and Rosie a couple of days later. They were all dolled up, frocked and suited, and heading out to dinner together. Their faces puckered in commiseration the moment they saw her. Rosie opened her arms and gave Dolly a massive hug.

"I. Am. *So*. Sorry," she said. "No mother deserves that. Least of all you."

Dolly couldn't work out what they were talking about. It became clear, soon enough, that they had spotted Pippa and Geordie "groping each other", as the professor put it, outside the front door to Number Seven, and were consequently well up to speed with what Rosie referred to as Pippa's "unfortunate romantic situation".

"It won't last," Rosie said. "Don't you worry! Girls go through these phases, don't they?"

"May I ask," said Derek, "where, exactly, is *Mr Dolly Greene* at this juncture?"

"He's in Ealing," said Dolly. "With a new wife. And a new family."

"Hmmm," said Derek. "Well, don't you think he might want to weigh in?"

"Weigh in, how? What's he going to say? Anyway, he and Pippa don't really talk."

"Well, if *he* won't weigh in, Dolly, and do the fatherly thing, then I'm more than happy to put myself forward. As father-proxy. As it were. If it would help. Only say the word!"

Dolly thanked him politely, and changed the conversation. She asked him if there was a date yet set for the next Residents' meeting.

"You may well ask," said the professor. "And I'm glad you did."

It was taking longer than he or Rosie would have liked, he said, for two reasons: Terry-at-the-end would never answer his front door. And Isabelle Ferrari/Lucky Crystal had informed Derek ("can you actually believe it?") that she wasn't keen to get involved.

"Maybe it's not so surprising," said Dolly, who had yet to exchange more than the tersest of greetings with her new neighbour. She leaned forward, dropped her voice. "She's not terribly friendly, is she? Mind you, it might be more than that. To be fair. She might be a supporter of squatters' rights. After everything that's happened to her, she might be very political . . ." In the meantime, Dolly couldn't deny that her own initial pro-squatter stance was feeling somewhat tested, now that her daughter's emotions were involved.

"Yes, I bet!" said Derek. "I should think you've changed your tune a bit, have you? Don't you worry, Dolly. We're getting pretty close to identifying the property's owner, and once that's done and dusted, it's all guns blazing! That louse'll be out of Tinderbox Lane and, I sincerely hope, out of poor young Pippa's knickers, before you and I can say 'Peter Pan'!"

Dolly ground her teeth politely, and moved on.

A couple of weeks passed, and despite Rosie and the professor's best efforts, nothing much changed. Gigi, Trek and Geordie slowly made themselves more comfortable at the end of the lane, and Pippa's relationship with The Louse gathered steam. They spent a lot of their time at the squat, but seemed (so far as Dolly could tell) to sneak into Number Two to use bath and bed as soon as Dolly went out. And poor Dolly, so wretched about the cold front which had settled between her and Pippa, and so desperate not to antagonise her daughter, made a point of staying away and allowing her space. She stayed with Raff at the motorhome, which was cramped and uncomfortable, and came with a python.

But she had to go home at some point. There were clients to see — and clothes to wash.

The first time she met Geordie he was walking down her stairs naked but for a dressing gown which belonged to Dolly, and which was unfastened at the front. The sight of his bare skin didn't have quite the effect it had on Marina. On the contary, Dolly was infuriated. His presence in her house was the reason she'd been keeping away. But even so, *really* . . .

To be fair to Geordie, he looked appalled when he saw her. He froze — they both did. Finally he

70

remembered himself, did up the wretched dressing gown and said:

"You must be Mrs Greene."

"I must, mustn't I? And you must be Geordie. And that, unless you happen to own the same one, which I doubt, must be my dressing gown."

He pulled it tighter around him. "Oops."

"Yes."

"It's very nice to meet you, Mrs Greene . . . Actually I was just saying to Pippa it would be nice to meet you and now — here we are. Meeting."

"We certainly are. Perhaps you should get dressed . . . Where's Pippa?"

Pippa appeared behind him at the top of the stairs, looking dishevelled and embarrassed, wrapped in the household duvet.

"Why don't you both come downstairs," said Dolly coolly, "and we can have coffee together."

It wasn't an enjoyable or relaxing coffee break for any of them. But it was in everybody's interests that they got along — and Geordie was as aware of this as any of them. He collected his wits while he was dressing, and by the time he came downstairs he was on full charm offensive.

First he apologised for the "unfortunate" manner of their meeting, and then — clever lad that he was — set about asking Dolly a stream of intelligent and well-mannered questions about the Tarot.

"I would love to have a reading one day," he said. "Would that be possible?"

"You can't afford it," Pippa said quickly. "Forget it."

71

"On the contrary," interrupted Dolly. "As a friend of Pippa's, Geordie, I would be happy to give you a reading for free."

"What?" Pippa looked aghast. "Why? You never give my friends readings for free."

"They never ask."

"Well — nor did Geordie."

"Yes, he did. And I'm offering him a reading for free. Right now. How about that, Geordie? I don't suppose you've got much going on this afternoon, have you? Of course you haven't. Let's do a reading right now!"

"Mum . . ." It was the last thing Pippa wanted. "This is silly. I thought you said you had a client . . ."

"I said nothing of the kind! My next client isn't for another hour." She stood up. "So come on, Geordie. On your feet! You said you wanted a reading. Put your money where your mouth is! Or don't, actually. As I say, this one's on the house."

"But Geordie doesn't really want —"

"Oh I don't know about that, Pippa . . . I think I really do, actually," said Geordie, sounding languid and amused. "If your mum's up for it, so am I! Thank you very much, Dolly — can I call you Dolly? — I would love to have my cards read."

He stood up.

"Mum!" Pippa cried desperately. "Stop! You know he doesn't believe in any of it!"

"It didn't occur to me that he might," said Dolly, grimly. "Come on then, Geordie. Let's see what the cards have to say about you."

As he trotted behind Dolly through the kitchen to the broom cupboard beyond, he turned back to Pippa and grinned. Like the thing was a joke. Pippa did not smile back.

Idiot, she thought.

CHAPTER
NINE

Geordie disliked not being on top of a situation. And being a clever young man, he rarely wasn't. But the tone of this little encounter — which three minutes ago had seemed like a jape, something to be witty about to his friends later — had quickly taken a more solemn turn, and though he would die before he admitted it, he was a little frightened. The smell of incense scratched at the back of his nostrils and Scary Tarot Lady, sitting opposite, was looking dour and scary indeed. He had chosen the cards in silence, as she instructed. She was gazing at them intently now, not speaking a word, and it seemed to him suddenly that he had made a dreadful mistake: as if his fragile, important future was now lying brutally exposed. He fought the urge to cover the cards from view, or even to crumple them up and run.

It was all nonsense, of course.

He wore a silly smile in case she looked up — in case his friends could see him through the tiny window with the silk blind across it, above the back door. After a while, when the silence became unbearable, he asked her:

"So. *Quid mihi futurum est, fortuna loquitur?*"

"Is that Latin, sweetheart?" said Dolly, without looking up.

"It is, actually . . ." He laughed self-consciously. In that little room, with the cards between them, it had sounded unexpectedly pretentious.

Another long silence. She could sense his great discomfort and yet Dolly, normally so kind, felt no inclination to set him at ease. He had strutted into her broom cupboard like a lamb to the slaughter, quite convinced he would emerge from it the victor: and now here he was, talking to her in Latin, and here were his cards, *telling her all sorts of things* she would have preferred not to know . . . but which she needed to know to protect her daughter. There were other matters on display here too: a lonely childhood . . . a cold and clever mother. No sign of any father at all (or not on the table). Dolly set herself many rules — moral as opposed to commercial — when reading for her clients: rules that forbade her from saying some things and compelled her to say others. But this was different. He was not a client, he was a freeloader. A freeloader who had strutted into her broom cupboard thinking he could outwit the wisdom of the universe, while wearing her dressing gown, squatting in her street, and *sleeping with her daughter*.

. . . The Seven of Swords and the Nine of Cups lay one on top of the other at his core: pleasure and deceit, deceit and pleasure — he was having a fine old time with her beautiful, precious daughter, and if he wasn't deceiving her explicitly, or not yet, he had every intention of it — rather, no intention of *not* . . .

"It's all about you, isn't it, Geordie?" Dolly muttered.

"Well — yes. I would have thought so. After all I'm having my cards read." He leaned against the back of his chair, crossed his legs, and prepared to feel more relaxed in the situation.

Arrogant little sod. She would have liked to empty a glass of water on his head. But she couldn't do that. Obviously. She had a duty — not just to her daughter, but to the cards. And they were telling her things, and she needed to listen . . . He'd been cruising through life lately, cruising through life since the day he was born, really — learning the talk, but not feeling a thing . . . *Cruising for a bruising*, as they used to say at school . . . And yet, beneath it all . . . She turned over the Knight of Cups, and then the Four of Swords — yes, there was a heartbeat in there; feeble and yearning, waiting for the magic kiss that might bring him to life.

Dolly smiled. "A sleeping beauty," she muttered. "I know you don't feel it — you don't feel a thing, do you, Geordie? *But you're not dead yet.*"

He laughed, of course, because he had to. And yet she'd touched a nerve. Sometimes he wondered about that very thing: he wondered whether he was missing out on something — whether he was somehow not really a whole person, or if everyone felt as little as he did and, when they talked about "love", "joy" and "sorrow", whether they were all just pretending. He didn't know. He never knew. But then, when he thought about it too intently, he realised that he must be able to feel something, because fear would come bubbling to the surface — fear and the most terrible loneliness. Dammit. Scary Tarot Lady was good! She was like that famous interviewer — who was it? — who could always make his subjects weep. Geordie felt his eyes stinging. *How humiliating!* He uncrossed his legs and crossed them again. He cleared his throat. Said nothing. And began to feel better again.

Dolly turned over three more cards.

The Devil.

Death.

Justice, reversed.

And slowly exhaled. She looked up at Geordie . . . saw the silly, innocent smirk stuck on his handsome face. *Poor boy*, she thought, *cruising along with that cumbersome brain of his. He doesn't have a clue.*

"Goodness," he said. "You look like you've seen a ghost."

She said: "No. I'm looking at you, Geordie. Trying to find some words that might hit home — that might just persuade you to listen."

"Try them in Latin," he said: it was meant to be self-deprecating; a boyish acknowledgement of his earlier prattishness. But she didn't smile.

"Geordie," she said carefully. "The cards are suggesting to me that you may be heading for stormy weather ahead."

"*Twas a darrrk and storrrmy night*," he said. "*And the wind was blowing a'gale . . .*"

"What you're getting into right now —"

"*And the captain said to Antonio, Antonio tell me a tale!*"

She ignored him. "Whatever it is you're getting yourself into right now, you're not equipped to deal with it. Are you listening? You're out of your depth. Do you understand me? You're young. You're innocent, though you may not think so. This thing you're embarking on — the stakes are very high. Much higher than you can understand. It's not as simple as you think."

He stared at her. What was she talking about? Not Pippa, surely? They were just having fun . . .

Dolly shook her head. "And no, I'm not talking about Pippa. Though by the way, I can tell you now, it's not going to end well."

He nodded politely. Geordie's relationships with women didn't really involve "beginnings" or "ends", in any case. Or not as far as he was concerned. They came and went — ebbed and overlapped and flowed.

"But as I say, I'm not talking about Pippa. I'm talking about something else, Geordie . . . something you're embarking on. You're not equipped to deal with it. It's bigger than you are and it's going to . . . it's going to blow up in your face. It's going to be nasty unless you're very careful. Do you understand? Is there something in your life you can relate this to?"

What the hell was she talking about?

Finally, in that big brain of his, the connections were made. He groaned. Christ, he was stupid! And for a moment there, she almost had him! What was he doing in this stupid cupboard anyway, listening to this nonsensical drivel? Was he a fourteen-year-old girl?

He stood up. "I think I understand you, yes," he said, and then he laughed. It was a disagreeable laugh. "Gosh, you must think I am very stupid."

"Far from it," replied Dolly, slightly perplexed. "Although there are so many different ways to measure it . . ."

"Well, Mrs Greene," he said, leaning across the table towards her, "how about you measure it like this: the house at the end of your road is not the first property I've squatted, and it won't be the last . . . and I am — believe me — *well aware* of what I am 'getting myself into'. A lot more aware than you will ever be. So you can rest assured, that I, and my crew, and the entire network of London crews we have at our disposal — are more than 'equipped' to survive the legal brickbats and petty, bourgeois snobberies of Tinderbox Lane." He shook his head and laughed, hardly able to believe the absurdity of saying it. "I can tell you this. It'll take a lot more than a Tarot reading to frighten us off."

He made the mistake, dramatically speaking, of pausing to see how she responded to his speech before stalking out of there. Dolly burst out laughing.

"What's funny?" he said. "I don't see anything very funny . . ."

"You are," she said.

"No. *You* are, Mrs Greene. *You* are the funny one."

"If you say so." She was till chuckling as she collected up her cards. But he was right — it wasn't funny, not really. He hadn't listened. He wasn't ready to listen. Whatever it was that was coming his way was going to hit like a thunderbolt — and it was too bad. As

79

she straightened the cards and fitted them into their box, a single card plopped out of the pack.

She turned it over already knowing what it would be.

Sometimes images have more impact than words, and the image of the Tower card was designed to alarm. In the blackest of skies, lightning can be seen striking an upper floor. The Tower is crumbling, and two figures, their mouths open in terror, are tumbling head first towards the rocky ground below.

Dolly left the card lying there for a moment, to ensure that Geordie saw it.

As he gazed at the card, she felt his fear, and she felt for him. She didn't like him — not at all — but he was still human. He was young, and he was important to her daughter. "How about you climb down off that high horse of yours," she said, "and stay for supper?"

"What?"

"Stay for supper. You look like you could do with a decent meal." She smiled. "I'm a good cook."

He was confused. And disconcertingly tempted. Supper in a real house, with hot water and heating and clean corners and full bookshelves and matching plates and actual adults to talk to . . . was something he'd not experienced for a long time. Something he despised, of course. On the other hand — *every once in a while* . . . "I don't think so."

"Risotto," she said. "You won't get a better risotto this side of the Thames."

Geordie said, with great dignity: "Actually, I'm mostly vegan. Anyway, I'm busy."

"Stay for supper," the Scary Tarot Lady said again. It sounded like an order this time. In any case, he told himself he didn't have a choice.

CHAPTER
TEN

So Dolly called Raff at work and advised him not to come for supper that night after all. It would have been too uncomfortable. Geordie and Pippa would have been insupportable, and Raff, in his taciturn way, wouldn't have been much better. It had become clear to Dolly that her police-sergeant boyfriend felt as antipathetic towards Oxford-educated anarchist squatters as Oxford-educated anarchist squatters felt towards police sergeants. It would not have been enjoyable for anyone.

As it was, the evening passed in a civilised haze. Dolly, Pippa and Geordie discussed the ebb and flow of trade union powers — which nobody knew enough about for an argument to develop — and how to cook the perfect risotto. Geordie, who could be very charming, ate three helpings and told Dolly that it wasn't simply the best risotto this side of the Thames, but the best risotto he had eaten in his entire life.

And though Pippa longed to know what had gone on between them in the broom cupboard, neither was willing to say. Finally, at about nine-thirty — not very late, really, but just late enough for it not to be impolite — Geordie and Pippa slipped away. They were going to drop in on a pal of Geordie's who lived around the corner, and probably stay the night at Number Seven.

Left alone, Dolly pondered Geordie's cards. She was about to pull them out again, spend more time meditating on their meaning, but then Raff called. He'd just finished a shift and he wondered "what Dolly was up to", so she invited him over.

Late the following morning, while Dolly was in her broom cupboard with a client, she heard the front door banging, and, with a lifted heart, knew that Pippa had come home. It meant the coldness between them was beginning to thaw at last. Or, at least, that Pippa was no longer avoiding her.

She was sitting on the front garden wall, smoking a rollie, when Dolly shepherded her client out of the door twenty minutes later. "There you are at last!" Pippa said, slightly too soon, and very slightly louder than Dolly would have liked. "I thought you'd never get rid of her!"

They hugged each other, and that was that. It seemed that a truce had been called.

"So guess what?" Pippa began.

"I can't . . . Have you got time for some coffee?"

Pippa had a lecture in a couple of hours, and a shift at the pub that evening, and yet more job applications to complete — but she definitely had time for coffee. "So listen to this," she said, unable to contain the gossip a moment longer. "You remember that Russian girl whose cards you read the other day? The one who was waiting for you when you got back from holiday?"

Dolly paused, Nescafé jar suspended. "*Well!*" she exclaimed. "And isn't it peculiar you should mention it? Of course I remember her! Believe it or not, I dreamt about her last night! She thought her boyfriend wanted to murder her. And yet she was still desperate to marry him." She laughed. "I dreamed about them going on a long cruise, and the ship falling off the edge of the world."

"All right — well, she did!"

"Did what, Pipps?"

"She married him!"

"*No!* How do you know?"

"Because I saw her again last night. The boyfriend — and by the way, FYI, Geordie calls him 'Killer Kayle' . . . Turns out he and Geordie are quite good friends."

Dolly pictured the beautiful Russian girl with her ferret eyes, gazing out from inside that anorak . . . so young, so stubborn, so unhappy . . . "Geordie calls him Killer Kayle? Why?"

"Because everybody thinks he killed the old woman who used to own the flat — I mean the flat that . . . I thought you said Marina told you all this stuff in the reading?"

"I'm not sure," said Dolly carefully. "What did Geordie tell you?"

"So the flat that belongs to Kaylin — it's around the corner from here, on Eddison Grove. And it was left to him by this lonely old woman who died — and I can't tell if Geordie's joking, or what, but in any case, she doesn't seem to live there now. Whether or not he killed her, who knows . . .? But Kaylin definitely does live

84

there now, along with that Russian girl, and a whole lot of old-lady junk which couldn't belong to anyone but an old lady; and yet the flat seems to belong to him. Or so he says . . ."

"Slow down, Pippa . . ."

She didn't. "We all went round there last night. That's where we went after dinner —"

"Sorry — 'we' being . . .?"

"Being *me, Geordie,* and his two housemates: Trek, who's pretty cute, actually, in a public-school sort of way. Geordie says he's secretly loaded. And the other one — don't laugh — she's called Gigi. She's sweet. *Very* left wing. They all go round to Kaylin's to wash, because the flat's got hot water and a bathtub and so on . . . And we went round there last night after the risotto, for a — well, for a drink — all right? And who should be sitting there, licking her paws like an evil cat that got the cream — *that horrible Russian girl!*"

"Marina?"

"*Yes,* Marina! Wearing a ring on her wedding finger — which Geordie said Kaylin probably snaffled out of the old lady's jewellery box before he did her in . . . But I think he was joking. He actually said it to Kaylin's face —"

"Bit rude," observed Dolly.

"Well — but I'm pretty sure he was joking . . ."

"I hope so . . ." Dolly said. "And what did Kaylin say?"

"Nothing. He wasn't making much sense by that stage . . . at all, in fact." Pippa frowned. "He was boasting about the flat being his, how it was worth all this money and so on. And he was pawing at Marina — which was gross . . . really gross. He was groping her — literally at one point he had his hand in her bra, as far as I could tell, and she was just sitting there, chatting away with Trek — absolutely ignoring him. Like it wasn't actually happening." Pippa shuddered. "Repulsive man. So anyway . . . That's that! Marina married him! She got the guy! Not much of a catch, frankly. But, you know. He's on the property ladder, isn't he?"

Dolly smiled. She was picturing the girl's cards, remembering how adamantly devoid of celebration they were, how certain Dolly had been that there would be no marriage. Something wasn't right. And in Dolly's experience — it was unlikely to be the cards.

"By the way, I think Trek's shagging her," Pippa added, after a pause.

"What — who? Who's Trek again?"

"I told you, Trek's one of the squatters. He's actually in a relationship with Gigi, the girl squatter — but Gigi's quite a free spirit. So it's all a bit tense."

"So Trek is sleeping with Gigi?" Dolly said. "Is that important?"

"No! You're not listening. Trek and Gigi are in a *relationship*. But I think he's shagging Marina. Or if he isn't, she definitely wants him to — Geordie kept teasing Trek about his private wealth . . . And every time Geordie mentioned it, Marina sort of purred and edged up towards him — I mean, *Trek*. Kaylin was comatose on the sofa by then — which is apparently a pretty normal state of affairs — so *he* didn't notice. But I think he's suspicious. Because earlier, when . . ."

Pippa paused, and thought better of whatever it was she had been intending to say. "And Gigi too. I think she was subtly getting quite pissed off about it, which was a bit much considering how free-spirited she is. And as for *Trek* . . . well, obviously, Trek was having the time of his life!"

"What nice friends you have, Pipps."

Pippa laughed. "I'm just telling you the gossip, Mum. I thought you'd be interested."

And of course she was. Not so much about Gigi and Trek, but the news about Marina was more than interesting — it was shocking.

"Are you sure it was the same Russian girl?"

"Of course I am! Anyway she recognised me."

"And are you *certain* she got married?"

"*Yes*, I'm certain! Of course they got married. She wouldn't stop talking about it . . . Poor girl. Geordie says she's only doing it to get legal status here. Which is obviously true. I mean it's got to be . . . That and for the flat, of course. But I mean, even so . . . things have to be pretty desperate to want to marry a man like him."

Dolly nodded "He certainly doesn't sound like a great catch . . . It's just so strange . . ." She leaned across the breakfast bar and surprised Pippa by taking hold her hands: "And having met this man, Pippa, do you think he's a killer?"

Pippa took her hands back, embarrassed by Dolly's intensity. "Well, *I* don't know! I only met him once."

"Come on. You've obviously considered it."

Pippa frowned. She didn't like the question. She'd only wanted to share the gossip — didn't want the responsibility of really thinking about what might be going on in that flat. It was too creepy. "Honestly," she said, after an unhappy pause. "I can't work it out. He's like a little rat —"

A ferret.

"He's got these little ratty eyes — and it's like — no matter how messed up he is on whatever, or if he's laughing, or if he's groping Marina . . . it's like he's always on the case — you know what I mean? He's got the coldest, most calculating little ratty eyes . . . So . . ." Pippa shrugged. She laughed self-consciously. "Maybe I'm getting carried away. But it's a weird set-up in there, that's for sure. Not happy . . . *Nasty*. He's a nasty piece of work, Mum. But whether that makes him a killer . . ."

Pippa had excluded a few elements from her account of the evening: the drugs, mostly. And the impassioned political discussions, which she had enjoyed but which she knew would make Dolly roll her eyes.

Kaylin, before he checked out of conversation altogether, didn't think much of his friends' diatribes either. He was more concerned about a meet-up scheduled with a supplier later in the evening — before closing time, on a bench overlooking the river, outside the White Hart pub. He had forgotten about it, or so he said. The man had called him, apparently irate, and from his sofa-throne, his hand inside Marina's shirt,

Kaylin had soothed the man accordingly: Marina was on her way. She would be with him in a few minutes.

"You're sending her out there on her own?" Geordie asked him. "Are you sure it's safe?"

And Kaylin had shrugged. "He likes her." He glanced across at Marina, who was on her feet already, wrapping herself in the anorak, and gave her a weaselly smile. "Doesn't he, love? Doesn't like dealing with me. Plus . . . she's so gorgeous, she gets a discount. Gotta be Marina. Isn't that right, love?"

She didn't reply. She took the money he handed her and with quick fingers and beady black eyes began to count the notes.

"Most of it's there," he said. "Tell him he can have the rest next week, yeah? He won't mind, if it's coming from you."

"But you can't . . ." Trek stood up. "She can't go out there alone. While we're all sitting here. It's not right."

"It's fine," said Kaylin, an edge to his voice that hadn't shown itself before. "Sit down, mate. You're not going anywhere with her . . . Off you pop, love. Quick as you can." He grinned at her. "I'll keep your seat warm."

Pippa, until this point, had been feeling somewhat intimidated by the political passions and casual drug-taking of the evening, and yet she heard herself speaking up: "It does seem a bit weird," she said. Kaylin turned to look at her, almost, Pippa thought, as if he were focusing on her face for the first time. As if he'd forgotten, until that moment, that she was in the room. Pippa turned to Marina: "Why don't I come? I'll keep you company, if you like?"

Kaylin said: "I don't think he's into threesomes, love."

Pippa blushed. Marina gave a drab, unkind little laugh.

There was an awkward pause. Only Kaylin and Marina seemed at ease with the situation. Geordie — to his credit — stood up. In a tone that sounded casual and yet didn't brook dissent, he said: "I'll go with you, Marina. I'm not into threesomes . . . not ones involving park benches and bad-tempered drug dealers, at any rate. I'll wait up on the road for you. All right? That way the guy gets the pleasure of your company without me wrecking the mood. And, y'know, if there's any trouble, I can . . . raise the alarm."

"Very noble!" said Gigi, remembering why she fancied him. "I'd go. But I don't think I'd be much use . . ."

Kaylin lost interest. As long as it wasn't Trek, he didn't really care: and as long as the meet-up went ahead, and he didn't have to move from his seat. "Whatever. Hurry up, though. The stupid twat won't hang around for long."

They returned forty-five minutes later, by which time Kaylin was out for the count. Geordie was mid-sermon: something about the evils of profit maximisation principles. At the end of it, by which time he was back in his seat, his arm wrapped around Pippa, Marina let out an impatient sigh.

"But I don't give you a fuck about it," she said.

Geordie smiled. "I think," he said, "you mean, you don't give *a* fuck about it. But you should, you know. If you believe in justice, and I believe you do."

"I mean," she said, smiling at him. "I don't give *you* a fuck about it. Your politics ideas are bad. I like man who make money for woman, not talk talk talk: make all the poor people live *behh*, like him. Poor and stupid. *You* are stupid. No clotheses, no holodays, no hope. This is disgusting to Russian girls now."

Gigi giggled. "Looks like you got yourself a convert, there, Geordie."

"Yep! Job well done, Geord," added Trek. Annoyingly. He was irritated he hadn't gone with Marina himself. But then they all rolled another big fat joint. And the evening moved on.

CHAPTER
ELEVEN

Not surprisingly, perhaps, Pippa was suffering from quite a nasty hangover. It hadn't kicked in over coffee with her mother in the morning, but by late afternoon she was feeling rough. Not ill so much as dispirited. She was always a little depressed after a big night, and this afternoon was proving to be no exception. Fortunately — or so she thought — she had a shift at the pub this evening. It would keep her busy, and keep any gloomy thoughts at bay.

But then the pub cancelled her at the last minute. She was back from college and heading out to work when she got a call saying she wouldn't be needed. It was bad news on two fronts. She needed the money. And now she had no plans for the rest of the afternoon or evening. Her mother was out. She called Geordie. But he wasn't replying to any messages — as usual. And nor was her usual fail-safe, her closest friend, Nicole. Everyone seemed to be busy. It was only 5 p.m., and it looked very much as if she would be stuck at home for the evening: all alone with her post-high low, and nothing but her wretched thesis for company.

Pippa had thought a lot about Marina's situation through the day: hadn't been able to think about much else, in fact, except the weird, possibly murderous, set-up at Eddison Grove. Whatever the truth, it was hard not to come to the conclusion that Marina was stuck in the middle of it, somehow: a victim (though she couldn't see it) of a mighty unfair world. Pippa decided she felt sorry for her.

She gazed at her laptop. The words *macro-environmental factors: effective competitive analysis* gleamed cruelly back. There was no chance she'd be able to concentrate, not while the mysteries of Eddison Grove continued to linger in every corner of her mind. Perhaps Geordie and co. were over there, right now? Perhaps they were all getting high together, and she was missing out on a party? She didn't feel like getting high in the middle of the afternoon. But she definitely wanted to get out of the house.

When Marina looked down from the first-floor window to see who was ringing the doorbell, she assumed Pippa had come to buy weed. She opened the window and asked her if she knew how to get in. Pippa had seen Geordie doing it — it hadn't looked hard. So she delved for the chisel, lying in the bush beside the door, and a moment or two later, was climbing up the stairs to the flat. Kaylin was on the sofa, fast asleep, and Marina was in full war paint, a beautiful, dead-eyed alien in her sparkly earrings — and that ridiculous anorak. No one else was around, Marina told her, and she was on her way out.

"You want buy weed?"

Pippa said, "Errr — well, I haven't brought any money."

"They why you come? Kaylin not give credit."

"Actually I was just dropping in to see if Geordie and co. were here. But I guess they're not."

"No."

"Oh." Pippa glanced around her. It was a horrible, creepy flat: it smelled of must and cannabis. But it could have been lovely . . . if you cleared out the clutter, redid the heating, electrics, window frames . . . everything, pretty much . . . It needed money spending on it for sure, but the estate agents of Barnes would have been unanimously enthusiastic about its potential. The place must have been worth a fortune. "Well never mind . . . Are you very busy, Marina? Don't suppose there's a cup of coffee going?"

The question took Marina by surprise. She had no expectations of friendship here in England, least of all with another woman. But something seemed to shift when Pippa said it, as if that simple question — that tiny act of friendliness, if not of friendship — had plucked a chord in her stony, lonely little heart. In any case, Marina shrugged, in stony Russian fashion, and took off the anorak again. "You want milk, sugar?"

They perched opposite one another, sipping instant coffee — not in the sitting room, where Kaylin lay comatose on the sofa, but in the middle of Marina's unmade bed, which served as a sort of unsavoury island amid a surrounding sea of stale-smelling clothes.

It was awkward from the start. Marina had no conversational skills whatever — and Pippa's early

94

gambits: "It's a bit chilly isn't it?", "How's married life?!?", "Shame about the roadworks on Hammersmith Bridge" — were met with solemn, monosyllabic responses and deafening coffee slurps.

Pippa decided to up the ante. Mention the elephant in the room — the thing that had been haunting her all day and night. She said: "It's a bit weird, isn't it, the way Geordie calls Kaylin 'Killer Kayle'. Don't you think?"

Marina shrugged. "Kaylin he don't like."

"I'm not surprised! . . . It's a bit weird, though, isn't it?" Pippa said again.

Marina gazed at Pippa: "You are asking, is it true?"

"What? No, of course not!"

"You want to know if Kaylin kill Mrs Linklater?"

"Mrs — ? No! God, no . . . I mean he didn't — did he?"

Marina smiled. "No, of course. Anyway it's not important. The old lady she is dying soon anyway."

"What do you mean?"

She laughed. A dead little laugh. Pippa couldn't tell if she was teasing her. "Maybe he push her along with the pillow, squeeze down." She mimed the action. "Maybe he make a help for her. Sometimes this life, when you are old." She gave a small shrug and its apparent carelessness took Pippa's breath away. "You are happy when someone help you make it over."

"You think that's it? You think Kaylin did her a favour?"

She said: "But I tell your mother this already — it is not so important. You are missing important point."

". . . which is?"

Marina's cool eyes rested on Pippa a moment longer, and then she seemed to lose interest. She said: "Anyway, I am searching Geordie. Like you. He must to give me money for bath. He and his friends. Where are they?"

"Geordie? I don't know." Pippa wasn't ready to let the subject go quite so easily. "So, Marina — are you saying you don't mind being married to that guy, even if he killed someone?"

Marina said: "I have not say that, no."

"But if you think he killed her —"

"I have not say that."

"But if you *don't* think he *didn't* kill her . . ."

"Pardon?"

Pippa laughed. "I mean — don't you worry at all? If maybe he did kill her . . . that, you know, once a killer, always a killer and all that."

"How you know this?"

"It's an expression, isn't it?"

"No. I have not heard this." Marina finished her coffee. She stood up from the bed, and reached for that massive anorak again. "I go now," she said. "I look for Trek and Geordie and — the girl. Please tell it to them."

Pippa took a final gulp of coffee and followed Marina out of the room, tripping on a tangle of extension leads between door and corridor as she went. "Christ," she said. "All these wires, Marina! It's a bloody death trap!"

"Next time you want Kaylin weed," Marina said, "you bring money, yes? No money, no weed. Just coffee." And she smiled. And there it was: something sweet in her smile — as if, deep inside that anorak, beneath all that war paint, was a human heart, and a sense of humour, and a need for friends.

But now wasn't the time. Marina ushered Pippa along the corridor, past the slumbering Killer, and followed her down the stairs and out onto the street. At the end of the road they went their separate ways, Pippa to her thesis and Marina to her basement cloakroom in Mayfair.

No more than a minute after Pippa had settled back at the breakfast bar and opened up her computer, there was a bang on the door.

It was only six o'clock. The evening might yet be saved. Praying it wasn't Rosie Buck and/or the professor, she went to answer it, and found Geordie standing there, looking shifty (Pippa assumed because he was hoping to avoid her mother). He said he was trying to avoid Marina.

"She wants to get money off us for the hot water," he said, eyes roving past Pippa into the room beyond. "It's bloody ridiculous . . . Is she here?"

"No. Why should she be?"

"Oh — that's strange. Trek said something about you guys having tea . . ."

"How would he know that?"

Geordie grinned, ruefully. "He's a bit obsessed . . . I think he spotted you both coming out of the flat."

"Oh? So why didn't he —"

Geordie glanced behind Pippa, nervously. "Is your mum home?"

"No . . . D'you want to come in?"

His eyes swivelled back to Pippa's face. "Your mum's not around?" Another big grin. "You bet I want to come in."

So.

After that — brief but sparkling interlude of intense reciprocity — Geordie took a bath, as he always did when at Pippa's, and Pippa sat on the edge of the bathtub and chatted. They talked about Kaylin.

Geordie hadn't known him for long — only for a couple of years, since he arrived in London. He was Geordie's friendly dealer — nothing much more than that, initially. But then they spent a bit of time together, getting high, and, said Geordie from the bathtub, "Well, you know, it's nice to have a civilised relationship with your dealer, isn't it? He was the one who told us about the empty place on the lane. He's pretty cool. He's a good guy."

"*Good?* Are you sure about that?" said Pippa.

Geordie, rinsing suds from his thick, dark locks, sent a sharp glance at Pippa through the bubbles. "What do you mean?"

"Well — you call him Killer Kayle. You must have a few reservations?"

"It's a joke," he said coldly, and dunked his head underwater.

Pippa considered this until he re-emerged. "It's not a very funny one though, is it? Anyway, I don't believe you. It's not a joke. Marina thinks he did it."

"Bollocks. No she doesn't."

"I think she does."

"Bullshit."

"Not bullshit, Geordie. He's weird. The whole set-up is weird. Don't pretend you haven't noticed . . . He lies on that sofa, ordering Marina about, treating her like a cross between a slave and a prostitute . . . And then he passes out. What's with the passing out? What *is* that?"

"He does it all the time."

"Has he got narcolepsy?"

"I don't think so, no," Geordie said. "I think it's the roofies." He laughed. "I actually think Marina drops them in his tea, to keep him quiet. Just to get a bit of peace."

Pippa absorbed this. She was torn between laughing — after all, Kaylin deserved nothing better — and calling the police. "Geordie, if that's true, that's pretty fucked up."

"Oh, nonsense! It's *funny*, Mrs Grundy. He deserves it. Don't be such a prude."

"She's *doping* him. Don't you think you should do something about it? Say something?"

"It's between them."

"Geordie, if he was giving it to her, it would be tantamount to — I mean, everyone would assume it was date-rape. You can't just go around drugging people to keep them quiet. It's disgusting!"

Geordie guffawed. "Trust me. I don't think she's date-raping him."

"I'm saying if it was the other way round, he'd be locked up . . ."

"So what? What's it got to do with us? He's a pain in the arse. Have you seen the way he talks to her? She deserves a break — don't you think?"

"Of course —"

"Anyway, I suspect he half knows she does it. He's a lazy bastard — I should think he's quite pleased."

"That's ridiculous."

"Really? How so? Think about it: a girlfriend who does everything; cleans the house, earns the money, looks sensational, cooks the dinner, fucks like a rabbit on heat (so he says) . . . *and* administers roofies, free of charge, so he can spend the rest of his life sleeping it off . . . Forgive me for being crude, Pippa. *But where's the downside?* It's pretty much every man's wet dream. He doesn't deserve her."

Pippa stood up, offended and — as had perhaps been the intention — jealous. "Every man's wet dream she may be, Geordie. But your friend had better watch his back. The way Marina was talking about the old woman this afternoon, I wonder if it wasn't her who did her in. And now she's married to your friend, she's got everything she needs from him. She hasn't got much reason to keep him alive, has she? You should tell him, next time he's too bloody lazy to make his own tea — it may be his last."

She left the room.

His laugh followed her down the stairs. ". . . that's right, Pippa. Blame the little foreign girl, why not?"

"Don't be pathetic."

"And then you wonder why women can't get ahead in this country!" he shouted after her. "It's not men

100

keeping them back, it's *women like you!* Jealous, petty-minded, racist, misogynist . . . Always ready to cut your own sisters down to size."

She ignored him, returned to her computer and tried to concentrate on her work. He joined her soon afterwards, fully dressed, looking rueful and smelling of Dolly's soap.

"Sorry," he said. "Think I got carried away there . . ."

Pippa didn't look up. It was going to take more than that.

"I was a prick — I was being an idiot. I'm sorry, Pippa. Really, I am." He contorted himself over the breakfast bar so that his head obstructed her view of the computer keyboard, and he smiled. "Please, Pippa . . . forgive me?"

She pushed his head away.

"I just feel for her a bit. That's all. Watching the way Kaylin treats her. It's so awful . . . and then you, going for her like that. She's a sweet girl. Really, she is, when you get to know her."

"I'm sure she is," said Pippa, not certain at all. "Let's just forget it."

"Please let's," he said. "And I really am sorry . . ."

". . . I've got a lot of work to do. Shall we catch up later?"

"*Definitely,*" he said.

But they didn't catch up, not properly. Not ever again. Though they didn't know it that afternoon, it was the beginning of the end. Their days of intense reciprocity were done.

CHAPTER
TWELVE

Three and half weeks previously, when Professor Filthy first knocked on her door to suggest forming an Association to remove the squatters on Tinderbox Lane, Lucky Crystal, aka Isabelle Ferrari, had been on her way to the lavatory. She was, in any case, a woman who liked privacy, disliked and distrusted men, and who did not appreciate neighbours dropping in willy-nilly. And so, to hasten his retreat, she had declared herself a communist, who believed passionately in the redistribution of wealth and in the right for the homeless to occupy property when and wherever they could . . .

It turned out she believed it a lot less passionately, however, when her bladder was empty and the property being occupied turned out to be her own. Maurice Bousquet's bequest to her was a gift that just kept on giving . . . It now appeared that he had left Isabelle not just his own small cottage, but four or five other properties in the area, including Number Seven Tinderbox Lane.

On discovering this, Isabelle had told Rosie (when they met on the lane) that she would have to set aside her poetry-in-Brazilian, at least for the time being.

"With wealth comes responsibility," she complained to Rosie, who nodded like a fluffy bunny should. "My properties have been neglected, and they need my attention. Every one of them. As far as Number Seven Tinderbox Lane is concerned, rest assured I intend to *push ahead with proceedings*, as you would expect." But what did she mean by "*proceedings*"? the professor asked Rosie when she reported it back. Rosie couldn't tell him. She could tell him, however, that Isabelle was now more than amenable to a meeting of the residents. She had asked Rosie to ask the professor to organise one as soon as possible.

Professor West received this welcome news while on a two-night conference in Communications Engineering at the University of York, but he tapped out an urgent message for Terry Whistle from his hotel room, emailed it to Rosie to print, and ordered her to hand deliver it, and if necessary to "lean on his ruddy doorbell until the little bugger comes to the door and grabs it out of your hot little paw."

That wasn't Rosie's style. She posted it through the letterbox. Fortunately for her, Terry read it and responded at once. He emailed Derek to express his disgust at the situation, of which he had been quite unaware until now — and to assure him that he would be available for a meeting at any time.

A date was set three days hence, on the evening of Derek's return. Rosie got cooking. And in the meantime Isabelle Ferrari, responsible woman of wealth that she now was, surveyed her growing empire, considered carefully which of the many "proceedings"

103

open to her would be most effective in which corner, and pushed ruthlessly ahead.

"Where have you been, wifey?" whined Kaylin. His head was propped on the armrest of the yellow draylon sofa. He lifted it a fraction so she could see that he was frowning. "I've been worried sick."

Marina didn't reply. It was early afternoon, and she was back from her cleaning job, as usual. She headed straight for the stashbox under the sofa where he was lying, opened it up and folded a handful of notes into the bundles.

"What's that then?" he said, watching her.

She didn't reply.

"Marina, love . . . I've been feeling very strange today," he sounded plaintive, like a child. "I think we should call a doctor."

Marina locked the box and put it away. She looked at him for the first time. "How you feel strange?" she asked.

He screwed up his face. ". . . Tingly," he said. "All over tingly. It's not right, is it? Like my hands and feet are numb. I think I'm having a heart attack."

"This is not heart attack," Marina said. "Maybe you need exercise. Fresh air. Go for walk."

It took a moment for her words to sink in. "You *what*?" he said at last. "Piss off. It's fucking raining." He wriggled his tingling fingers, and winced. "Bet you'd call the doc if that rich kid told you he was tingling . . ."

"What rich kid?"

"Tractor — Tonker Toy . . . whatever his stupid name is. You'd be all over him, untingling him all over . . . silly tart."

She shrugged — and headed to the kitchen. A copy of their marriage certificate had arrived in the post this afternoon. She carried the unopened envelope in her hand — she wanted to have a proper look at it without Kaylin breathing down her neck. "Maybe have bath," she said. "Hot bath sometime help with circulation . . . You want tea?"

He laid his head back on the sofa arm and closed his eyes. "Paracetamol, love. My head feels like a hundred fucking footballers are jumping all over it . . . with studs on . . . you know?"

She didn't reply. He hadn't expected it. He sank back into self-pitying silence, and waited for — well, nothing really. Whatever Marina did next.

The flat's tranquillity was interrupted — rudely interrupted — by an aggressive hammering on its front door — not a knock so much as a kick, immediately followed by a woman's voice, smoky and authoritative, educated — and slightly foreign.

"Open this door, please. We know you are in."

Marina heard it from the kitchen. *Immigration? Police? Where was the stash? Where were her papers?* She glanced at the kitchen window. It was only one floor up, perhaps she could climb out?

Another thump on the door, and then Kaylin's voice, more plaintive than ever:

"*What the fuck?*"

THUMP!

And then, quite clearly, the turn of a key, and the door downstairs slamming open.

". . . Marina! MARINA! They've got keys! They're coming up! What the . . ."

Marina hesitated. Should she make a run for it? She could — she could climb out of that window without any trouble at all — land on the front path and run like hell. Be gone. But then again . . . From the kitchen, she tiptoed into the short passageway and peered into the sitting room. Two strangers stood at the foot of Kaylin's sofa: a fat, middle-aged black man with a neck that was wider than his head, and beside him a glamorous woman in her fifties with a fragrant air about her: long, dark, glossy hair, heavy golden jewellery, patent black stilettos, suit trousers, fitted cashmere sweater . . . and — of course — a fucking amazing body.

"You are not Mrs Linklater," stated Isabelle Ferrari irritably. "Who are you?"

"Who am *I?*" snarled Kaylin. "Who the fuck are *you?*"

"Where is Sheila Linklater, please?"

"Fuck off. Sheila's on holiday. Now get the fuck out of my flat. Before I call the police."

She laughed at that: looked across at the fat-necked guy and they shared a chuckle. "Actually this is my property. And you are living in it illegally. What is your name, please?"

"You *what?*" gasped Kaylin. "How dare you come barging in here?"

Isabelle shook her glossy locks, and the stale air was, for a moment, filled with the sweet smell of

106

Chanel No. 5. "I don't like lawyers," she said. "And I don't want to involve the police unless I have to . . . I'm sure you don't want it either." She seemed to sense another presence in the flat. She half turned her amazing body towards the corridor, and caught the beady eye of Marina peering at her from behind the door. "Come!" she ordered Marina. "Come join us."

Marina edged into the room.

"This property," Marina said, "he belong to us. My husband and me. Call the police if you want. Or I call him." The two women eyeballed one another for a moment until, without breaking the contact, Marina indicated Isabelle's fat-necked companion. "Who this man? Why you come here disturbing us?"

Isabelle Ferrari didn't answer the question. There wasn't any need. Instead she said: "This flat does not belong to you. Sheila Linklater, who previously lived here, was permitted to do so by the previous owner of the flat, for reasons . . ." She paused: she had no idea. It didn't matter what reasons, anyway. "For business reasons. Anyway, the property belongs to me now." She held up a bunch of keys, as if to prove the fact. "And I am ordering you to vacate. You have . . ." Again she paused: took in the hostile ferret eyes of the young woman, and the man still lying on the sofa with his mouth open . . . He was, she thought, the embodiment of everything that was decrepit, entitled, soft and despicable about the people of this ghastly country . . . She had been planning to give them a month — but the sight of him made her change her mind. "One week."

"You w-what?" stuttered Kaylin. "You can't do that! It's my property. Sheila left it to me in the will — before she went on holiday. And unfortunately died."

Isabelle shook her head. "It wasn't hers to leave."

". . . I've got rights . . ."

"Maybe you do. Maybe you don't."

Marina stepped up. "Of course it our property. How dare you to say it? Kaylin — show her the paper. Now. Show her Sheila's will."

Kaylin looked flustered: "Pardon . . .? I told you. It's with my solicitor. In my solicitor's office. Along with a lot of other stuff . . ." He paused to relight his rollie. It took a moment, because his hands were clumsy. First he dropped the lighter, then he couldn't make it work.

"You can't show me any papers," said Isabelle, after it was obvious he had no more to add, "because you don't have any." She turned to Marina. "I don't know what he's been telling you, darling, but . . ." She laughed. "The flat belongs to me. And you need to vacate it by the end of the week. Is it clear?"

"No," said Marina.

Isabelle shrugged. "Well then, of course, I can involve my lawyers." She looked knowingly from one to the other. "If that's what you prefer."

Marina said: "I am married!" It sounded pathetic.

Isabelle said: "I am happy for you."

"This is our apartment. You get out."

Isabelle said: "He's been lying to you, my darling girl. This is not your apartment." She turned to her large companion, and addressed him briefly in

Portuguese. He nodded. She turned back to Kaylin and Marina: "So. We are going to take a look around."

"Like hell you are," said Kaylin. But he didn't leave his spot on the sofa. "Get out of my flat!"

They left a few minutes later — there wasn't much to see.

At the top of the stairs, Isabelle paused to examine a damp patch on the wall, and muttered something again: another instruction in Portuguese. Again, Fat Neck nodded.

"This," she said to Kaylin, "was a courtesy call. Please vacate my property by the end of the week. I hope you understand me."

"Not a chance," he said carelessly. "We have rights in this country . . . y'know." He laughed. It sounded a bit loose, as if his lips and voice weren't in sync. As if he was very stoned.

She took a last look at him and stepped onto the stairway.

"*Vacate your property indeed!*" he muttered to himself. "You're gonna have to kill me first . . . fucking dyke . . ."

The door slammed. And Kayle's head flopped back onto the arm of the sofa. The room was spinning. He was going to be sick.

CHAPTER
THIRTEEN

Rosie's kids had decorated the kitchen table with Easter bunnies made of cotton wool and toilet roll for the Tinderbox Lane Residents' Association meeting, called to render homeless their young idealistic neighbours. Rosie said: "It's that time of year again!" And everyone agreed that the kids and the bunnies were adorable.

ITEM NUMBER ONE on the Association's agenda needed to be dealt with before the meeting was even called to order: Does anyone present have a nut allergy?

Terry Whistle, the beardie dude from Number One, said he wasn't actually sure. Professor Filthy assured him that, in which case, he was more than likely in the clear, and Rosie was quick to reassure him that she'd not included nuts in any of the snacks laid out between the bunnies, only that India (7yrs) had been eating nuts earlier, so there may have been a few nut residues mixed in with the bog roll and cotton wool.

Having been lavishly complimented on their remarkable creativity, the children were dispatched to the media room, to watch *Frozen* for the 678th time, and the adults of Tinderbox Lane settled down to business.

Present at the summit were:

— Professor Filthy (chairperson)

— Rosie Buck (hostess, mother, Easter Bunny monitor)

— Dolly Greene (peacekeeper and psychic)

— Pippa Greene (squatters' friend and firebrand)

— Terry Whistle (unknown quantity: possibly the local idiot)

— And finally, of course, smelling of Chanel and making it difficult for the gentlemen to concentrate, Isabelle "the body" Ferrari. She was wearing reading glasses, carrying an expensive fountain pen, and scowling. Nonetheless, she smelled wonderful and her shirt was slightly transparent.

Raff Williams had declined to come — despite Professor Filthy's efforts. He was not, after all, a resident; also, lately, when the subject of the squatters came up, he and Pippa couldn't help arguing, and that would have made things disagreeable for everyone.

"May I say," began the professor as soon as everyone was correctly seated, "what an honour it is to have Ms Ferrari with us this evening. As you will all by now be aware, she is not only a resident of Tinderbox Lane, but the owner of the property in question. Among several other properties, so I understand! Mr Bousquet was certainly a dark horse, wasn't he? No offence intended . . . Anyway, Ms Ferrari — the *gorgeous* Ms Ferrari," he amended, quite unnecessarily, "perhaps you would like to kick us off with a progress report. Has an eviction notice been served at the property or is that still in the works?"

111

Isabelle nodded. "Firstly — I want to thank you from my heart. I have learned in my life there is nothing more important than good neighbours, and I feel blessed tonight, by your friendship and support."

"Not at all!" beamed the professor.

"Oh goodness, it's the least we could do," beamed the bunny monitor.

Dolly, Pippa and Terry, who'd done nothing so far but turn up to eat Rosie's nut-free canapés, each, in their own way, felt a little uncomfortable. This was the first time Dolly had met Isabelle for more than a barely polite greeting, and so far she didn't like or trust her any more — possibly even less — than she liked or trusted the trio of young squatters next door. Her "friendship and support" were by no means guaranteed. And Pippa, of course, was never meant to be here to offer support, but most adamantly to fight the corner for the soon-to-be dispossessed.

As for poor Terry — moments before Isabelle arrived, Professor Filthy had informed him, in a noisy whisper, of her previous career, and honestly he was paralysed; couldn't catch her eye, hardly dared to look away from the bog-roll bunnies. His groin was sweating, and he felt very conscious of the odour that seemed, suddenly, to be rising off his trainers. At that instant, friendship and support were the least of his concerns.

Isabelle Ferrari seemed oblivious to this — oblivious to all currents, all thought, feelings, hopes and dreams — except her own. The people were gathered here at Windy Ridge *for her*. The house next door belonged *to her.* The loathsome squatters needed to be ejected, For Her.

She'd dropped in on them two days previously, fat-necked Brazilian lackey in tow, but somehow the visit had failed to have the impact it had had on Kaylin and Marina. Far from being intimidated, the Oxford graduates had been arrogantly conscious of their "civil rights" — to the point where they seemed, almost, to be gunning up for the fight. Isabelle had called her lawyer immediately afterwards and — as she now informed the group — eviction papers were to be served on the squatters tomorrow. If they refused to answer the door, which they probably would, the papers would be gaffer-taped to the property and photographed for the court.

"But what if someone comes along and unsticks the gaffer tape?" asked Pippa. "Just because you photographed the documents, doesn't mean the residents actually receive them."

"Too bad for them," said Isabelle, cool brown eyes resting on Pippa. "The papers will have been served. Then it's just a matter of the hearing."

Pippa smiled. "It may not be as simple as that."

Isabelle smiled. "I think it will."

"No — not if it's a commercial space."

Isabelle's smile thinned. "But it isn't a commercial space," she said.

"But it might be," replied Pippa, staring right back at her. "It's got those north-facing windows, hasn't it? Someone in the Bull's Head where I work was saying they distinctly remember it was an artist's studio once . . ."

"Well, dear . . ." Isabelle paused. "I'm sorry, what is your name?"

"My name is Pippa. I live next door to you. And I came to this meeting to ask you *why*? Why are you so determined to throw these people on the street?"

"Now look here, young Pippa," interrupted the professor. "Really this is neither the time nor the place . . . for that sort of thing. If you've only come here to be obstructive —"

Pippa ignored him. "Until last week you didn't even know the house was yours," she continued. "You don't need it! After everything you've been through in life, I would have thought you might be a bit more generous."

"And what have I been through, dear?" asked Isabelle, her chilly eyes resting on Pippa's young, animated face. "What do you mean by that?"

"Well I don't know . . ." Pippa blushed, out of her depth. "I'm just saying . . . can't you at least give them a chance? What if they agree to do the place up? Make it nice so you can sell it — can't you just . . . you know . . . share some of your good luck? Is it too much to ask?"

A silence fell. Everyone waited. Dolly muttered something inaudible.

Pippa glanced at her. "What, Mum? What did you say? Come on! Don't tell me you don't agree with me. At least a tiny bit . . ."

But Dolly shook her head. "I'm sorry, darling. I wasn't listening . . . just — someone walking over my grave. Bad news must be on the way! What were you saying? *Is there someone at the door?*"

"I don't think so, Dolly," said Rosie. "Are you all right?"

Dolly noticed her daughter, looking defiant under the gaze of their disagreeable new neighbour. *Isabelle Ferrari disliked younger women . . .* And no, there was no one at the door . . . Dolly focused her attention. Her daughter appeared to be under attack. What had she missed?

Isabelle, laughing disagreeably, was saying something to Pippa: ". . . I admire your ideals, young lady."

"Thank you," Pippa said. "I wish you shared them . . . And by the way, you may think you have the law on your side, but you shouldn't underestimate what you're up against. There are squatters all over London and, you know, one call from the guys next door and they'll all be down here. Fighting for the crew. It's how it works. It's a whole, massive network. You can't just trample over these people and expect them not to fight back. You can't."

Isabelle's eyes bored into Pippa.

She more than disliked younger women, actually. And it wasn't sexual jealousy — quite the opposite. Isabelle had endured more than enough male admiration over the years (if admiration was the word: and no, it wasn't). She despised the men who drooled over her. She despised all men. But it hardly mattered any more. She was rich. Their lust, waning or otherwise, was irrelevant. Her feelings about her own sex, on the other hand, were more toxic and less easily dismissed. A young woman, like Pippa, who had never needed to indulge the repellent, unkind fantasies of men, who had no inkling of their true nature, tended to awaken the worst of her demons. A young woman, like Pippa, whose gentle life lent her the confidence to turn up in this house with no make-up and dirty hair and impose her spoilt, self-righteous opinions on her elders and betters, who had no concept of how lucky she was, or how worthless her sense of fair play in the real world . . . made Isabelle's stomach turn with jealousy and bitterness and sorrow: which three, combined, felt quite akin to hatred.

"Would you like to know what I have learned," murmured Isabelle, "'after everything I have been through in this life', as you put it?"

"Yes . . . Of course I would," said Pippa.

"You bet we would!" shouted the professor, keen to ease the tension.

"I have learned," she said slowly, deliberately, looking around the room, "that nobody cares about the poor."

"*Exactly!*" cried Pippa. "That's my point exactly!"

"Without money, one is nothing. One might as well be dead. You, my dear," she said, looking back at Pippa, "have had an easy life. I can see that. It's written over that young, pretty face. You can afford your English-girl ideals . . . for now. But you'll realise, in time, how worthless they really are. Nothing but noises. Because at the end of the day, *nobody cares*. Money is the only thing we can trust."

Dolly laughed. "Well, that's a bit depressing," she said. Isabelle opened her mouth to reply, but Dolly continued. "Seriously, Isabelle, if all you've learned from your own difficult life is how to make life difficult for everyone around you, then I suggest you haven't learned anything worth passing on."

Pippa grinned. Her mother's plain speaking had, over the years, been the cause of so much mortification, but moments like these made up for it.

Isabelle's glossy lips curled into another of her disagreeable smiles. "The *Tarot lady* speaks!" she said. It so happened that Isabelle's mother had been fond of the Tarot. Isabelle's mother had been into all sorts of peculiar, occult practices — the Tarot being the least of them. And if there was one thing Isabelle despised almost as much as men, and fortunate, fresh-faced young women (and squatters, and welfare scroungers and lawyers and politicians and police and . . .), it was people, like her mother, who believed in magic.

"I do speak," said Dolly. "And by the way, you may think my daughter is young and idealistic — well, after listening to that claptrap, all I can think is thank goodness someone is, frankly —"

"HAS EVERYONE GOT ENOUGH TO DRINK?" asked the professor.

They did.

"NO, BUT ON A SERIOUS NOTE, ISABELLE . . ." In his experience, nothing lightened a potentially awkward situation better than laying on a bit of high-decibel flattery. "Now that Pippa's brought it up. We're all of course *agonisingly* aware of what a dreadful, appalling life you've had —" he sent a meaningful look at Dolly "— first in Brazil and then —

you know, *here*. And I do wonder — I think we all do: you're such an exceptionally classy lady, if I may say. Such a *classy lady* . . . Isn't she, Rosie?"

"Oh, absolutely!"

"Don't you think so, Dolly, though?"

"Depends how you measure it," muttered Dolly.

"And I don't think I need to ask if Terry agrees with us!" the professor persevered. "Isn't Isabelle a classy lady, Terry?!"

But Terry couldn't speak. He'd suddenly noticed his shoelace was undone. So Derek turned back to Isabelle. "Bottom line, Isabelle, Rosie and I keep asking ourselves how a lady like you — so educated, so, you know, like the sort of lady we might encounter at a dinner party: how could you stand it, being a — well, you know — doing *what you did* in recent years? How did you survive?"

Isabelle didn't seem to realise at once that a question had been asked of her. She gazed at him with her cool brown eyes.

"Serious question, Isabelle," he tried again. "How on earth?"

Isabelle's eyes roved from one resident to the next until, inevitably, they returned their steely lock on to Pippa. "What has to be done, has to be done," she said.

Silence fell round the table.

And then came the knock on the door.

"*Goodness me*," said Rosie. "I wonder who that is?"

It was Raff, in uniform. Bringing bad news.

An adult male had been discovered, electrocuted to death by electrical charger, in a bathtub at a flat on

118

Eddison Grove, SW13. Police were attending the incident now ... Unfortunately the caller, having raised the alarm, had refused to remain at the scene. All efforts were being made to trace him or her, of course, but the mobile they had used to make the report was using an unregistered SIM card. "At this time it's not clear the identity or even the gender of the caller. In the meantime ..." Raff, standing at the threshold of Rosie's oatmeal kitchen, removed his hat. He looked at Pippa with utmost sorrow and gentleness: "The caller insisted that Pippa Greene of Tinderbox Lane would be able to identify the body."

CHAPTER
FOURTEEN

It's often the case, thought Dolly, watching her daughter check her phone for the umpteenth time in a minute, that the tougher a person appears on the outside the more fragile they are in their hearts. It was especially true for young people, of course, who put such a forlorn premium on appearing not to care. Pippa could seem hard, with that sharp tongue of hers, but she wasn't hard. She was brave. And never more so than at the mortuary that morning.

Dolly accompanied her, of course. Mother and daughter had sat side by side in the mortuary counselling room, listening as an attendant explained that there would be no need to look at the actual body. He could show her photographs, if Pippa preferred. Pippa said she did. So he reached for a file. Before passing it to her, he warned her of what to expect — some skin discoloration, burn marks, singed hair, slight blistering and bruising; nothing too horrifying, he assured her, and then he opened the file and slid a photograph of the deceased, face down, over the table.

It was quite unusual for a body to be found in a bath and for no one to know its identity, so any information she had, the attendant said, was going to be welcome.

He leaned in as she turned over the photograph, waiting for Pippa to speak. She didn't: not for some time. "I'm sorry," he muttered after a while. "I know this is upsetting. Can you tell us the individual's name?"

Pippa continued to stare down at the image for what felt like an age. Her chin began to tremble, and tears rolled down her cheeks. And then, disconcertingly, she started to laugh.

Dolly said: "Pippa? What's funny?"

"Nothing," she said. "Nothing is funny . . . nothing. I'm so sorry."

Dolly craned in to see the picture. "*OH!* . . . Oh, *well!* . . . That's a relief, isn't it?" she said. "I assumed it was going to be . . . Who is it, Pippa? Do you know him?"

Pippa looked up from the photograph to the mortuary attendant who was still waiting, tactfully. "He's called Kaylin," she said finally. "So far as I know. But I don't know his surname. We only met a couple of times. I hardly know him. I'm not really sure why I've been asked to identify him. Whoever it was who gave you my name — I don't know why they thought I might be able to help . . ." She slid the photograph back across the table, hugged her coat around her and stood up. "But I'm sorry. I can't help any more than that. I think I had better go home."

They offered to show her the physical body, which was lying in a room next door, "just to be sure" — but Pippa was adamant. There was no need. She recognised the face, but she barely knew the man. She didn't know

121

his surname, and she wanted to go home. She would have given them Marina's mobile number if she'd had it, but she didn't, so she gave them Geordie's instead.

"They're old friends. Sort of. Or anyway Geordie knows — knew — Geordie knew the guy a lot better than I do. Did . . . But I'm not even sure Geordie knows his surname, either. You really need to talk to his girlfriend."

Pippa and Dolly took the bus home. It was a beautiful, clear spring day outside; the sort of day that puts a bounce into every Londoner's heart and step. But not in theirs, not on that morning. The still, grey gloom of the mortuary stayed with them, and they spent most of the journey in silence, Dolly almost exploding with the effort not to ask questions, and Pippa in a world of her own. This was the closest she had come to death — and now that the initial, wild relief that the body in the morgue wasn't Geordie's had subsided, she was hit by the horror of it all, and by the guilt, too, which follows news of any suicide, no matter how remote.

It seemed odd — shocking — that Kaylin would have killed himself . . . He may not have had much to live for, but even so. It felt — odd. The act of suicide required something . . . courage, maybe? Self-awareness? Some sort of will power or discipline that the Kaylin she had met completely lacked.

The mortuary attendant told them that Kaylin had died of low-level electrocution, his mobile phone having been found in the bathwater beside him, its charger still attached to the jumble of archaic plug extensions on the bathroom floor. It had been a long, slow cook as opposed to a sudden violent shock, he said. Hence the lack of much facial scarring in the photograph. Nor had he been dead for long when he was discovered, hence the lack of bloating . . . Pippa wondered what drugs had been inside him at the time of his death: she imagined him passing out in the bath, and the phone slipping slowly through his fingers. Perhaps he'd had a skinful of roofies inside him. Perhaps he dropped his mobile into the bath by mistake, and he had simply been too out-of-it to pick the thing up again. Or perhaps —

Perhaps, perhaps.

But that was too frightening to contemplate.

She broke the silence to break the train of thought.

"He was pretty hopeless," she said to Dolly. "He probably dropped the phone in the bath . . ."

"I should think so," said Dolly. "That's what they said, isn't it? Mind you, with these iPhones, you would have thought there might be a sort of cut-out mechanism. It's amazing, when you think about it, that more people don't get killed like that every day. How many people look at their mobile in the bath? Millions, I should think."

Pippa shrugged. "Yeah, but his was charging, wasn't it . . . Plus I should think he got the mobile off someone dodgy. I bet it wasn't the real thing. Plus — seriously — I don't think the electrics in Kaylin's flat would have passed many safety tests. I don't think *anything* in that flat would have passed any safety tests

— it looked like the place hadn't been touched since the 1950s . . ."

"Well, well," muttered Dolly, vaguely. Her mind was whirring with unwelcome questions. She had never met Killer Kayle, of course — so what did she know? Nothing. Except that everything about everything felt wrong, and Marina's cards were haunting her. "I'm just so sorry you had to get mixed up with it." She put an arm round Pippa's shoulders. "You wonder where Marina is . . . at a time like this."

And they said nothing more after that, because they were both thinking the same thing, and neither much wanted to voice it.

CHAPTER
FIFTEEN

Gigi was gone. She was helping out at a pop-up bike repair workshop in Elephant and Castle, near where she and the others had used to squat, and where most of their friends still did. Having spoken with Trek the night before, she had decided it would be expedient, given her preciously guarded status as an Unknown Person, to stay away from Tinderbox Lane until "things settled down". Geordie and Trek, meanwhile, less sensibly, were barricaded behind Trek's metal door at Number Seven, drinking neat vodka at two in the afternoon, and trying to work out a plan. Should they stick around? Or should they go?

Geordie's mobile rang. He glanced at it guiltily — but didn't move to pick it up.

Trek said: "Is it Pippa again?"

"Never mind Pippa," Geordie said. Pippa was not important. Never had been, really, or not to him; never anything more than an expedient and enjoyable bang buddy. Not that he didn't like her — he did, very much. He liked going to her cottage and eating the food in her fridge, and washing himself in her clean bathtub. And he liked the sex, obviously. It occurred to him that he might have to break a rule of a lifetime and be kind, and actually, explicitly *dump* her . . . At some point in the near future . . . But not right now. Right now she was the least of his problems.

"She's probably back from the mortuary," Trek said. "You should answer it, Geordie. She must be out of her mind with worry."

"You should never have involved her."

"I realise that. But what else was I supposed to do? She was the only person I could think of who was kosher. I couldn't exactly give them your name, could I? And I didn't know who else . . ."

"What about Marina?"

"Marina . . ." Trek fell silent for a long time. "Apart from the fact that I don't have a number for her — do you?"

Geordie shook his head.

"Anyway — she's an illegal immigrant, for Christ's sake. She's even more vulnerable than we are. I wouldn't do that to her. Any more than I would to you or Gigi . . ." Trek pictured his father, the excruciatingly fair-minded Right Reverend Bishop of Newport, and his sweet, innocent ma, the bishop's wife, so loving, so respectable, so *decent*. They knew their son was politically active and they were proud of him for that. But they knew nothing about how active, let alone how unlawful. For crying out loud, they didn't even know he smoked! If they had the faintest idea about the realities of his life . . . "Jesus, Geordie, what the fuck have I done?"

"I don't know, Trek. What have you done?" There was an edge to his voice — Marina-related. He wondered, among other things, whether Trek had had sex with her.

Trek didn't seem to hear him. "I wish I'd never gone in there, Geordie. The sight of that naked body . . . Christ . . . I wish I'd just turned around and walked straight out again. Why didn't I just turn around and get out?"

"It's the question I'm asking myself."

Trek pulled the vodka bottle out of Geordie's hand and took a clumsy glug, drenching his chin and T-shirt in the process.

Why hadn't he turned around and left? He was an Oxford graduate, for God's sake. With a future. Next year, under his real name, in his real life, he was enrolled on a law conversion course and he was going to qualify as a lawyer: a lawyer who fought for the underdog, who would help people. He was going to make the world a better, kinder, fairer place. That had been the plan. *And now this.*

"But what was I supposed to do?" he asked again. "Just leave him, lying there in the bath? I couldn't do that."

"You should've done that."

"I couldn't do it."

"Right. And now they're going to ask, how did you get into the flat in the first place."

"You know how I got into the flat. Same way everyone got in. I knew Kaylin would never answer, and Marina wasn't in —"

"How did you know Marina wasn't in?"

"I assumed . . . I don't know . . . What does it matter? Because she's never in. She's always working. Unlike that lazy bastard boyfriend —"

"He's dead, Trek."

"I know he's fucking dead! I fucking saw him in the bath, didn't I?"

"Was he dead when you got there?"

"What? Yes, *of course he was!* What do you think? For God's sake, Geordie —"

"So how did you get in?"

"You know how I got in! I used the chisel. Did the twist and shove routine, same as everyone else . . . *Oh fuck.*"

"You forced an entry."

"*Fuck fuck fuck fuck . . .*"

"I'm only asking it because they're going to ask you, Trek — *what were you doing in there in the first place?*"

"You know what I was doing! We discussed it! The same thing everyone is doing in Kaylin's flat."

"Calm down."

"Oh Jesus, Geordie, what am I going to do?"

"You were in the flat to score some . . . illegal narcotics. Correct?"

"Yes it's fucking correct! You know that perfectly well. I was on my way up to see you guys at Elephant, wasn't I?"

"Nothing to do with Marina then?"

"*Marina?* What are you talking about?"

"Were you banging Marina?"

"Was I . . .? *NO!* What the hell, Geordie? Next you're going to ask if I fucking killed him."

Geordie said: "Did you?"

"*Fuck you.*"

Geordie held his friend's gaze. "I'm asking you, Trek, because they will, for sure. If the stashbox is missing, they're going to want to know."

"What stashbox? What are you trying to say? *No.* I did not kill the stupid, useless bastard. Far as I'm concerned he was as good as dead already, lying on that sofa all day and night, ordering that poor girl around. And no, I was not 'banging Marina', as you put it. Were you?"

Geordie smirked and shook his head. "Sadly not." Just then his mobile struck up, once again. Again, he glanced at it, but he didn't move. "As you can see," he added, "I have my hands full already."

"Since when did that stop you?" muttered Trek. "Anyway, you should answer it," Trek said. "The poor thing — just answer it, won't you? Tell her you're okay. Or something. You can't let her keep ringing like this. It's not fair. Send her a message. She'll be round here any second if you don't. With her mum's Tarot cards, I don't doubt . . . *And I can't see her.* Not after what happened last night. You can't tell her."

"You're quite right, I can't," Geordie said coldly. "I'm still not exactly clear what did happen last night . . ."

"You *know* what happened . . . I went to the flat. I saw the — I saw Kaylin. I called the police, and I gave them Pippa's name — but there's no need to tell her that. There's no need for any of us to be involved with any of this. We just have to . . . Please, Geordie, are you listening to me?"

Geordie had taken up his phone at last, and was tapping out a message to Pippa:

Can't talk. Shit-and-fan situation. Just had terrible news. Will call later — G

He sent it and paused, head down. He was thinking.

"I won't tell Pippa you gave her name to the police," he said. "Why would I? But you've got to face the fact the police are going to find you eventually, no matter what. You made the call."

"*So what if I made the call?* Geordie, think about it. There's no record of us here. Nobody knows our names. 'Trek' doesn't even have a surname! He doesn't exist. Plus — I whispered. And I put on an accent . . . I don't think they would have known if I was even male or female. I was quite careful."

"You called on the landline?"

"There isn't a landline. At least I assume . . . I didn't even look for one . . . I called on my phone. But my phone isn't traceable. Obviously. I've got another phone for family and shit . . . But the one I use as Trek . . ."

"Two phones? Two-phones Trek? How very chic of you," Geordie said, coldly. "And how clever. To be so many steps ahead."

"Well of course . . . You've got to have two phones, haven't you?"

"No, Trek. I have just the one phone. I find the one quite expensive enough. Sometimes I forget — you're not really one of us, are you? This whole thing is a sort

130

of lower-class sabbatical from real life; a jolly old jape before Mummy and Daddy buy you a jolly nice little flat and —"

"Give it a rest, Geordie. Please. Just this once, try not to be a cunt. *This is serious.*"

"Your language is appalling," muttered Geordie. But his mind was buzzing. Trek was quite right, of course. There was no reason any of them should have to be involved in this, if they were clever about it. "I think you should get out of town. Go home to your parents. Or go abroad for a while."

"What about Gigi? I can't just leave her . . ."

"Don't worry about Gigi. I'll look after her."

"Yeah, of course you will."

Geordie took the vodka bottle back from his friend. "Trek," he said. "I mean it. We're all better making ourselves scarce round here for a while. But you, especially. And I promise, I won't touch her. I'll look out for her."

Trek said: "Or maybe she'll agree to come with me? We could set up a squat in . . . somewhere else. Copenhagen . . . Or Rome. Marseille . . . Ha! How about Marseille? Supposed to be great down there. Fancy coming along?"

But Geordie wasn't listening. In fact, on closer examination, Trek realised his friend looked terrible — actually quite distraught.

"Geordie? Are you all right, mate?"

"Hm? Me? Yes, of course."

"You look a bit rough."

"Yes — well. I suppose I was just — I was thinking about poor old Killer. I liked him. In a way. It's a shock, isn't it? I mean — one day he's here, the next he's gone. I've never really known anyone who's died yet. Have you? Maybe we could have helped him."

"Helped him, how?"

"I don't know . . . Not die."

"I don't think so."

"We had some good times together. I was fond of him," Geordie said again.

"Really?" Trek was surprised. "I wasn't."

"He had his faults, but he was a good guy . . ."

"Not really. I don't think so."

". . . of all the people in the world to do themselves in, I would never have believed . . ." Geordie fell silent.

Trek hesitated. "So . . . it hasn't occurred to you that maybe — I mean *maybe he didn't* . . . kill himself?"

Geordie said nothing.

Trek persevered. "Seriously . . . have you seen Marina lately? I know I haven't."

Geordie, jolted out of his grief, looked coolly at Trek. "Why? What are you suggesting?"

"You know what I'm suggesting. It must have occurred to you, Geordie. She had motive enough. And opportunity. And I don't think anyone would exactly blame her."

"*It was the Russian hooker wot dun 'im in!* Is that what you're saying?"

"I didn't say she was a hooker."

"And maybe it was Colonel Mustard. With the candelabra." Geordie stood up. "And maybe, Trek, just maybe it was *you*."

"Funny."

"Not funny. You were the last person to see him alive, after all."

"He wasn't alive. For Christ's sake. *I told you.* His body was all disgusting and nude and he had weird lines all over him and . . . he was fucking *dead*."

"So you say."

"Piss off, Geordie. Don't make things even worse than they already are."

"You're the one suggesting foul play."

"I wasn't. I was just —"

"We should get moving. Pippa'll be round here any second, as you say, and you're right, you shouldn't be here . . . I won't ask where you're going, all right? That way I won't know if anyone asks, will I?" He smirked disagreeably. "And I don't believe I have your rich-boy second mobile number, thankfully."

"I'll give it to you."

"Don't. When you want to come back — send a message. And we'll let you know the situation, all right? Somehow I doubt we'll still be here. That crazy fucking landlady . . . And now, with all this." Geordie and Trek stood opposite one another. Gigi had hung thick, dirty blankets at the windows to keep out prying eyes. They were drawn closed, as always, keeping the room in semi-darkness, and spread around the boys' feet, unheeded through the tobacco smoke, was the detritus of last night's dinner, this morning's breakfast, and a week's worth of beer cans and cigarette butts. "You want me to give a message to Gigi? I can do that, if you want . . ."

"No. Thanks. No — I'll get a message to her. Maybe I'll send a letter . . . like the olden days."

They hugged each other awkwardly. It was by far the most affection they had ever shown one another, and more than either really felt. They quickly pulled apart, embarrassed.

"See you around then," Geordie said, clearing his throat, staring at the floor. "Good luck."

He looked, Trek thought, as if he wanted to cry. Which made two of them. The world that they had always been so confident of putting to rights had never seemed a darker and more frightening place.

CHAPTER
SIXTEEN

Marina wandered Oxford Street, shivering with cold despite the anorak, at a loose end, but unwilling to waste money in a coffee shop while she waited for work to begin. Not for the first time, her mind meandered back to the Tarot reading on Tinderbox Lane. She'd told herself not to believe a word of it — what a waste of £50. But the woman had turned out to be right, hadn't she. There was never any marriage: never anything to celebrate. Nothing. Kaylin admitted as much shortly after the landlady and the fat-necked man left the flat on Eddison Grove . . .

Marina remembered it — standing in front of him, demanding answers, shaking with rage. His head had lolled back onto the bathtub edge, and he groaned with the disagreeableness of it all, with the effort that would now be required to stop Marina from bawling at him. It was as much her fault as his, he told her, for having been so dozy as to believe him. Hadn't she known all along that it was all codswallop, that they were both just playing a game? He explained to her that the marriage, like everything else, had been — well, a charming *idea*. A romantic drama, if you like . . . They'd been through a lot together, her and him. Of course the flat had never been his.

And he had laughed. *Laughed* . . . Marina felt her rage swell once again as she imagined his face in that bathtub. *No*, he told her, *maybe in Russia you could buy a bride over the Internet "for forty rupees or whatever"*, but in good ol' Blighty, things were a bit stricter. There were licenses to apply for; passports to produce . . . *heh heh*.

"*. . . but come here, baby . . . don't look so serious. There's more to life than boring old marriage certificates. Why don't we go overseas? Let's go away somewhere where the sun's . . . y'know . . . always yellow. Wouldn't that be great? Come here, love, for goodness' sake. Don't stand there scowling at me — you're giving me nightmares . . ."*

His head lolled this way and that as he spoke, as if he couldn't be bothered to hold it upright while he smashed her codswallop fantasies into pieces. He seemed not to care what he was saying, to have no sense of the effect of his words. Something snapped inside her.

And, yes, of course she had known that the "marriage" was a piece of nonsense — she was not so stupid. But it had been an almost marriage; a step towards the real thing, a pretence of a pretence that the two of them held together. Marina had not analysed her feelings about the online marriage. (It wasn't her style.) All she knew was that a sham online marriage was better than no marriage at all. It was a step towards ultimate victory: a concession from Kaylin — a

136

warm-up, an acceptance that this was where things were headed, a statement of intent: a step towards a step on the property ladder. Whatever it was didn't matter now. The marriage was not the deal-breaker. Nor even, on some bewildering level, the truth about the flat . . . It was Kaylin, with his head lolling this way and that, laughing at her dreams, after all they had been through together. After all she had done for him. She had hated him, at that moment, with every cell of her beautiful, young, ambitious body.

And now here she was — sleeping in the ladies' toilet at the Mayfair club she worked in; paying the early-morning cleaner a tenner in hush money. After everything, all the work, all the effort; all the straddling, sucking, licking and massaging; all the cuppas prepared and cleared away, she was never further from her flower-decked Californian wedding canopy, her dinner-jacketed fiancé on bended knee. Never more alone.

Not that she dwelled on it. Self-pity was not in her make-up any more than feeling pity for anyone else. She'd had the foresight, at least, to have taken the cash from the stashbox with her. There had been almost two thousand pounds in there, and it gave her breathing space. And next time she moved in with a man she wouldn't be so careless. She wouldn't waste her efforts on anyone without real money, and a real job. And a real office, and a real suit . . . Her mind began to wander. To every cloud, there was a silver lining.

In the meantime, she'd left the flat in such a rush; she'd not been thinking clearly. There was stuff back there she needed — her passport, for one. And the old woman's jewellery . . . And the rest of her clothes. She needed to get back into the flat somehow — and soon. She would have to hide, and watch, and wait, until she knew it was safe.

CHAPTER
SEVENTEEN

Dolly was at her breakfast bar, replying half-heartedly to her few — depressingly few — enquiries for readings. She was thinking about Raff and wondering whether, if she called him, he would be more pleased or irritated to hear from her. Their relationship, which had seemed so unequivocally joyful in St Lucia, had taken something of a dive in recent weeks. It wasn't simply the reality of day-to-day life that was wearing the friendship away — they were muddling along with that. In fact, in some ways, the difficulties of finding time and space alone added to the preciousness of the time they did have together.

It seemed ludicrous, but the problems between them were rooted in the situation at Number Seven. Pippa and Raff couldn't seem to be in the same room without a political argument ensuing — and of course it was always Pippa who started it, who needled at Raff until, finally, he reacted. Dolly disagreed with many of Raff's opinions and almost all of Pippa's, which seemed to grow more aggressive and revolutionary every day, but she tried her best to arbitrate. It wasn't easy, and — worse than that — it wasn't fun.

Dolly didn't want to take sides. Above all, she never wanted Pippa to feel unwelcome in her own home. The more argumentative Pippa became, and the more Dolly longed for Pippa to leave Raff and her in peace, the more guilty she felt, the more she compensated by supporting Pippa . . . and the more tense it became between them all, and the more Raff stayed away.

This afternoon, for example, was Raff's afternoon off. Pippa was meant to have gone to college, but after a sleepless night, and a morning at the mortuary, she had decided to give it a miss. And so here she was, sitting at home at Tinderbox Lane, kicking her heels, checking her phone, itching for some kind of salve that Dolly's maternal presence clearly didn't provide. It was difficult.

Pippa's phone bleeped. She grabbed it

Can't talk. Shit-and-fan situation. Just got terrible news. Will call later — G

A second later, Pippa was on her feet. "I think I'll head out, Mum."

"Oh!" said Dolly, trying to sound dismayed.

"That was Geordie — he's obviously heard the news. *Finally*. Sounds like he's in a bad state." She smiled at her mother. "I'm being a nightmare, Mum. I know I am. But I'll get out of your hair now."

"Don't be so silly!" said Dolly. "You're never a nightmare, Pipps."

Pippa laughed. "Liar." She patted her pockets for tobacco and headed for the door. "I think he's really upset," she said. "I'll go over there now. See how he is."

"I should think he's in a bit of shock, is he?"

140

"Definitely."

"Is he *asking* to see you?"

"I'm just going to pop in. Check he's all right . . . He probably doesn't even realise I know what's happened yet."

Dolly would have liked to get Pippa out of the house, but not as much as she wanted to protect her from Geordie and his insalubrious friends, one of whom clearly had been responsible for giving Pippa's name to the police. "I should leave him be," she said. "If he wants you, he knows where to find you, after all. I should just let him get on with it."

Pippa stared at her mother. "Get on with what?"

"Get on with . . . whatever he has to get on with. Do we know who it was who gave your name to the police yet?"

Pippa's smile faded. "No. You know we don't."

Dolly said nothing, kept her eyes on her computer, shrugged innocently.

"What are you trying to say, Mum?"

"Nothing."

"Why do you dislike him so much? What's he ever done to you?"

Dolly said: "He hasn't done anything to me. And I don't dislike him. Well — okay. I don't *like* him much. I think he's arrogant. And I don't think he has your best interests at heart. That's all . . . but, as I know you're about to remind me, you're an adult now, and it's none of my business. So. I'll put a sock in it." She smiled. "Do whatever you feel is right, Pippa. By the way," she added (deftly rebooting), "I wanted to ask your advice about something."

"Really?" Pippa sounded unconvinced. "Advice about what?"

"Not now. When you get back. If you have a moment . . ."

"I have a moment now, Mum. What advice do you need?"

"Well . . ." Dolly sighed. "I'm just looking at these emails — and it's getting a bit desperate, really. Only one reading booked today and one tomorrow — I was thinking maybe . . . But listen. I don't want to keep you. If you have to go, please —"

"Mum. I want to help you. As we both know, Geordie's survived okay without me until now . . . I'm sure he can survive another twenty minutes." They smiled at each other: it was the first time in a long time.

"I was just wondering if I should resuscitate those Tarot Talks I did at your college — they made a bit of money, didn't they? Do you think I could do them again? Maybe offer a sort of intermediary course as well — or maybe just another beginners' course? I was going to ask Derek about it — but, bless him, he's fairly useless. I really need your help."

It seemed like a lifetime ago. The fairly useless professor had found a room for them in the faculty, and Pippa had put posters up all over the college. Dolly had made a few hundred pounds out of it. Pippa felt a wave of nostalgia for the friendship she and Dolly had enjoyed, before the boyfriends came and messed it all up.

"Great idea," she said. "Why not? And why stick to the college? There's the community hall in Barnes . . . Or the library on Castlenau. Or one of the pubs — they do themed evenings at the Bull's Head. We could ask them . . ."

For a moment it was lovely. Like old times. And it would be again of course. But first there was this: a knock on the door.

Dolly opened it and found Geordie standing there. He was hardly recognisable as the young man who'd swaggered through Dolly's house wearing her dressing gown not so long ago.

"Good Heavens," exclaimed Dolly. He looked terrible. "Are you all right, sweetheart? Do you want to come in?"

He shook his head. *Adamantly not, of course!* And yet — there was something about Pippa's mother, something reassuring, and imperturbable, and grounded, and just then it made him long to accept her invitation. Suddenly, more than anything in the world, he wanted to come into her neat, pretty house, which smelled of fresh coffee, to be invited in and to make himself comfortable in that brightly coloured, clean armchair. And to be told by her that *Everything was Okay*, and Kaylin wasn't really dead, and the world was just as easy to understand as it had been yesterday. "No, no, I won't come in," he mumbled. "I don't want to disturb you. No, I was just —"

"Don't be silly," interrupted Dolly. She pulled the door open a little further and stood back to let him in.

143

"Pippa's just here. I'm sorry about your friend, by the way. Would you like some coffee?"

"Wait there," Pippa said, standing behind her mother, fidgeting nervously. "I'll get my jacket." But by then he was already through the door.

He slumped in the brightly coloured armchair, muttering thank yous, and then fell silent.

"D'you want some coffee?" Pippa asked him again.

He shook his head.

"You sure?"

"No, thank you, Pippa. Thank you very much."

"Well, I've just made some," said Dolly quite gently. "So if you change your mind . . ."

"I'm really sorry about Kaylin, Geordie," Pippa said. "It's awful . . ."

He nodded.

"When they told me — when Raff told me — there was someone dead in the bath, I thought it was you. All last night, I thought it was you who was dead."

That seemed to take him by surprise. He lifted his head. "Why?"

She shrugged. "Why else would they have asked me to identify the body? Plus you were always taking baths at that place. So I assumed . . . Have they called you yet?"

"Who?"

"The mortuary guy. Has he called you? I told him to call you. I couldn't think of anyone else. I haven't got Marina's number. They needed someone to identify the body — I couldn't. I hardly even know his name. I said they should ask you."

144

Geordie looked aghast. "*Why would you do that?*"

From her place by the kettle, on the far side of the breakfast bar, Dolly watched her daughter blush — as if it was she who had done something wrong. "Well he's a friend of yours, isn't he, Geordie?" Dolly said. "Pipps didn't even know the man's surname. She was trying to be helpful."

"Yes," Geordie nodded, with a visible effort. "Yes, of course. Sorry. Sorry, Pippa."

"We weren't sure why Pippa was asked to identify him in the first place, frankly," persisted Dolly. "She hardly knew him, after all. Do you know?"

"Do I know why she was asked to identify the body?" Geordie looked at Dolly, and then at his hands. "I didn't even know she had been. That's awful."

". . . Well she *was*. And I was wondering who would have suggested her name. As someone to do that particular job. It seems so odd — don't you think? Who would have suggested her, do you think?"

Geordie took a moment to reply. Through the silence, Dolly continued to stare at him.

He thought he could feel her eyes on him, burning into his heart and soul. "Yes, it's very odd," he said at last. "I can't think who would have done that." He glanced at Pippa. "And horrible for you, Pippa. I'm sorry. What were–?" He stopped, unsure what question to ask — or which to start with. "Did they–? Was it–? Do they know who made the call yet? Was the person male or female?"

"They don't even seem to know that, apparently," Dolly said, still watching him. *Did she imagine it, or did he seem relieved?* "So it's a mystery. At the moment. No doubt they'll get to the bottom of it eventually . . . It wasn't you, was it?"

"Mum, what kind of a question . . ."

"I'm just asking."

He smiled. "It wasn't me, no. Thanks for coming out with it, though — asking me straight. Thank you. I appreciate that."

"Don't mention it," Dolly said.

Another silence. Geordie longed to fill it — with anything at all — but for once, his giant brain would not come to his aid. He couldn't think of a thing to say. He was aware, only, of Dolly, leaning against the sink at the back of the kitchen, shuffling her bloody Tarot cards. She hadn't taken her eyes off him since he walked in.

He turned to Pippa. "I'm really sorry, Pipp," he said at last. "Things have been a bit messed up since I heard the news. But I should have called you earlier. I know I should."

"I called you last night. Loads of times," Pippa said. "As soon as I heard. But you wouldn't pick up."

"Yeah, I know — I'm sorry."

"I thought it was you," she said again. "I thought it was *you* who was dead in that bathtub."

"I'm sorry. Really, I'm so sorry. I had no idea. Obviously. If I'd any inkling you were thinking — something like that — of course I would have called . . . We would have talked."

"So where were you?" Dolly asked him abruptly.

"What's that?"

"Mum —"

"Well, I think it's fair to ask. Isn't it? Pippa was beside herself, Geordie. She thought you were dead! She must have called you a dozen times . . ."

"Mum, please . . ." Pippa laughed. She turned back to Geordie. "She's got a point, though. Where were you last night? What were you doing that was so all-consuming you couldn't check your phone the entire night?"

Geordie smiled, for lack of a good answer springing immediately to mind. His brain still wasn't functioning properly, not at its usual lightning speed. Either that, or the situation was more complicated than any it had previously been asked to navigate. In truth, his memory was a bit fuzzy on the question of his activities the previous night, due to having taken quite a lot of mind-altering "illegal narcotics", as he called them. Ketamine, MDMA, cocaine, grass . . . He had been up in Elephant and Castle with Gigi, that much he knew, at an all-night eviction party and on the hunt for a bit of intense reciprocity with some previously untested female flesh . . . This was the truth. But he didn't want to admit to it, obviously. Certainly not in front of Dolly. And yes, of course he had checked his phone last night — and yes, of course he had noticed, through the narcotic fuzz, that Pippa had been trying to call him. At the time he had not felt under the slightest obligation to return the call — why would he? His attention was elsewhere: he was doing something else. The thought of calling her, from the middle of a party in Elephant and Castle, genuinely hadn't crossed his mind.

He gave them both a sheepish grin. "I was at a party," he said. "On the other side of town . . . I was a bit drunk."

"Hmm," said Dolly. She pulled out a card, turned it over: just as she expected. It was the Seven of Swords. The two-timer's card. The cheater's card. *What a creep!* How could Pippa not see through him? "Well that would explain why you're looking so rough this morning, I suppose."

"I think it would," he said. "I'm sorry, Pippa. If I'd known for a second . . ."

"Forget it," Pippa snapped. She could see her mother, staring at her damn cards. She knew what her mother was thinking, and it was humiliating. "Forget it. It's not a big deal. It doesn't matter."

"Thank you," he said, sending a look Dolly's way. Not that she noticed, she was busy flipping her cards, one after the other. *The Seven of Swords, and then The World . . . and then the Three of Cups and the Three of Swords . . . and the Ten of Swords and the Ace of Cups reversed* . . . "What matters," he continued, "is that Kaylin died. It's a shock. A horrible shock." Again, he looked from one Greene to the other. His hangover probably wasn't helping, but the sight of Dolly in the corner of the room, flipping those cards, learning things about him . . . made him suddenly very angry. It seemed to him to be an outrageous intrusion of his privacy. He forced a laugh. "What are you doing over there, Dolly? You're freaking me out a bit. Are you finding things out about me? It's rather unnerving, you know."

148

Dolly, still turning cards, didn't reply. She may not even have heard him.

"*Mum*," Pippa said. "Please. Can you stop? People really hate it when you do that and I don't blame them."

"Are you off somewhere?" Dolly said suddenly. It wasn't clear to which of them she was speaking, but when no one replied, she looked up from the cards, to Geordie. "Are you leaving Tinderbox Lane, Geordie? Maybe . . ." She sounded hopeful. "Have you come to say goodbye?"

Geordie laughed. "No, Dolly, I'm not off anywhere, you'll be disappointed to hear. No, I haven't 'come to say goodbye'. I came here because my friend has died, very suddenly, in horrible circumstances . . . and I was feeling sad. And I wanted to see Pippa . . . If that's all right with you?" He turned to Pippa. Tried to smile.

There were beads of sweat on his forehead, noted Dolly.

"I don't think your mum likes me very much," he made a stange, hiccupping sound that was meant to be laughter. It had come out sounding more emotional than he wanted.

"Of course she does," said Pippa.

"Well," Dolly said. "No, I don't. Not really."

This unsurprising and, he recognised, well-earned confirmation that the Scary Tarot Lady, who made such good risotto, didn't really like him, was — on that dreadful day — the final straw for him: the piece of news that wiped away the last of his bravado. Before their eyes, his entire body seemed to shrivel. He curled his back and bent his head into his hands and stayed like that, for what felt like an age, doing and saying nothing more.

When Pippa reached over to put a hand on his shoulder, he didn't raise his head. "This is awful," he kept saying. "This is awful. This is awful . . ."

"It's not *that* awful," Dolly said, more gently. "It doesn't really matter whether I like you or not. I don't suppose you like me much, either. If you think about it. What's *awful* — is that you have lost a friend."

"I have," he said. The words were muffled through his delicate hands. "I've lost a beautiful, beautiful friend . . . Oh God, Dolly — Pippa. *Everyone.* EVERYONE — *I've lost a beautiful friend.*"

This outburst took everyone present by surprise. Pippa had no idea he felt so strongly about Killer Kayle. Dolly had no idea he was capable of feeling so strongly about anyone. It must be the shock, decided Dolly. He may not have been the ideal boyfriend for her daughter — but he was still young, and human. This was probably his first encounter with death. And suicide, if suicide it was, was always especially horrible . . . Pippa wrapped an arm around his shoulders. Dolly took pity, and put away her cards. They were trying to soothe him, trying to make him feel better, and it seemed to be working. He was just apologising for "behaving like a twat" when a second knock on the door made them all jump.

Dolly went to answer it, hoping it might be Raff. He'd been on duty last night — and apart from a text message this morning, wishing Pippa luck at the mortuary, she'd heard nothing from him since he left them on the doorstep of Windy Ridge yesterday.

But Dolly didn't find Raff on the doorstop, looking handsome in his sergeant's uniform. She found no one at all. She looked up and down the lane. There was no one to be seen.

"That's strange," she said. "Was there a knock or did I imagine it?" She looked this way and that once again, and then down at her feet. A small package lay on the step, scrappily wrapped in plain brown paper. No address and no stamps. Dolly picked it up, and the package partially unfastened in her hands.

She carried it to the breakfast bar without a word and slowly pulled back the paper.

"Oh my goodness," she said quietly. "Oh dear . . . Look at this."

Lying in the midst of the packaging, glistening with moisture, there lay a heart, pierced, like a pin cushion, with twenty or more pins. Between the pins, tied around the centre and knotted into an untidy bow, was an electric coil — a phone charger, and attached to the coil, like a gift tag, was a Tarot card.

Gingerly, Dolly flipped over the card, and gave a grim chuckle. Well of course. Scrawled in gold pen across the image of the Fool were the two words:

YOUR [sic] NEXT

"Oh for goodness' sake," muttered Dolly. "What is this nonsense? Who the hell?"

The three of them stared at it in horror.

"Do you think it's human?" whispered Pippa.

151

"It's too big," Dolly said. "Human hearts are much smaller."

"Well — what is it then?" Pippa asked. "Who the hell put it there? Do you think it's meant for you, Mum? Or for me?"

Dolly shook her head. "I don't know, Pipps . . . The Tarot card would more likely be aimed at me, wouldn't it? But the phone wire . . ."

"Makes you think of Kaylin." Pippa glanced at Geordie. "They found him with the phone charger . . . You know that, right?"

"Yeah. Yeah." He nodded, eyes fixed on the gruesome delivery. "I know that. I'm aware of that."

"It's got to have something to do with that, hasn't it? Too much of a coincidence . . . Which means it's aimed at me, Mum."

"Nonsense!" said Dolly — too quickly. "Of course it isn't aimed at you, darling. Why would it be? It's aimed at me."

"Are you *stupid?*" burst out Geordie. "*IT'S AIMED AT ME!*"

Pippa laughed. "Of course it isn't. Why would it be? It's been delivered to us here at Number Two."

"BUT I'M HERE! CAN'T YOU SEE ME? I AM STANDING HERE!"

Good heavens, thought Dolly: all those brains and not an ounce of grit. Pippa must at least begin to see through him now? "Calm down, Geordie," she said. "It's only a cow's heart . . . Just someone being silly . . ."

152

"A COW? *ONLY A COW?* HOW DO YOU KNOW IT'S ONLY A COW ANYWAY?"

"Because, Geordie, like you, I went to school. And unlike you, apparently, I paid attention in biology lessons."

He stared at her, not yet convinced, and yet longing to be. Finally, he said: "I don't understand how you can be so calm."

Dolly wasn't calm. Far from it. But she couldn't show panic, not with Pippa standing beside her, thinking the package was for her.

"Who put it there?" Pippa asked. "Who would have done that?" She leaned in to peer at it more closely, but Dolly pulled her back.

"I wouldn't touch it," she said. "There might be fingerprints."

Time to call Raff, she thought. She picked up the phone, and noticed as she did so that the front door was still open. More than that, there were footsteps outside.

CHAPTER
EIGHTEEN

"*Well hello, Dolly! How nice to have you back where you belong.* Fabulous film. Have you seen it? Highly recommended. How are you this morning, Dolly? How's Pippa? Is she OK after all the dreadfulness?"

All this he managed to cram in between Dolly's garden gate and her front door.

"Only us!" he said. "Can we come in?"

It was Professor Filthy and Mrs Frosty, out on a walk together, they said, ostensibly en route to deliver a letter to Terry — "Residents Association business . . ." — really to find out what had happened with Pippa, after last night. Had she been to the mortuary yet?

"She's fine," said Dolly. "It was a bit grim at the mortuary of course, but thankfully it turned out she didn't know the person needing to be identified. Or not that well, anyway." Dolly wasn't unhappy to see her neighbours. On the contrary, they brought a bit of noisy normality to a situation which was clearly in need of it. On the other hand — things being as they were, with Geordie, hated squatter, on the edge of tears in the living room, and a pierced cow's heart with what might be construed as a death wish attached to it lying on the breakfast bar, she wasn't sure she wanted to invite them in. It appeared they were coming in anyway.

"Do we know who it was then?" Rosie asked, leading the way, causing a slight traffic jam by pausing politely at the threshold to wipe her feet. "Who was it? In the mortuary, I mean. It wasn't anyone too special I hope?"

"Budge up, Mrs B," said Derek. "You're blocking the door."

By then Rosie had looked up from her scrupulous foot-wiping and noticed, first, Pippa and Geordie — and, finally, the package on the breakfast bar between them. "Oh it's you," she said, first glowering at Geordie. And then, "*What's that?*"

"Well, if you'd get out of the light," said the professor, sounding tetchy, "I might be able to tell you."

"Is that a cow's heart?" Rosie said, still not moving, rooted to the spot.

"*Out the way!*" said Derek, giving her a childish shove and sending her flying, while simultaneously taking a single lanky step into the middle of the tiny room. He glanced at Geordie — who, without another word, slipped past him and Rosie, and stepped out onto the street.

"Are you all right, Geordie?" Dolly called after him, "Where are you going?"

He muttered something inaudible, head down, waved a hand in the air and kept on walking. A second later Pippa had grabbed her jacket and run after him.

By which time Derek had spotted the open parcel on the breakfast bar. He stooped over it, prodding it curiously with his big hand. "What the —?" he boomed. "My giddy aunt, Dolly! What's going on here?" He flipped over the card. "That's one of your Tarot thingummies, isn't it?"

"Certainly is," Dolly replied. "Don't touch it though . . . I think maybe they can test it for fingerprints."

"Fingerprints, hmm? Good thinking, Dolly . . . Well I never. Who would have thought? 'YOUR NEXT' . . . 'YOUR NEXT'? Ha! Some idiot can't spell. Do we know what this is, Dolly? What's it doing here? Is it something to do with you?"

Dolly told him what she knew — which wasn't much. She didn't know who it was from or who it was for. But Geordie, who had left in such a hurry, seemed to be convinced it was for him . . .

"Yes, I was surprised to see him in here," Rosie said. She wrinkled her face and gave a dainty shudder. "Nasty young man. Is Pippa okay? Not too upset?"

"Scarpered pretty sharpish, didn't he, soon as he spotted us." The professor laughed. "Not funny, mind you. Not when you're young. These things can be very painful. Isn't that right, Dolly? We've all had a relationship or three go south on us, I'm sure. I bet that heart of yours has been broken more than once, hmm?"

Dolly wasn't certain what he was talking about. Nor did she much want to discuss her personal emotional journey with him at that particular moment. Ever, in fact. She gave a non-committal smile, and directed attention to the other heart, glistening in its damp packaging on her counter top. "So the question is . . ." she said.

"Quite right," boomed the professor. "Never mind that young scoundrel . . . Question is, *who sent this to whom, and why?*"

They considered this in silence for a while.

"Someone with an interest in Tarot cards, perhaps?" suggested Rosie, tentatively.

"Hmmm," said the professor. "But you only have to have watched *Live and Let Die* at some point in your life to know about these Tarot cards, of course . . . Another classic, by the way. They don't make James Bond like the old days." Neither woman responded. "Added to that, of course, Mrs B, you know, whoever it was — whichever illiterate it was who plonked this nasty little package outside our friend's door, they really only had to know that *Dolly* was interested in the Tarot cards. And you only need to look on the Internet to discover that."

"Yes," Rosie agreed solemnly. "That's a good point, Derek. I see what you mean."

"Time to call the sergeant, I should think!" declared Derek. "If you haven't already?"

"Yes — I was about to. Actually it only arrived a few moments before you did."

"Oh?" said Derek. "Tell me more."

"There was a knock on the door. I answered it. But there was no one there. No one, anywhere to be seen. And this parcel on the doorstep."

". . . interesting . . ." said Derek, rubbing his chin. "And you answered the door immediately you heard the knock, correct?"

"Of course."

"And there was definitely a knock, was there? You heard the knock?"

"Well, I think so."

"And yet the lane was completely clear just now, when Rosie and I were walking along it, moments ago. Did you see anyone, Rosie? I don't think you did. Well. Then whoever it was, must have been exceedingly sly. They must have," — he poked his head out of Dolly's front door — "either disappeared into one of the houses, and run out through one of the back gardens, or jumped over the wall into the bus station . . . which," he said, "would imply that said 'Somebody' must have been moving pretty damn fast — am I right? Which, if my instincts are correct, inevitably leads one to conclude . . ."

Dolly laughed. "You sound like Hercule Poirot, Derek. All you need is the French accent."

It was perhaps the elevated tension, induced by the heart on the breakfast bar and so much death in the air, but at Dolly's remark, Rosie emitted a noisy and unRosielike snort.

"What?" he demanded, glaring from one to the other. "What's funny?"

"Nothing," said Rosie. But they were both still laughing.

"Seriously, ladies. I think you're being a little childish. I'm simply trying to help us get to the bottom of this — really very disagreeable delivery."

"Of course you are, Derek," said Rosie. "We're just being silly . . . Please. Carry on."

158

"And by the way," he added, "without wishing to be pedantic, Dolly, the great Hercule Poirot is of course Belgian, rather than French. So if I was *really* wanting to sound like Monsieur Poirot I would be affecting a *Belgian* accent, which is slightly different."

"Good point," said Dolly. "Forgive the interruption. I was only teasing."

"I wouldn't normally object," he said, "but in this case I feel —"

"Oh belt up," said Dolly. "It was a joke, for heaven's sake. If you have any idea who might have delivered this horrible object to my door I would love to hear it, Derek. In the meantime, I'm calling Raff, and handing this —" Dolly indicated the bloody package "— unpleasant piece of nonsense over to the police. Pippa thinks it might have something to do with the body they found in the flat on Eddison Grove last night. She may be right."

Rosie's eyes bulged. "Really, Dolly? *How?* You still haven't told us anything about it. Who was it, in the end? Derek and I were wondering if it was that dreadful little squatter chap — but obviously not, since we've just seen him in your house! So who was it?"

"Nobody really knows," Dolly said. "And I'm still not sure what any of it has to do with Pippa. The body actually turned out, weirdly enough, to belong to the boyfriend of a remarkably disagreeable Russian girl who came to me for a reading a few weeks back." Dolly shuddered. "So it's all very mysterious . . ."

"Good God! You don't mean that *gorgeous* young Russian girl?" Derek glanced at Rosie. "The one I spotted on the lane the day you came to dinner. And I impressed you all with my fluent Russian language."

Dolly said, "Yes. That was the one."

"Oh well, then. Goodness. That changes all sorts of things. She should have said, shouldn't she, Rosie?"

"Probably, Derek, yes," agreed Rosie.

"I should say so," the professor continued, his confidence returning. "The big clue, of course, is in the spelling mistake. Add to that her now-evidenced interest and knowledge of Tarot cards; her close link with the tragic circumstances up the road — did the fellow in the bath die accidentally, do we know? *Or did she kill him?* You bet she killed him, the little minx! And on top of all that, before you interrupted me with your amusing comments about Hercule Poirot, Dolly, I was about to point out that any individual able to deliver that package and disappear at such lightning speed has got to be pretty young and pretty damn athletic . . . Don't you agree? Do go ahead and call the sergeant, Dolly. I, for one, would be interested to have his input. However, I suspect, ladies . . ." He stopped, twirled an imaginary moustache, and said: "Ze case of ze cow heart is now cloz-ed! Find the Russian girl! That's my advice."

Rosie didn't laugh. She was staring at the upturned card, a look of unhappy confusion on her face. "Am I being super dopey . . .?"

"Oh come on, Mrs B, make an effort!" cried Derek, rolling his eyes. "She's only written two words on the ruddy card."

"Is it — *your?*"

Derek put an arm around his landlady. "Oh dear, oh dear," he said, chuckling. "Maybe it wasn't the Russian strumpet, Mrs B! Maybe it was you! Have you been leaving cows' hearts and illiterate death threats on our neighbours' doorsteps without telling me?"

"Don't be so silly," said Rosie, blushing deep red.

"Only *joking!*" He looked across at Dolly. "I think another residents' meeting is in order, don't you, Dolly? Never mind squatters at Number Seven. I think we need to organise some adult literacy classes!"

But she was already dialling Raff, and just then he picked up. Dolly, in search of privacy, took her phone into the broom cupboard and closed the door.

CHAPTER
NINETEEN

He was on his way to an incident, so he said he would send a colleague to pick up the heart. But he was pleased to hear from her. He promised he'd find out what he could about both situations — pierced animal hearts and the death of Kaylin — as soon as he returned to the station, and they agreed to meet for dinner that night. Dolly offered to come round to his motorhome and cook pasta — but Raff said he was fed up with the caravan. He wanted to show her some brochures for properties in the area; and he wanted to take her to dinner.

"Property brochures! I say! I'd love to have dinner with you, Raff . . . I thought you might be feeling a bit fed up with me," Dolly added, "after the last couple of times."

Raff laughed. "Fed up with you? Not in a million years, Dolly. I thought you were feeling a bit fed up with me."

"Not me, Raff. Never . . . It's been difficult, though. Hasn't it? With Pippa and everything . . . That silly boyfriend of hers . . ."

He didn't reply. His car was speeding down Mortlake High Street, sirens blaring, his partner Ollie at the wheel. He shouldn't have been on the phone at all. Added to which, he wasn't sure what to say: no, the boyfriend wasn't silly? No, Pippa wasn't the most argumentative young person he had ever encountered? He said he had to go, and promised to be round at Tinderbox Lane to fetch her by 7.30 latest. "You're all right, though, are you?" he asked her.

"*Me?* Yes, of course I'm all right."

"Not too shaken up with this nasty Juju business?"

"I don't think it is Juju, Raff. Not really. It feels too sloppy."

"Well — good. You're the expert, Dolly."

"In fact," she said, looking at the package again, "I reckon whoever sent it just happened to be passing a butcher shop and thought — you know — *why not?* Perhaps I shouldn't bother handing it in to the police after all? Perhaps I'm giving it more weight than it deserves?"

"Of course you should hand it in," he said. "I'm sending someone round right now — all right? They should be with you any minute." He smiled into the phone. "I could talk to you all day, Dolly, as you know. But I've got to go. There's a madman with a penknife on the loose on Sheen Lane . . . Calling everyone Mohammed and threatening to kill them."

"Shame," muttered Dolly. "Angry world, we live in. Be careful, won't you?"

Raff's patrol car had arrived at its urgent halt. "Certainly will. See you later then, Dolly."

"Don't get stabbed! Please be careful!" she shouted, but he had already hung up. Raff was always careful, anyway; after nearly thirty years on police patrol, one angry drunkard with a penknife he could handle.

Dolly spent the rest of the afternoon inside, reading for two return clients and waiting for an officer to turn up and take the wretched heart away. By the time Raff arrived she had washed her hair and put on some lipstick, changed into a silky shirt and some new, inexplicably flattering black corduroy jeans, and was keen to get out the door.

"How was the crazy penknife man? Did you stop him in his tracks?"

Raff had diffused four or five no less toxic situations since then, as well as poking his nose into the situation *viz* the death at Eddison Grove — about which he was brimming with news. For a moment he couldn't even think what she was talking about.

"How was who? Ah!" he said, and laughed. It occurred to him that he had laughed more in these last few months with Dolly than he had in the last twenty years put together. Not that anything was particularly funny. But she made him happy. (Especially when Pippa wasn't around.) "Yes. We stopped him in his tracks. Thank you for asking. He is — or was, last I heard — safely behind bars, back at the station, awaiting a solicitor."

It was a gentle spring evening: not too cold. Neither of them had a car, in any case. And they had plenty of time. All the time in the world. Pippa had left a message to say she was staying the night with Nicole, which meant that Dolly and Raff would have the house to themselves.

Dolly had reserved a table at a pub a twenty-minute amble along the river, and they set out down the lane towards supper. As they walked past Number Seven both tried, surreptitiously, to peer through the window. Downstairs, Gigi's blanket blocked any clues as to what might have been going on inside, and there were no lights on upstairs: the house seemed very quiet.

"I think they may have left," Raff said softly. "One of my colleagues dropped by this afternoon — couldn't get any reply."

"Maybe they have." Dolly thought about the cards she'd pulled this morning. They had certainly suggested that Geordie, at least, would be moving on. And the house did indeed seem very quiet. "Geordie was round at our house this afternoon, after we came back from the mortuary."

"He was?" Raff sounded interested.

"In a dreadful state. Very upset about his friend. He used to go round to the flat to have baths all the time, according to Pippa. Though how he managed to fit them in, between all the baths he took at my place, I don't know. Anyway . . ."

"Maybe the water ran hotter for longer at yours," Raff said.

Dolly smiled. "Possibly."

"Or maybe you had better cleaning products . . . You definitely had a nicer bathroom."

Raff pictured the scene: that scrawny body in that filthy, ancient bathtub. The bathroom at Eddison Grove

165

looked as if it hadn't seen any cleaning products for decades. "He hadn't been in the bath for long," Raff added. "When we found him. There were no signs of bloating. The body was in reasonably good shape . . ."

"Oh, yes?" said Dolly faintly. She and Pippa had only seen a photograph of the dead man's head and shoulders. It hadn't occurred to her to think about the rest of his body. "I must say, his face looked pretty normal," she added. "I mean — brownish. A couple of blisters on his neck . . . And the hair was singed . . ." She shivered. "There we go, talking about death again. Let's talk about something else! How's Sam doing?"

"Ah! *Sam*," Raff smiled at the mere mention of his son, "Sam is doing very well, Dolly! Thank you for asking. He's doing very well indeed. On Cloud Nine, as a matter of fact. He's just been offered a terrific teaching job at Berkeley University. In California."

"No!"

"Indeed he has!" Raff's pride in his son was so great, it made his voice waver, which made him laugh. He cleared his throat. "Amazing though, isn't it?" he said. "Who'd've thought?"

"You'll miss him though."

"Of course I will. But we can go and see him, Dolly. We could go together, if you liked. Have you ever been to California?"

Dolly had not. And on her current earnings, nor would she. But it was a beautiful idea. "I'd love to go one day . . . if Sam doesn't mind."

"Sam definitely won't mind! Sam still talks about that shepherd's pie you made him back in the spring.

Anyone would think it was the only thing he's ever eaten under my motorhome roof."

It was a good pub; small and unpretentious, and usually fairly quiet. But you were never entirely safe in this part of London. This evening there were a couple of noisy bankers in expensive leisurewear at the bar, competing with each other about their sons' off-piste skiing skills, so Dolly and Raff decided to eat out in the garden, where there were outdoor heaters, and Raff could update Dolly on his news in peace.

And he had plenty:

Firstly, that the dead man's identity remained unconfirmed.

2: There was no official record either of Kaylin or Marina living at the flat on Eddison Grove.

3: The utility bills and council tax were in the name of a female in her eighties, name of Sheila Linklater, and were all paid fully, and up to date.

And finally, "Listen to this, Dolly . . ."

4: *Sheila Linklater was also still drawing a pension.*

"Oh dear," said Dolly. "Well, that's alarming. Because I'm fairly certain Sheila Linklater is dead." She thought about it for a while. "Geordie used to call Kaylin 'Killer Kayle'. Did you know that?"

Raff didn't.

"Well," Dolly said, "I think maybe someone ought to talk to Geordie. He probably knows more than he's letting on."

"Easy to say, Dolly. He appears to have gone AWOL. We were looking for him at the house this afternoon, as

167

you know. There was no one answering the door, and he's not answering his mobile. Are you certain Pippa gave the mortuary the right number?"

Their food arrived. But the barman must have misheard their order over the noise of the off-piste skiers, because they brought Dolly the wrong dish; and there was a discussion as to whether she should settle for the steak and kidney pie they thought she'd ordered, or wait for the salade nicoise she had asked for.

"Oh, forget the salad!" Dolly said, smelling the pie. So it was a while before she and Raff could return to the matter in hand.

"Where were we?" Dolly said. "One old lady, almost certainly dead; one unknown man, definitely dead. One unknown squatter with a mobile he won't answer. One unknown Russian girl — missing . . . Where the hell is she?"

"We're looking for her . . . inasmuch as we can. But we don't really know who we're looking for. This is the thing with illegals — squatters, immigrants, whathave-yous. They tend to exist below the radar. One more thing, Dolly. Which might surprise you." He smiled. A little more delving had revealed the true owner of the flat on Eddison Grove.

"The old woman owned it!" said Dolly. "That's what all the fuss was about."

Raff shook his head. "Actually," he said. "It was owned by your old neighbour, Maurice Bousquet. Which means, of course, that it now belongs to the appalling Isabelle Ferrari."

168

She absorbed this in silence, remembering all the times Maurice had pleaded poverty, all the times he'd complained about not having enough money to go home to St Lucia to see his family. "He was a secretive old bugger, wasn't he?" she said. "If I'd known he was such a rich man I might have made a play for him."

"Very funny," said Raff. It reminded him of the property brochure print-outs he had, folded away in his coat pocket . . . Hardly for Buckingham Palace, any of them. Perhaps, he thought, he would bring them out another day.

CHAPTER
TWENTY

The mood at Number Seven Tinderbox Lane that evening was tetchy and bleak. Trek, the idiot, had done nothing all day, not since Geordie had left him this morning. Frozen by his own terror, he had lain on the sitting-room floor, in the dark, surrounded by the ashtrays, stale food and empty beer cans, and drunk himself semi-comatose. When Geordie left, the bottle of vodka had still been three-quarters full. Trek had swallowed it all, and was now lying in a senseless, drunken heap, trying to sleep it off.

Gigi was back. She'd snuck home from Elephant and Castle, but only to clear out her stuff. She'd had enough of the Tinderbox Lane experiment: Kaylin's death had been — figuratively — the final nail in the coffin. She wanted to rejoin her old crew again. But she couldn't quite bring herself to abandon Trek as he slept there, lying in his own vomit. So she was trying to wake him — without sympathy or success.

Geordie, meanwhile, was stretched out on the sofa, as usual, ignoring them both. Having quickly got shot of Pippa, he'd spent the day trudging through the West End, not noticing where he went or why he went there, and growing increasingly paranoid and miserable.

170

There were moments when he thought he spotted Marina in the crowd and he would understand that this was what he was actually doing: searching for her. But then, like a mirage, her image seemed to disappear back into the swarm, and he would trudge on again, as aimless as before.

This time last week, he would have said he had the measure of Marina: a beautiful, lonely girl in a hostile city, working hard to find a place for herself in the world. Geordie had even gone as far as to discuss her unhappy plight with Kaylin . . . not that Kaylin had much to say on the matter. Now — after everything that had happened — he kept asking himself, what did he actually know about her, after all? That horrible pierced heart kept flashing up in his mind. What else might she be capable of? He didn't like to imagine.

All day, as he tramped the streets, he'd been checking his mobile to see if she had called. But of course she hadn't. Why would she? Pippa had called (he hadn't answered), and the mortuary had called, or the police, or whoever. They must have tried him at least a dozen times. But he had no intention of answering *those calls*. God knows. Just thinking about it made him panic.

In the end, he'd done the only thing he felt he could under the circumstances, because his big brain wasn't thinking straight. He scribbled down a few important numbers from his mobile contacts, removed the sim card, bit it — and threw his phone into a nearby bin. The end.

Except then he'd had to buy another phone. Which had basically wiped him out, financially. (But at least it had stopped the mortuary from hounding him.) And now he was hungry, dreaming of Dolly's risotto, and trying to formulate an intelligent plan on an empty stomach was not proving as simple as he would have hoped. Gigi and Trek weren't helping, either.

"For fuck's sake," he said, sliding his new phone into his pocket and standing up. "Gigi, he's not going to budge. He's an idiot. If he wants to lie there and piss his future away until the police come and scoop him off the floor, there's not much either of us can do about it, is there? Trek, you fucking moron. Wake up."

Trek grunted, curled his meaty body into a tighter ball, and continued snoring.

"We can't wait for you, mate," Geordie said. "We've got to get out of here. All the shit about Kaylin . . . Fuck only knows what skeletons he's got in his closet, but we don't want to be involved in it. We don't want to be caught up in this shit. Can you hear me? Trek, you stupid cunt —" Geordie gave him a hefty kick in the ribs. "Wake up! We've got to go."

Trek didn't move. Geordie and Gigi stood over him, waiting, each of them wondering, silently, whether they might simply leave him there after all. Except he was dangerously drunk. What if he died? What if he choked on his own vomit and died?

Trek was many things, chief among them, according to Geordie, *a total fucking idiot*. But he was also somebody's son, somebody's brother and, above all, their friend, and they knew they had to look after him.

Somehow, they were going to have to drag his vast and inebriated body onto its feet, and transport it all the way up to Elephant and Castle.

"We need a shopping trolley," announced Gigi.

"No. What we need is some ice-cold water and some black coffee."

There was a thump on the door. Geordie and Gigi turned towards it, and simultaneously noticed their error: Trek's metal barricade, so assiduously built and installed, hung wide open. In their united anguish, fretting over their stupid friend, neither had remembered to close it, and now it was too late. Whoever it was out there wasn't waiting for them to answer the thump: they were coming in. There was another thump; an ear-splitting crack — and the old wooden door that separated the squat from the world beyond split half open. Gigi and Geordie watched helplessly, in the semi-darkness, as the head of a sledgehammer hit the door with one more almighty blow, and then another, until there was nothing between the young squatters, their landlady, and her hammer-wielding henchman, but splintered pieces of wood.

Isabelle, glossy-haired and perfumed, set one dainty, pointed boot over the threshold, and then the next. She paused at the door, flicked on the light and coolly surveyed the scene. Her lackey — the fat-necked friend — stepped over the debris to join her. She muttered something to him in Portuguese. He nodded, and stepped into the room.

And like Colonel Mustard, Geordie noted, the man was holding a piece of lead piping.

CHAPTER
TWENTY-ONE

Dolly and Raff didn't spot the broken door when they passed by a few hours later. Fat Neck had tidied it up before he left and of course Tinderbox Lane had no street lighting. Added to which, Raff and Dolly, happy in each other's company, and reassured that Pippa was spending the night elsewhere, were headed home to Number Two with other matters on their mind.

In fact, nobody noticed the state of the door until seven o'clock the following evening, when Pippa went to call.

Raff had been barely awake when he crept past at the crack of dawn, en route to the motorhome, where he'd left his uniform for work; Rosie didn't notice it as she ushered her children into her husband's white Range Rover for the school run; the professor, singing along to his iPod Wagner, didn't notice it when he left for college that morning; Terry Whistle hadn't stepped outside since the weekend; Dolly had a client booked mid-morning and another mid-afternoon, and didn't venture beyond her front garden all day; Pippa, who had spent the night away, went from her friend Nicole's flat directly to a double shift at the pub; and as for

Isabelle . . . she would have been unlikely to raise the alarm.

As was her wont on Tuesdays and Thursdays, Rosie went directly from school drop-off to the gym, where she did a few gentle press-ups on one of the high-tech press-up machines, took a short walk on one of the running machines, and felt quite pleased with herself. She spent the rest of the morning in the café upstairs, eating muffins, drinking cappuccinos, changing into her day clothes, blow-drying her hair, and reading the *Daily Mail*. At noon, just as she was preparing to leave, Derek texted, inviting her to join him for lunch. He said he would "swing by" and take her up West.

"Ooh," Rosie thought. Her life revolved around the school gate, the gym, and the Waitrose on Sheen Lane. Central London might have been a foreign country. But Derek told her he'd noticed there was a promotion on Le Creuset cooking pans in the kitchen-supplies department at the John Lewis on Oxford Street, and he thought she might enjoy it.

He thought quite right. Rosie was delighted by the idea. So he swung by the gym, where Rosie, thankfully, was fully made-up and having a good hair day, and they drove up to Oxford Street together.

But Derek's research hadn't been as thorough as it should have been and it turned out the Le Creuset promotion had taken place the previous week. So they left John Lewis and went for a wander up Oxford Street instead.

"You forget how crowded it is," Rosie said.

"Don't you just," replied Derek absently. He was feeling annoyed, wondering how John Lewis could have been so incompetent. As has been noted, he was a very tall man, also an impatient one, and he towered over the milling shoppers, hardly able to contain his irritation at their slow walking pace.

"I should hate to come up here with a pushchair," Rosie was saying.

"Mm-hm," he replied, from high above her head.

She was having trouble keeping pace with him: there wasn't space on the pavement for them to walk side by side and he didn't seem to take this into account. He had his hands in his Barbour jacket pockets and he was striding ahead, constructing a letter of complaint to John Lewis, or possibly to Westminster Council — when he could have sworn, through a gap in the traffic, that he spotted her. She was on the other side of the street, wearing that stupid anorak with a furry hood, head down, dodging between kerb and road: like everyone else, trying to find a space to walk along the pavement. Derek stopped short, causing minor inconvenience to pedestrians behind him. He raised a long arm and pointed:

"Rosie!" he shouted. "Look!"

But by then, the gap in the traffic had closed, and he was pointing at a bus.

"What is it, Derek?"

"For crying out loud, Rosie. It's that dreadful girl — the Russian strumpet everyone's looking for! Come on!" He lurched into the street, and after a moment's confusion, Rosie followed. But they couldn't get far due to all the buses.

"Call the police!" Derek yelled, mostly to Rosie.

But it was pointless. By the time they had navigated their way through the traffic, the girl was gone.

". . . literally. Vanished into thin air," he said to Dolly, later that evening, over a glass of wine. "Isn't that right, Rosie? Rosie didn't even see her, did you, dearest? The good news is, I don't think she saw us either. Did she, Mrs B? I mean she couldn't have. Frankly. There was a bloody great bus in the way . . ."

"Even if she did see us, she probably wouldn't have recognised us. To be fair." Rosie said. "I've certainly never spoken to her. Have you?"

That was at about six-thirty. Rosie and Derek had come charging down the lane, bottle in hand, fresh from the West End (via the off licence) to tell Dolly the news. Once again, they had hurried past the patched-up door at Number Seven Tinderbox Lane without pausing to look.

"It's a fair point, Mrs B," Derek acknowledged. It was true that he'd never spoken to the Russian girl either — although he could have done, of course, due to the Russian he learned at university. Nonetheless he believed that he and Rosie were "rather distinctive" and that, had she happened to look their way, she would definitely have known them, "and very probably, run like hell".

"What's she doing in Oxford Street?" Dolly wondered. "Are you certain it was her?"

"Which is a great shame," Derek continued, ignoring Dolly's questions. "Because there are a few things I'd like to say to her, I can tell you that. Numero uno . . ." He took a slurp of red wine. "Where the hell are you hiding, young lady? And numero duo, did you kill that chap?"

Pippa turned up from her double shift not long afterwards. Dolly was kind, seeing her daughter's sad face. She poured her some wine, asked after Nicole and her day at work and Pippa made an effort to appear cheerful. But it hadn't been a great day. The pub had been quiet and she'd received two email job rejections in the afternoon. (She'd wasted a whole day filling in the application form for one of them.) And despite having called him a hundred times, she'd not heard from Geordie since yesterday. Now she was wondering if there was something wrong with his mobile. Either he'd been disconnected or he was blocking her calls. In any case, he certainly hadn't tried to call her. She'd made a point of not looking up from her phone when she walked past his front door on the way home this evening and now . . .

. . . here were Rosie and the professor. To delight her.

"You'll never guess who Mrs B and I spotted up in the West End this afternoon, Pippa," Derek said. "I was just saying to your mother — really, if I'd only been that tiny bit quicker, we would have had her."

"Who did you see?" asked Pippa, politely.

"Have a guess!"

"Che Guevara?"

A pause, while Derek registered that she was joking. He gave a belt of laughter. "Ha! Che Guevara's not a she, you muppet! Ha-ha-ha! You are a one, Pippa Greene! Ha-ha-ha *Che Guevara* indeed!"

Pippa's mind wandered. *Perhaps there was something wrong with her phone? Maybe that was the problem? Maybe Geordie was desperate to speak to her but for some reason couldn't get through?*

". . . can you believe it?" the professor was saying. "Stuck behind a bloody great bus! We tried our best to catch up with her, Pippa, but frankly, she's a quick-footed little thing. Isn't she? One minute she's there, next minute she's gone! It's all very suspicious, though, isn't it? What do you think, Pippa? Do you think she had anything to do with that poor chap getting electrocuted in the bath? It wouldn't take much, would it? And with the Russians . . . you can't trust them. They're all crooks. And they love violence."

Rosie said, "That's sounds a bit racist, Derek."

But Pippa wasn't listening again. Her mind was on Geordie, and the stillness that had emanated from Number Seven as she walked self-consciously by. Maybe, after all, she had inherited a little of her mother's sixth sense — or maybe she was just looking for an excuse to go calling on him . . . But something hadn't been right. It had been too still. Too silent.

"Has anyone seen them today?" she asked suddenly.

"If by 'them' you mean your *squatter friends*, I'm pleased to say not," answered Rosie, pouring herself another glass of wine. "No. They've been very quiet

179

today . . . Well. We've been out most of the day, I suppose . . ."

There was a novel on the breakfast bar: something earnest lent to Pippa by Geordie: *Close to the Knives: A Memoir of Disintegration*. She'd not even opened it. She picked it up now. It was a paltry excuse — but she felt she needed one. If not to knock on his door, then at least to get out of this one.

"Oh dear," she said. "I promised I'd return this to Geordie." She stood up. "I'll do it now."

"My goodness, Pippa!" bellowed the professor, rolling his eyes. "Come on, girl! You can do better than that! That must be the most pathetic excuse I've heard all year."

"Darling, are you sure it's a good idea?" Dolly said. "Why don't you give it back tomorrow?"

"I won't be long, Mum. He may not even be in. I'll probably be back in a minute."

"Honestly, love," said Rosie. "He can survive without his silly book for one evening . . . There are so many super men you could choose from — a gorgeous girl like you! Why are you wasting your time on a horrid little man like him?"

"Well said, Mrs B!"

"Thank you, Derek."

"You can do better, Pippa!" Derek shouted after her. But she was already gone.

CHAPTER
TWENTY-TWO

Number Seven Tinderbox Lane was dark and silent, just as it had been since yesterday. Gigi's grubby blanket still hung at the front window, blocking any view, and, as usual, there were no lights on upstairs. Even then, standing outside, feeling half intimidated, half repelled by that horrible, dirty blanket, and staring at the wretched house, it took Pippa a moment to notice the door: split down the centre and removed from its hinges — leaning in several bits against the door frame.

She hesitated. Something bad had happened in there. She knew it. Just as her mother would have done. And just like her mother, though she sensed danger, her feet moved towards the house. She pushed open the garden gate.

"Hello? Anyone there?"

No reply.

She paused at the front door. It was dusk outside, but inside it was pitch black, and it frightened her. She wanted to run away, and yet her feet wouldn't move.

"Hello?" she called again.

"Hello there, Pippa," came a friendly voice from behind her. Pippa jumped.

It was Raff. He was dropping in on Dolly on his way back from work.

"I don't think they're in," he said — stating the obvious. He looked at her more carefully. "You all right?" he asked. She didn't reply at once. "Pippa? Are you all right?"

"I think something's happened. Something feels very wrong."

Raff said: "Something's always felt very wrong about that place. But you know my opinions on that. Oh —" He noticed the door, at last. "Hello, hello . . ."

"I've not heard a word from Geordie all day. Raff . . . will you —" Pippa paused. She gave an awkward smile. "Would you mind very much coming in with me? I'm not sure if I want to go in there on my own . . ."

So they went into the house together. Raff pushed away what was left of the door and, side by side, they stepped into the darkness. The place stank of stale food — sour milk, old curry — cigarette smoke, spilled alcohol. Pippa's foot hit against something solid, heavy — soft — and she tripped slightly, skidding in something damp and tacky as she recovered. The room also smelled of vomit.

"Hello?" Pippa called out. "Anyone here?"

No reply.

"*Hello?*"

Raff flicked the light switch. Nothing. He pulled out his torch.

The place was a wreck. It had been a wreck before — but this room hadn't simply been neglected, what there ever was of it had been vandalised: the sofa was upturned, there were books and papers and pieces of broken glass scattered over the floor. Raff's torch travelled along the filthy floor and dirty white walls — but there was only debris left behind — the takeaway packaging and upturned ashtrays; an empty bottle of vodka on its side; beer cans; a pool of drying vomit. No possessions. No personal effects. No sign of continued life. And there on the walls — Raff's torch swept over them once and then returned: there were fat smears of black — or dark brown —

"Blood?" whispered Pippa.

"Could be," said Raff.

"Oh Christ. Oh fuck — *what's happened to them?*"

"Looks like they had a visitor," said Raff. "Someone who scared the living daylights out of them, by the look of things. I should think they've scurried off back to wherever it was they came from."

He made it sound run of the mill.

"But — that's blood! How do you know they're all right?"

"I don't, Pippa."

"What do you mean, *you don't*? Aren't you going to — use your radio? Call in some of your police friends? People can't just *do this* . . . There's blood! For all we know — they're *dead*, Raff."

Actually, the thought had flitted through his mind. There was something wild about Isabelle Ferrari, aka Lucky Crystal, which made almost anything seem possible. Especially so, considering what became of her other sitting tenant . . .

He dismissed the idea. Because of course — what Pippa didn't realise — this sort of lawless eviction of lawless squatters was, indeed, *run of the mill*. It's what happened in the world beyond the law, where girls like Pippa didn't generally venture: shit happened. Raff turned his torch towards the front door. "Come on," he said. "Let's get out of here."

"What? *No!* We've got to deal with this! There's *blood . . .*"

"I'll call it in," he said. "You go on home . . ."

She hesitated. It was what she wanted to do most in the world. But she felt bad, leaving him there.

"Go on!" he said. "Tell your mother I'll be there in a minute."

". . . Thank you, Raff."

He smiled. "They come in handy sometimes, don't they," he said to her as she headed out the door. "Your fascist police service." Raff chuckled at his own joke. "Maybe not completely evil, after all, huh?"

She ignored him and walked slowly, sadly back onto the lane, Geordie's earnest novel still in her hand.

Something had attached itself to the tacky vomit on her shoe: a small piece of paper — folded, and slightly crumpled. She tried to wipe it off without touching it, but it didn't want to budge. And so, with dainty fingers she bent down and gave it a tug.

There was something written on it: a few scribbled words in small, spiky handwriting. There wasn't enough light on the lane to read it so she pulled out her lighter. The paper smelled of sick and it took a while for her to decipher the handwriting . . . She had never seen

184

Geordie's handwriting — but this, she knew, had to have been written by him. Written by him — and addressed to her.

   . . . Doubt thou the stars are fire. Doubt that the sun doth move. Doubt truth to be a liar. But never doubt I love.
   I AM SO SORRY IT HAS TO BE THIS WAY

A farewell letter? Is that what it was? A farewell to her? She felt her eyes stinging — Geordie had never finished the quotation. Not the first night. (She'd looked it up when she went home.) And they had never spoken of it again — never spoken of love at all — of course not! And now . . . it was too late. Now there was blood on the wall — and he was gone.

CHAPTER
TWENTY-THREE

She was wrong about the blood. It turned out to be a mixture of lentil masala and vomit. But she was right that he was gone. And for a week, with no squatters to squabble with or over, life on Tinderbox Lane settled back into something like normality. Terry Whistle, at Number One, stopped calling Richmond Council, and returned happily to his mysterious IT consultancy work, which so rarely involved venturing outside. And Professor Derek West took Rosie out to dinner and declared his enthusiasm for her in a way that made Rosie giggle and blush, and feel happier and sexier than she had in many years. The following day he rented a police inspector uniform from a fancy dress shop in Hammersmith, and spent his first, blissful night in her large bed. (He moved back to his own bedroom before the kids woke up.)

Isabelle Ferrari, having previously been somewhat elusive, became quite an obstreperous presence on the lane. She posted a lightly perfumed, handwritten letter through all her neighbours' doors, to update them:

Friends,
You will no doubt be delighted to hear that the Law Brakers[sic] who were residing illegally at my

property, Number Seven Tinderbox Lane, have returned to the filthy cave from where they came. This means that the property is now vacant again, and improvements may commence . . .

She reported that her builders would begin repairs at once, and that the house would be put on the market as soon as the work was done. She signed off, "Thanks be to God", which was a bit rich. In any case, when she wrote "at once" she meant it. By the time her neighbours read their letters, work had already begun.

She was now spending several hours each day on the site, communicating with her builders in noisy, imperial tones — in a language presumed to be Portuguese by everyone except Rosie, and the top of the lane looked like a bombsite. When the professor confronted her on this and asked if she might perhaps ask her builders to be a little tidier, she waved him away without even making eye contact. She told him it would be finished soon, and to be patient.

"Or would you like me to leave it as it is, so squatters come back?"

It was a reasonable question, he thought, however rudely delivered. Professor West was not afraid of many people, but something about Isabelle Ferrari unnerved him. He'd heard from Dolly that the chap-in-the-bathtub had lived in a flat which also belonged to her — and it posed a few uncomfortable questions . . . Especially when you put it together with the sudden disappearance of the trio next door. So he rubbed his hands together and said:

"Lovely jubbly, Isabelle. Good to know you're on it! Just as long as it doesn't drag on . . ."

But by then Isabelle had already glided away to yell at her workers, and he was left there, talking to himself.

Pippa cropped short her beautiful long hair. Never a good sign. She was miserable. Nothing much was going right in her life, but she focused her unhappiness on the disappearance of Geordie. She kept his note, sick-smeared though it was; and brought it out at intervals through the day.

Its significance grew with each unfolding. She tried to imagine at what point he had written it, and whether he knew, as he wrote it, that she would find it there, lying in the drying pool of vomit. More than that, she wondered whether she should search for him. Maybe he was waiting for her now? Maybe he had left clues in the house that she was too dim to pick up?

Or maybe he had moved on. Forgotten all about her. Had no interest in ever seeing her again.

And she still lived at home with her mother.

And her best friend Nicole had just been offered a great job in environmental planning and marketing — meanwhile Pippa still hadn't been called in for a single interview.

And her hair was too short.

And if Geordie really loved her he wouldn't have simply buggered off like that.

Except maybe he had no choice?

And she was broke.

And she couldn't find a decent job.

And she still lived at home with her mother.

And her hair was too short.

And she was going to get old and fat and soon she would die and nobody would care and . . .

So on.

Over breakfast, a week after the disappearance (and five days after the lousy haircut) Dolly happened to mention that Raff was looking at properties to buy in the area — and Pippa burst into tears. Dolly — to her shame — didn't even notice. She had her back to Pippa, was preoccupied trying to squeeze badly cut bread into the toaster. She was wittering about the cost of property; what Raff might or might not be able to afford and how nice it would be for Dolly when he and his pet python finally moved out of the motorhome . . . She turned around and spotted a tear rolling off the tip of Pippa's nose.

Dolly left the toaster, stopped talking at once. She waited for Pippa to speak.

"Ignore me," Pippa said. "I'm being an idiot."

"Of course you're not," said Dolly. "There's me, banging on about Raff, and it's been a horrible few weeks for you." She put an arm around Pippa's shoulders. "Do you want to talk?" she said. "Or do you just want to cry? Or both?"

Pippa continued to cry.

"Actually," said Dolly, "you can cry as much as you like — but you have to talk to me, Pippa. I presume this is mostly about bloody Geordie? Of course it is. You still haven't heard from him, I presume?"

"No."

"And have you tried to call him?"

"Of course I have . . . I think the line's been cut off."

"All right. So . . ." Dolly wasn't sure what to say to this. The man was a lightweight. A creep and a bastard, and for making her daughter feel like this, she wanted to kill him . . . And now, thankfully, he was gone. Pippa would forget about him eventually. It had been such a short affair . . . If she could just be called in for a single job interview, it would be such a help. But she couldn't say that. She said: "Where the hell is he then?"

"I don't know."

Pippa pulled the scrap of sick-stained paper out of her pocket and dropped it onto the counter. And as Dolly picked it up, the cards he had pulled during their reading drifted into focus: the Three of Cups reversed, the Three of Swords, the Tower . . . She couldn't read the tiny handwriting without her glasses . . .

She squinted at it. A tiny, illegible black scrawl, and then in capitals:

I AM SO SORRY IT HAS TO BE THIS WAY . . .

Which way? What was he talking about?

"Did Geordie write this?" Dolly asked.

"Of course he did!"

"How do you know?" Dolly smelled the paper. It still smelled vaguely of vomit. "What makes you say so? Is this his handwriting?" She reached for her glasses.

"Yes! Of course it is!"

Doubt thou the stars are fire. Doubt that the sun doth move. Doubt truth to be a liar. But never doubt I love.

"Are you certain he wrote this, Pipps? It doesn't sound like him."

"Mum, it's Shakespeare!"

"I know that."

"And yes it does sound like him! Mum, that's what he said to me the first time we met! The very first time. When I was sitting on the doorstep outside Windy Ridge!"

"*Really?*" said Dolly. "It was a bit forward, wasn't it?"

"No! Yes — I mean *no*. He didn't say the last bit. He said the bit before — we were looking at the moon."

"Hm . . ." Dolly's head was aching. Something didn't make sense.

"Where did you find it?"

"I found it in the house . . . It was stuck to my shoe."

"Stuck to your shoe?" Dolly folded the paper and dropped it back onto the counter. "Pippa my love, are you certain this was written by Geordie? What about the other chap? Perhaps —"

"No!"

"But Pippa, a neat little quote like that — these things get shared, don't they? One person says it — another person hears it. It stays in the mind, doesn't it?" Dolly wasn't helping her daughter to feel any better. She knew this — but there was something about the note. Something distracting — and ultimately irrelevant. *It wasn't meant for Pippa.* Why was Pippa sobbing about it? Probably, reflected Dolly, because in her heart, Pippa knew this too. "Do you think," said Dolly, "do you suppose, my darling Pippa, that this letter was written by the other chap — whose name I can't remember — to another girl entirely?"

"*No.*"

"Either that, or do you think *possibly* — do you think it might possibly — just possibly — have been written by Geordie — to someone else? Darling Pipps — I just . . . Are you absolutely certain that you were the only person Geordie was seeing? Because I have to be honest with you, my love — his cards . . . From the very beginning, Pippa — his cards . . ."

"Please." Pippa held up a hand. "Please, don't talk about his fucking cards." And then she really started crying. Because of course Dolly was right. In her heart Pippa knew it perfectly well. This disgusting sick-stained sheet of paper — was nothing. A piece of nonsense — written by Geordie, perhaps. But never meant for her.

The Three of Cups, reversed. The Three of Swords. The Moon, reversed . . . the Tower . . . Someone else had pulled those same cards. Maybe not in that order. But Dolly had seen them, lately. Yes, Geordie had pulled them. But so had someone else . . . Dolly could have kicked herself for being so slow. She remembered exactly who it was. Last spotted in an oversized anorak, ducking behind buses on Oxford Street.

The police, according to Raff, were no closer to finding her. Maybe Dolly would have better luck. Pippa didn't need to know what Dolly planned to do next — but tomorrow, when Pippa returned to college, her mother was going to head out in search of Marina. The girl had a lot to answer for. Or maybe she didn't. Either way, Dolly was fed up with so many questions still hanging unanswered. She had a great deal she wanted to ask her.

CHAPTER
TWENTY-FOUR

Marina had last been seen somewhere near John Lewis, Oxford Street: possibly one of the most crowded streets in Europe. And she'd only been spotted for a second. And only by Professor Derek West, whose enthusiasm to be involved in the drama rendered his evidence less than a hundred per cent trustworthy. Added to which even Rosie, walking beside him at the time, hadn't spotted her.

However — a lead was a lead, and Dolly needed to start somewhere. So she stopped at Windy Ridge on her way up to the West End, to confirm the details.

The professor never seemed to do much work. Dolly found them both at home, drinking cappuccinos and eating home-baked muffins, side by side at the dining table. The professor had his laptop open at least. Rosie, as usual, was reading the *Daily Mail*. She looked happy — like a different woman from the one Dolly met when she and her vile husband first moved onto the lane. The professor looked like a cat with the cream. A perfect match, Dolly thought. She wondered what Rosie's husband might make of it, if ever he found out. She wondered if anyone on Tinderbox Lane would ever see him again.

They plied her with a freshly frothed cappuccino, and when she told them what she was doing that day, they insisted on coming along.

Reason Number One (said the professor): six eyes searching were better than two. Obviously.

Reason Number Two (said Rosie): it might be dangerous.

"By the way," added the professor, spraying blueberry crumbs onto his keyboard, "I know Mrs B didn't tell you at the time —"

"I didn't have the heart."

"She was meant to. We'd very much agreed that she would," said Derek, looking at her balefully. "Because this is the sort of thing neighbours are meant to do for each other. Isn't it, Mrs B?"

"But then when everything went so sort of pear-shaped, Dolly, I thought there really wasn't any point . . ."

"What?" Dolly asked. "What were you meant to tell me?"

Still, Rosie hesitated.

"We saw her, didn't we, Rosie, dawdling along by the river with that young man, Geordie."

"You saw Marina and Geordie together?"

"He was giving her the most dreadful googly eyes, wasn't he, Rosie dear?"

"He was," said Rosie, ruefully. "I felt awful for Pippa. But then I thought, well — thank goodness. Really. *For you*. And then everything went horrid, you know. With the chap in the bath and everything . . ."

Dolly nodded. Well of course. It made perfect sense. "When did you see them together?" she asked.

"If I remember rightly," said Derek, "it was the Wednesday. Before I went to York for the conference — because then we got back and there was the dinner immediately after, and Raff came by —"

"In his uniform," added Rosie.

"— and told us about the chap in the bath, and you and Pippa had to rush off home . . ."

"It didn't seem *right* to say anything at that point," Rosie said.

"Yes. I can understand," Dolly agreed. "It would have been awkward."

"That's why we were rather surprised when he was sitting in your front room just the other day!"

". . . yes, it was definitely on the Wednesday," Derek continued. "Because Rosie was in a rush, weren't you, dear? We wanted to go for a longer walk, round to Chiswick Mall, but then Rosie remembered India had a swimming lesson."

There were no swimming lessons today. Better yet, Rosie and Derek both had cars. (Rosie would never use public transport, because of the terrorist threat.) They set off for Oxford Street together in Rosie's luxurious Range Rover, Derek at the wheel, Rosie and Derek squabbling in a flirtatious manner about the faster route, and the most sensible place to park.

"Mind you, I think it's a wild goose chase," he said as the car edged along Hammersmith Bridge. "That is — we may or may not find her. I have a good idea which little side street she went down . . . But it may well be we're barking up the wrong alleyway altogether, Dolly. I was only saying to Rosie last night — *there's something pretty suspect about our Brazilian friend.* Don't you think? Rosie thinks so, don't you, dear?"

Rosie nodded. "And it's not because of her being a stripper or anything. It's not. I just think she's a bit peculiar . . . *Very* hostile. Not the sort of person you'd really trust . . ."

"I don't like her, Dolly," added the professor. "Not one bit. And I can't help thinking it's a bit of coincidence. She was landlady to the poor chap in the bath. She was landlady to those idiots at Number Seven, *all of whom have since disappeared.* Frankly, she makes Peter Rachman look like the Good Samaritan. And you know what else I think?"

Dolly, enjoying the luxury of riding in the back of Rosie's car, asked him to tell her.

"I think — and you'll probably leap down my throat for it, but the fact is — it's all very well, talking about Brazilian carnivals, and bum-lifts and pubic hair whatnots and all that —"

"Derek!" remonstrated Rosie.

"But there's more to Brazil than the fun stuff. She comes from a background where her husband was very probably murdered . . . if we are to believe anything she says. And then she spent all those years as a stripper. We're not dealing with — well, with someone *nice*. Like the wonderful Mrs Buck here. Or the lovely Dolly Greene," he added. "We're dealing with quite a tough little piece. Somebody gets in her way — she's going to put a bullet in their head! Or electrocute them in the bath. You know what I mean? That's the sort of world she's coming from . . ."

"Hm," said Dolly. "You may be overstating it, Derek. But I see what you're getting at."

"What I'm getting at," he said, "is here we are, off on the hunt for a few answers from the Russian strumpet. And I suppose it's in the back of all our minds that she murdered that poor chap in the bath. For her own dark reasons . . . Well — maybe she did. *And maybe she didn't.* Maybe it was Isabelle who did him in. So to speak. Maybe the bathtub chap was one of these 'sitting tenants'. And I'm telling you: where that lady comes from, '*sitting tenants*' probably get '*un*-sat' pretty damn fast. Know what I mean? *Whatever it takes.*"

"He's got a point, Dolly," Rosie said, peering under her seat belt into the back row.

"Possibly," said Dolly. But his theory didn't take into account old Sheila Linklater, now presumed dead, whose pension, it seemed, "the poor chap in the bath" had been claiming all this time. Rosie and Derek were shocked by this: as shocked by Dolly's failure to tell them about it earlier as they were by the news itself. The "poor chap" clearly deserved what was coming to him, Derek said. "*And more!*" But it didn't change his opinion that Isabelle was a nasty piece of work, and quite possibly capable of murder . . .

It turned out to be a fruitless but enjoyable outing to the West End. The three of them roamed along Oxford Street, Bond Street, South Molton Street and numerous side streets in between, peering under the hoods of anoraks as they walked, and found no one resembling Marina. Finally they stopped at Pret a Manger for a late lunch, and headed home, in good time for Rosie's school run.

They almost drove right past her. It was Rosie's beady eye that spotted her first. She was scuttling along the pavement by Sanders Funeral Directors at the bottom of Barnes High Street, just turning off in the direction of Eddison Grove.

"Derek!" she cried. "Derek! Look! The anorak! Isn't that . . .?"

"Yes, it is!" cried Dolly. "What on earth is she doing, back here again? Stop the car! No! Don't stop the car! Whatever you do, don't let her see us!"

Derek had the presence of mind not to screech to a noisy halt. As he parked up — too slowly, in Dolly's opinion — they could still glimpse her, scuttling into the distance.

"I think we should split up," said Dolly as they climbed down from the car. "If she sees all three of us coming she's going to know something's up. She'll run off, and we won't stand a chance."

"Good thinking, Dolly," Derek agreed. "Great thinking. Good to have you on the team."

"What?" Dolly stared at him.

But he'd moved on. "We should call the cops. Do you think a direct dial to the sergeant, Dolly? Or 999? Or both?"

"I have to fetch the kids," said Rosie.

"Come on, Mrs B! Forget the kids for once! We need you!" He pinched her bottom and she giggled.

Idiots, thought Dolly. The sooner she shook them off, the better. So she crossed the road, leaving them behind and dialling Raff as she walked. Raff didn't pick up, but she left him a voicemail, asking him to come at once.

Marina was at least fifty yards ahead of her, and walking fast, her head down. Dolly followed her as quickly and unobtrusively as she could. The street was quiet: they were the only two on it. At the end of the road, Marina turned left, away from the river and towards Barnes Pond. It occurred to Dolly that she didn't know exactly where Marina's flat was. Eddison Grove was a long road, stretching the length of the high street and beyond. By the time Marina finally came to a halt, Dolly was still twenty or more yards behind her, and out of breath. Marina paused at the door and glanced about her: on the lookout for something or someone, but not, apparently, for Dolly. She didn't notice Dolly, or anyway, gave no sign of it. Instead, she pulled out a small handbag, and began to rifle inside it. She rifled long enough for Dolly to catch up; long enough for Dolly to wonder if she was rifling at all, or simply biding her time, waiting for Dolly to pass on by. As Dolly drew even with her, Marina closed her bag and turned away towards the front door, her hand raised to the lock, as if to unlock it. Except, Dolly noticed, she wasn't holding any keys.

This was a mistake, of course. Behind her, Dolly stopped and turned into the doorway, blocking Marina's only escape route. She had no plan: only a lot of as yet unformed questions, and a desire to waylay the girl until Raff came: *if* he came.

Dolly said: "Oh! Hello! I thought it was you! It's Marina, isn't it?"

Marina looked — trapped. She looked terrified and uncertain. She said: "You are Tarot lady."

"I am! Well, I'm actually Dolly Greene. But yes — I'm the woman who read your cards a few weeks back. Is this where you live, then? How lovely . . . Funnily enough I was just on my way to calling on a friend a few doors up. And I *thought* it was you . . . So I thought, well — why not say hello? It gives me a chance to apologise, if nothing else! My daughter, Pippa — you know Pippa, don't you? She tells me you tied the knot. After all my dire warnings . . . So! As well as apologies, I think congratulations are in order." She was talking nonsense — clearly. She was saying anything that came into her head, just to keep the girl standing there. Never mind Raff, where the hell were Rosie and Derek? "And a refund, maybe? I don't often get things quite so wrong! How is married life treating you, Marina? Is it bliss?" Just then she remembered — the so-called husband was dead. And that if she knew Marina had married she would also have known —

There came the unmistakeable sound of footsteps thundering along the pavement towards them . . . Marina's expression had been hardening as Dolly's words piled up. At the sound of the approaching footsteps, and in less time than it took for Dolly to reach out her hand and try to grab her, Marina had

201

stepped around Dolly and run — onto the street and slap into the long, open arms of Professor Filthy.

"Well, well, well!" he said. "If it isn't our small Russian friend! And where are you off to in such a dizzy hurry, young lady?"

More footsteps. Dainty ones: totter totter totter, *pant pant pant* — and then there was Rosie, skidding to a halt beside them. "Well done, *Derek*!" she cried. "My have-a-go hero! You actually caught her!"

"I think, young lady," said Derek, staring down at Marina, a look of intolerable smugness on his large face, "you have a bit of explaining to do."

Marina wriggled in his arms, but she was indeed a small Russian (if not a friend) and he was very large. She stopped.

"Well then?" he said. "Do you want to begin?"

"Why you hold me in this way? Disgusting old man! I call police if you not let go."

"Pardon me," said Rosie. "He's not the disgusting one. You're the disgusting one, hanging around in our country, where nobody's invited you, being horrid, causing all this trouble . . ."

"Let go or I call police."

". . . stealing people's boyfriends . . . and that's the least of it, I understand. And by the way, we've already called the police, haven't we, Derek? So you needn't bother! What did you do to that poor chap in the bath? *Did you kill him?* Did you? And I suppose you killed that poor little old lady, too, did you? Whoever she was. And where did you put her, may I ask? In the deep freeze? Or in the rubbish bin, for the rubbish men to

202

collect? You probably flushed her down the toilet, knowing you. You should be ashamed of yourself."

"Slow down, Mrs B!" said Derek. "Let's not run away with ourselves. Remember — she may not have done anything."

"Oh, yes she has!" spat Rosie. "And don't forget that appalling — death messagey thingie, with the dead heart — the thing she sent to Dolly and Pippa. Don't forget about that! She should be deported. Bung her in a van and send her back to Russia where she came from. She's got the coat for it, haven't you, dear? Let the Russians deal with their own mess . . . And don't imagine there'll be colour TVs in the prison cells back in Slovia. Serbia. Sibraria. Whatever . . ."

Dolly put a hand on Rosie's arm: "I think we should let the girl speak . . ."

But Rosie hadn't finished. "Coming here, stealing other people's boyfriends . . . Just because you've killed your own. I've got no words for how disgusted I am by you . . ."

"That's enough, Rosie," Dolly said, more sharply.

"Well I'm only thinking of Pippa, Dolly," Rosie replied. "I should think if Pippa was here she'd want to give her a good *slap*."

"All right . . ."

Marina watched this exchange in silence, her emotions hidden behind that cold, hard, beautiful face. Finally, when everyone had stopped talking, and the professor had loosened his grip on her shoulders, just the tiniest bit, she laughed at them. It sounded hollow. "I don't know even what you are gabbling and shouting." She turned her haughty face upward, to look at Derek. "Disgusting man! Let go me. Or I call police."

"I will not let go, young lady," he said. "Not until you have explained what you are doing here. How that poor chap came to be dead in your bathtub; what happened to the poor old lady who used to live with you; and what possessed you to send that repulsive cow heart to my lovely neighbour here. And by the way. As Rosie says, you can stop banging on about the police, because they're already on their way.

Something seemed to be shifting behind the empty face — she looked confused . . . lost and confused — and then — nothing. The emptiness returned. She said:

"You are crazy. Everyone here, you are crazy. What are you saying about cow heart? And poor chap in my bathtubs? Who this man in bathtub?"

"Oh come off it!" said the professor. But he wasn't concentrating. He laughed in theatrical disbelief, looked across at Dolly and Rosie, so they could share the joke — and Marina, small and athletic and fighting for her own survival, grabbed that half-second of opportunity. She kicked him hard in the shin. He cried out in pain, released his grip — and she ran. Faster than lightning. She was already disappearing around the corner onto Terrace Gardens before Dolly, Rosie and the professor had collected their middle-aged senses sufficiently to go after her.

The three of them broke into what might loosely be described as a run — but they had already lost her, and really, they all knew it. And yet they kept running. Oh, how they ran. As they reached the end of the road and turned towards the river's edge, they saw her tiny figure four hundred yards ahead. She was sprinting — flying — up the steps to Barnes Bridge station. And they stopped. They could run no further.

They were bent double, hands on their knees, gasping for air and unable to speak as Raff's patrol car drew up.

"Hullo, hullo, hullo . . ." he said, looking at Derek, and trying quite hard not to smile, while his partner, Ollie, cracked up in the passenger seat beside him. "What have we got here, sir? Can I be of any assistance?"

"Never mind us!" Derek panted. "Catch her! Catch Marina! She's going towards the station . . ." As he spoke, they looked across the water. A commuter train was pulling out of the station, chugging north over Barnes Bridge, towards outer suburbia and oblivion.

A silence.

"Oops," said Ollie.

"Oops indeed!" said Raff. "I'll tell you what though," he added, leaning out of his window, looking at Dolly. "You may well be chasing after the wrong girl. That nasty package you had delivered last week. We've identified who sent it. Had her fingerprints all over it . . ."

". . . Marina?" Dolly panted.

"Nope."

"No?"

"It was Isabelle Ferrari, Dolly. Not a nice lady at all. She has a record as long as — well — if you'll forgive the cliché. But that lady has a record as long as my arm."

CHAPTER
TWENTY-FIVE

It was the day of Geordie, Trek and Gigi's eviction hearing at County Court: two weeks since they had disappeared without a trace now, and a week since Marina was last seen, flying up the Barnes Bridge station stairs, and then chugging into the outer beyond.

Life on the lane moved on.

Isabelle, still cruising under that Lucky star, had been formally cautioned, under the Malicious Communications Act, for delivering a dead heart to her neighbour's door. Needless to say, she did not appreciate quite how fortunate she was to have got off so lightly: if the card attached had been Death and not the Fool, she might have gone down for six months. In any case, she and Dolly continued to live side by side in silent, unacknowledged animosity. It was unpleasant for Dolly. She missed the good old days when she and Maurice Bousquet used to discuss the weather over the dustbins.

In the meantime, what with one thing and another, Isabelle had forgotten to inform her solicitor that the eviction hearing was no longer needed. She'd forgotten the squatters had ever even existed, until the solicitor called her mid-morning to confirm that said squatters, or "unknown persons" had failed to make an appearance at the courthouse, and that a legal eviction had — as expected — been secured.

Isabelle was standing downstairs at Number Seven when the call came through, in the middle of yelling at her illegal builder-slaves for lavishing unnecessary quantities of glue onto B&Q's cheapest kitchen units just then being attached to the back wall. If all went to plan, the property would be fully refurbished and ready for market within the month. In the meantime, no saving was too small, no shortcut too short. Whichever poor sap finally bought the place would have to start the full refurbishment all over again.

"What? Speak louder! What are you telling me?" Isabelle snapped into her phone.

"What are you talking about, 'County Court'? What 'hearing'? I didn't ask for any hearing. Why would I need an eviction hearing when I have no one to evict? I told you, the squatters have gone. Don't argue with me. I'm not paying you for this. Do you understand?"

So the squatters were gone, and nobody — except Pippa — felt much inclined to wonder where. Even for Pippa, the question was beginning to lose some of its urgency. That morning, at last, she had received an email inviting her for an interview. It was for a job as Sustainability Coordinator (£25,450 per anum) for a company, based in Battersea, which exported cardboard boxes. It wasn't that she cared much about cardboard boxes, although they had become a lot more interesting since the interview offer arrived, but — it was a job with prospects, and it paid enough for her to think about the possibility of renting a room of her own. Her heart was on the mend. Tinderbox Lane was on the mend.

And yet, there remained many unanswered questions: the whereabouts of Marina, being one; what had happened to old Sheila Linklater, being another. Eddison Grove ran between the river at one end, and the pond in the heart of Barnes village at the other: the flat that had belonged to Miss Linklater — or, rather, to Maurice Bousquet — was at the end closest to the pond, and Raff reported to Dolly that an application to dredge Barnes Pond for the remains of the missing old woman was currently "under consideration".

But resources were always tight these days. And since nobody seemed to have cared much about her, one way or the other, while she was alive; and since the same could be said for Kaylin, whom, it had now been confirmed, had slowly cooked to death in his bathtub with a skinful of roofies inside him, and whose death was being treated as accidental, there was an understandable lack of urgency about all aspects of either case.

On the evening of the day of the eviction hearing that Isabelle definitely hadn't ask for, Dolly, making her slow way back from the shops on Station Road, was feeling a little melancholy. Raff was having dinner with his son, Sam, and spending the night at his motorhome. Pippa was out celebrating the possibility of a job, and Dolly's closest friend, Sandra, whom she'd not seen since returning from St Lucia, was busy with yet another new man.

As she turned in to Tinderbox Lane, she was pondering, and not for the first time, the tragic fate of the unknown Sheila Linklater, who may have been lying at the bottom of Barnes Pond all these months and years.

It was dusk. The illegal builder-slaves had been sent back to their illegal dormitories, and the property at Number Seven was dark and quiet. She was thinking about how many other old women in south west London were perhaps being sent to similarly unremarked graves . . . How many other bodies might be discovered if they dredged the pond . . . let alone the Thames . . . Old women didn't have much flesh on them: attach a couple of stones to their frail, fat-free bodies, dump them in the river, and they would sink into the mud. Sink without a trace . . .

So water was on her mind. The sound of water being disturbed; the sound of splashing and lapping . . . gently, methodically splashing and lapping — around a corpse . . . Yes, that was it: the sound of the movement of water against the stillness of a corpse. The sound of a tap running. Water added to water. And a bath running. This was the sound that Dolly heard as she turned in to Tinderbox Lane, her mind elsewhere, at the bottom of Barnes Pond, and as she walked slowly, because of the shopping, past Number Seven's cheap new front door.

She looked up, glanced at the new door. It was closed, as expected. She noticed the lights were out and that the bottom window had been wedged open by an old, paint-stained plank of wood. Left by the builders, presumably, for ventilation. She could smell — not paint but plaster, was it? Cement? Whatever it was — the smell of fresh building works. There was nothing remarkable about the window being open, but why was a bath running when the lights were off?

Dolly glanced over at Windy Ridge next door: its double-glazed windows were tightly closed, and every light in the house was ablaze. But the noise was not coming from there. It was clearly coming from Number Seven. There was a bath running, slowly and quietly. So slowly, so quietly, she could hear the body inside the bath — a long, white body, the shape distorted slightly through the clear water . . . *She could hear it breathing.*

She stopped walking.

The breathing felt insufficient — too shallow and infrequent. It made Dolly want to fill her own lungs, and so she did, but the sound of the other breathing only grew louder; seemed to drown out everything else.

It was too loud. It made no sense. And it was no longer coming from the house. It was coming from behind her. She could feel the breeze in her ear. Someone was breathing into her ear — but not deeply enough. They were suffocating. She knew it.

She cried out. And without thinking further, dumped her shopping bags where she stood and headed towards the empty house.

The new front door was closed tight. But upstairs the splashing grew louder: and she was finding it hard to differentiate — between the water and the breathing —

The *breathing* —

210

And the water.

"IS ANYONE THERE?" she shouted, just as her daughter had, from that same spot, only two weeks before. "I'M COMING UP!" Nobody replied, and she could hardly hear her own words above the breathing, anyway. She looked again at the window, wedged open a few centimetres by the plank, tugged at it, pulled up the window and clambered in.

The room smelled of glue. That was it. Fresh paint and glue. She ran her hands against the walls and felt for a light switch — repaired now. It was working again. She found herself in a bare space; its dimensions identical to her own living room, and yet nothing like it. There was nothing here, except, to Dolly, a sense that something had happened: a cold cement floor, magnolia painted walls, cheap kitchen units at the back — the smell of paint and glue — and the sound of a bath running upstairs.

"Hello?"

She glanced at the stairs. The ground floor was open-plan, like hers: one small room with a small flight of stairs on one side. Dolly's stairs were carpeted with sisal. These stairs were bare, ingrained with years of filth. She should go up, *find out why the tap was still on.*

"Is anyone here?"

No reply. She crossed the room and climbed the short stairs — their width and depth so familiar and yet everything about them strange. At the top, the layout was the same as hers: in such a small space, options were limited. Directly in front of her was one cheap, new door, firmly closed; directly to the left, another, also closed. A bathroom and a bedroom. Just like hers. She opened the first door. Magnolia walls. Empty room. Space for a double bed.

She closed the door. The sound of breathing — stopped, as if someone was holding their breath. She opened the other door.

Magnolia.

Empty.

Nothing.

A bare room, and a new bath, unplumbed and still in its packaging, leaning vertically against the wall.

And the sound of the water — stopped.

Silence.

Dolly gazed into that small room for a while, confirming to herself that what she was seeing was what anyone else would see: a bare room, with a few pipes at the walls, and an unplumbed bath and toilet, still in their packaging. Nothing else. She swore under her breath. What was she meant to do with this then? This inescapable feeling of doom. Something had happened in here. Or something was about to happen in here — something — someone — somewhere. But what? Where? Why? *What was she meant to do with this?*

Downstairs, the front door opened. Dolly heard the lock turn and the door bang against the wall, and footsteps: light and sharp.

"Is that you, Dolly Greene? This is my private property. Come down here immediately, please, and tell me what you are doing in my property."

212

Dolly closed the bathroom door and turned back to the stairs. There were no banisters, she noticed. What had happened to the banisters? She said:

"Hello, Isabelle. I hope you're putting some sort of banister rail in here, are you? What happened to the original, do you know? We've got nice wooden banisters, haven't we? You and I. They got rid of them at Windy Ridge, of course. Put something modern in. But it's rather dangerous without *anything* . . ."

It was a habit of Dolly's, in moments of great tension, to say whatever came into her head. But Isabelle wasn't interested in banisters — then or ever. She asked Dolly again why she was in the house. And Dolly smiled at her as she descended the stairs, and her mind cast this way and that in search of a plausible answer. "Amazing transformation you've done here. In such a short time. Well done! When do you think you'll put the place up for sale?"

Isabelle said: "Why are you here?"

Dolly reached the bottom stair and stood in front of Isabelle. Her small-talk was wasted. There was no point in pretending that anything about this encounter could be civilised. The woman had sent her something akin to a death threat, attached to a cow's heart. And God knows — *who knew what else she might have done?* "I heard water running," Dolly said finally. "And I thought someone was in trouble . . . I thought . . ." She paused. "Actually, I thought someone was drowning in the bath up there . . . Like in your other property. I suppose I had that on my mind. And as I say, I thought I heard water running."

Isabelle glared at her, clearly unimpressed. "So you thought you would just come in?"

"That's right, Isabelle. The window was open. So I came in to see if there was anything I could do."

Isabelle said: "I don't believe you."

Dolly shrugged. "Well that's too bad."

"You didn't hear running water. There isn't any running water here."

"So I discovered."

"So. You are lying. What were you doing?"

"It doesn't really matter, does it?" Dolly laughed. "What do you think I was doing? Stealing your kitchen units?"

"Maybe."

A pause.

Dolly said: "Why did you send me that disgusting animal heart, Isabelle? It was such a nasty thing to do. Why would you have wanted to do that?"

Isabelle blinked. Somehow, the question took her by surprise. Since Dolly had never deigned to mention the incident until now, even after the formal warning, she had assumed that Dolly never would. Finally, she laughed. "The trouble with you English," she said. "You have no sense of humour."

"Well, no," said Dolly, "we do. But that wasn't funny. Why did you send it?"

Again, Isabelle hesitated. But she didn't really care. What did it matter anyway? "It wasn't for you. It was for your daughter. It was just a little joke, after her insolence at that silly meeting. And you called the police. How pathetic! It was just a joke."

"But jokes are meant to be funny," Dolly said.

"Maybe it wasn't funny to you —" Nor had it been to Isabelle, at the time. When she had the brainwave she was passing the upmarket butcher on Church Road, brooding bitterly about Pippa's soft life and sunlit future. She had ordered the heart, taken it home, bundled it up and fastened it, for lack of any string, with a spare electric coil, her entire body pulsating with malicious pleasure . . . but no laughter. The Tarot card, admittedly, had been a witty touch: a sideswipe at the mother . . . That had made her smirk. And the electric coil, on that day of days — had turned out to be pure serendipity! She and the universe clearly shared the same sense of humour.

But that was then. Now, Isabelle was beginning to find the whole topic quite tiresome. With polished red fingernails, she brushed the entire matter aside. "It was funny for me. You British are so soft, like little soppy puppies — boohoo — you take offence at everything. Who cares? Next time your silly daughter will learn to show some respect . . ."

"Respect for what — you?" Dolly laughed. "See? *That's* funny . . . Tell me, Isabelle; we've all been wondering. All your neighbours here on Tinderbox Lane. What, exactly, did you do to the three kids who were living here? What happened to them? Why did they disappear like that, overnight?"

But Isabelle had heard enough. She tossed back her head, and her lovely glossy hair caught the light, and that small, empty room filled, briefly, with the sweet smell of Chanel No. 5. She said to Dolly: "Get out of this house."

And in the back of Dolly's mind — no, just behind her, warm into her ear — came the sound of breathing again: shallow, resigned; the last, slow breaths of something that was dying.

"Get out." Isabelle said again.

Dolly didn't budge. She said: "And what about the other one? What about Kaylin? The man who 'accidentally' died in the bath? Did you have something to do with that, too, Lucky Crystal? Maybe you did. Maybe your luck's going to run out one of these days. I think it may."

Behind her, into her ear, the breathing grew fainter, sadder, weaker . . . Dolly looked into the woman's eyes and wondered quite what she might be capable of: quite what horrors she might have faced down before. There was not a flicker of fear or uncertainty in Isabelle's face. Nor even anger. Isabelle said nothing, didn't move her cold brown eyes from Dolly's face; and Dolly — whose skin was far too thin — felt Isabelle's coldness run through her like a blade. But she was damned if she would be the first to look away.

Someone was at the front door. Isabelle had left it ajar and someone was pushing it wide open; he was tall and lanky and loud —

"My goodness! What a transformation! This place was a *pigsty* last time I peered through the window. Bravo, Isabelle! Is everything all right, ladies? I saw the lights on. *Thought I'd better pop in.*"

216

"Everything's fine, Derek, thank you," said Dolly, her eyes still fixed on Isabelle. "Our friendly neighbour was just showing me round."

"Oh! Jolly good! Can I join in, then? I'd love to have a quick poke around upstairs if I may. Is it all done? Absolutely incredible, Isabelle, if you don't mind me saying. Your builders may be messy and I don't suppose our friends in Immigration would approve of them very much, but my goodness! They should be in the *Guinness Book of Records* for speed."

"We are just leaving," said Isabelle. "You will have to look another time."

"Oh go on — just the teeniest peep. I'll be half a sec." His long feet were already most of the way across the room. By the time he had finished the sentence one of them was already on the bottom stair.

"Unfortunately we are leaving just now," she said.

And the iciness in her voice stopped even the professor in his tracks. "*Really?*" he said.

"Yes, really. Please leave the property. Immediately, please. It will be on the market in a few weeks. If you're interested you can look at it then."

Dolly and the professor exchanged glances.

"Crikey," said the professor. "Well. All right then."

He and Dolly walked back out onto the lane, leaving Isabelle behind, casing her joint for other intruders, and locking all the windows.

CHAPTER
TWENTY-SIX

"Well I never!" declared the professor. "It doesn't happen often, Dolly. But words actually fail me. Isn't she *rude*?"

Dolly laughed. "She's not very pleasant, is she?"

"I thought she was finally extending an olive branch — after all that nastiness with the cow heart. But no! Not a bit of it! What is the matter with that dreadful woman? Was she really giving you a tour?"

"Not really, no."

"It's all very well," he continued (he never listened to answers), "but *lots* of people have a bad time in life. She's not the only one. It doesn't give them a free ticket to be odious for the rest of their lives. Don't you agree, Dolly? What a horrid woman! What are you up to, anyway?" They had come to a halt on the lane between Number Seven and Windy Ridge. "Do you want to come in for a drink?"

Indeed, she most certainly did.

Rosie was in the kitchen, cooking spaghetti Bolognese. As the professor described their encounter with Isabelle, Dolly spotted a bottle of sweet chilli sauce with its lid off beside the bubbling saucepan, and made a mental note not to be cajoled, under any circumstances, into staying for supper. It was one thing to eat fattening food. It was quite another to eat fattening food that was disgusting.

Rosie was appropriately appalled by Isabelle's rudeness. She wondered whether it might be a "smart move" to report her builders to the immigration authorities. Dolly and the professor assured her it would not be a smart move at all. "I should think the less we have to do with that lady, Mrs B, the better for all of us. We don't want any more dead hearts landing on any more doorsteps ... Not to mention any more dead bodies in any bathtubs, frankly. Are we any closer to knowing any more about that, by the way? The good sergeant tells us it's going to go down as accidental death, which is all very well ... but there must be *someone* asking a few questions. Wouldn't you think? Personally, I wonder what became of those young squatters. As you know, I wasn't a fan. But you can't help wondering ..."

Dolly didn't reply. Her world was back to normal now. The breathing, the running water — they had faded to silence. She would have loved to forget all about it. Pretend it hadn't happened. But, in her experience, it was never as easy as that. That was always the problem, when she had these — whatever they were called: moments when reality lost its expected shape? As often as not she hadn't the faintest idea how to react; there was always the same desperate sense of imperative — but to do what? She never knew.

Someone, somewhere was drowning. Perhaps. Someone somewhere was struggling to breathe. They needed her help. But who? And where?

"It's a bit flat," said Derek, handing her a glass of Prosecco. "We opened it at lunchtime, didn't we, Mrs B? To celebrate having found each other. Isn't that right, Rosie?"

"It is, Derek."

"I tell you what, Dolly. I'm the luckiest man alive!"

Rosie grinned. "Oh, stop it!" she said. "Anyway what about Raff? He probably thinks he's the luckiest man alive. So — you know. It depends on your perspective, doesn't it?"

"That's *right*, Mrs B! Well. I should think the good sergeant is the *second* luckiest man in the Barnes/Mortlake area. So. Now then, where were we? Isabelle Ferrari. What are we thinking? It's not very nice, is it, to have someone you suspect of murder living on your lane. Do you think there's anything we can do about it?" He raised his glass. "To Tinderbox Lane!" he said. "We got rid of the squatters — thank goodness. And we saw off the Russian strumpet — in a manner of speaking. In any case, I don't suppose she'll be coming back here in a hurry. Here's to getting rid of dreadful Isabelle!"

"To getting rid of Isabelle," repeated Rosie.

Dolly muttered: "Yes, it would be nice." But her mind was churning on other matters . . . And dammit that slow, sad breathing was back. She could feel her hair moving on her neck, with goose bumps this time, and through the fog, something was slowly, surely taking shape . . .

The Three of Cups reversed. The Three of Swords. The Seven of Swords. The debauched triangle; the lust that got out of hand; the heart that got broken . . .

220

How could she have been so stupid?

The heart that got broken belonged to Geordie.

Pippa never even had a look-in.

Dolly set down her glass: "I have to go," she said. "I'm so sorry. I have to *go*."

"What? Already? But you've only just arrived!"

"No I know, but —"

"Where are you going, in such a hurry? What's the big rush?"

"I just have to go." She had to go because nothing was clear, and everything was clear. And this feeling of dread just would not lift. And she knew from long experience that her only hope of seeing through *that* sort of confusion was to be alone with her cards. "I'll call you later," she said. "Wish me luck."

"Are you sure you don't want to stay?" asked Rosie. "I've made Bolognese."

CHAPTER
TWENTY-SEVEN

She was in her broom cupboard at the back of the house, burning mugwort and lighting candles. The house was empty and her mind was spinning, and that wretched slow, sad breathing ebbed and flowed, just behind her: sometimes so loud she couldn't hear anything else; sometimes, for a moment (which was more alarming) absolutely quiet.

By suburban south west London standards, Dolly Greene, tucked away in that broom cupboard, preparing herself for deepest meditation, was in full scary-witch mode, but that was fine. Nobody was around to be alarmed by it. She was alone, with her sprites and her ghosts and her precious Tarot cards. Sometimes, that was the only place to be.

She closed her eyes. Exhaled.

What was that?

A soft scratching sound.

Something was scratching on the broom cupboard window above her head.

She held her breath. There it was again.

The window looked out over the back of the house, of course. It was high in the wall — about eight feet from the ground — and in any case the silk hanging

222

over it obscured any view. Whoever it was out there —
Dolly couldn't see. More importantly, whoever it was
out there would have had to gain access to her garden.
They would have had to climb through the dank,
bramble-filled undergrowth and over the high metal
fence that separated Tinderbox Lane gardens from the
bus station beyond; or to have come in from one of her
neighbours' back gardens.

"Who's there?"

Dolly's words dropped into the silence. No one
replied.

"Is someone there?" she asked again.

Perhaps she had imagined it. Dolly's grasp of
physical reality at times like these was never a hundred
per cent certain.

Another scratch. Dolly had not imagined it. And a
familiar voice, whispering at her urgently:

"Open door! Please. Open door!"

"What do you want?"

"I need help. Please. Open door now!"

Last seen sprinting away from Dolly as fast as she
could run; now returning of her own volition. Driven
more by curiosity than any desire to help, Dolly stood
up and opened the broom cupboard back door so that
Marina and her anorak could come in.

The girl sat down without being invited. She plonked
herself back into her old seat, unzipped her anorak,
pulled down the hood, and waited. She looked terrible,
on examination: half starved, her hair so greasy it stuck
to her scalp, and her face as white as a sheet. Dolly was

torn between offering her soup and a shower and — well, not doing that. Not doing that won the day.

"You've got a nerve," Dolly said, sitting herself back down. "What are you doing here?"

Marina delved into her anorak pocket and brought out a packet of cigarettes — extra thin, extra long; just the sort of cigarettes a girl like Marina would smoke, thought Dolly irrelevantly, unkindly. Marina didn't ask if she could light up. Her hands were shaking as she did so. Her nails were bitten; the paint on them horrible and chipped. Dolly didn't much want her to smoke in here, but it would have been too petty, given the state she was in, to ask her to stop.

"What do you want?" Dolly asked her again. "You realise the police are looking for you?"

The girl exhaled a puff of smoke into Dolly's face. She nodded. "Also I know your boyfriend is policeman."

"Oh . . . you do, do you?"

The girl nodded, and smoked. It seemed she was considering how to start, and so Dolly waited.

"I come when I know house is empty. Just only you."

"All right . . . But I still don't know why, Marina. Why are you here?"

"Because I have not killed Kaylin! Why am I doing that? I have loved him." She looked — Dolly blinked, and looked again. And yes — Marina looked tearful.

Dolly's hands twitched for her Tarot cards. They were on the table in front of her. She picked up the pack — all but one. She missed the bottom card and it still lay there between them, face down. Marina, as if she knew it would help her, reached out a nail-bitten hand, and turned it over.

Sure enough — it was the card of mourning, the card of the greatest grief: the Five of Cups.

"*You* tell me he is dead. You and your friends. In the street. Before this, I'm not knowing he is dead. When I leave him he is not dead. He is dopey — bahhhh." Marina lolled her head in a dismissive imitation. "Stupid. But no he is not dead. He is in the bath and I leave him. How he have a phone in bath? How? When he never have a phone when I leave him there?"

Dolly waited, and nodded, her judgement suspended. She shuffled the pack, spread the cards into a fan across the table, and told the the girl to pick three.

The Three of Swords — *sorrow and pain*

The Three of Cups, reversed — *debauchery, love triangles*

And the Devil.

Again.

"You pulled those same cards last time you were here. Do you remember?" Dolly asked. She spoke louder than usual, because she couldn't hear herself properly; the breathing was back: whistling and wheezing through her head, driving her crazy.

"Of course I remember this. I remember very well. You said some things but I was not wanting listen."

"People often don't. Why are you here, Marina?"

"Because — I not killing Kaylin. You know this, with your cards."

But Dolly didn't know it. She looked at her cards, spread out between them. The Devil gleamed back. Yes,

225

the girl was grieving. But the cards were still ambiguous.

"You know I not killing Kaylin. And you can tell your boyfriend policeman. I am not killing him. I am just a girl. Very alone in the city. I am trying to have job, have life. I am only trying . . . Like every girl — I am only trying to have decent life."

And yet the Devil gleamed back.

Dolly said: "I'm sure you are, Marina. And I am sorry life has to be so difficult for you here . . . I really am." She needed to get hold of Raff. If she could keep Marina here, and somehow text Raff without Marina noticing. She had her mobile in her pocket. And a simple idea. "I'm going to try to help you, Marina . . . I need you to close your eyes and quietly shuffle the pack, all right?" she said. "Shuffle the pack. Keep your eyes closed. I'll tell you when to stop."

Marina glanced at Dolly suspiciously. She hesitated.

Dolly said: "You've come to me for help. You need to trust me."

With her eyes open, Marina picked up the pack.

"Close your eyes."

She closed her eyes.

Dolly texted Raff, COME NOW, and slipped the phone back in her pocket.

"All right . . ." Dolly said. "Let's leave the cards on the table for moment. You can open your eyes. First, before we go on — I have a few questions, Marina. If you wouldn't mind answering them . . ."

Marina nodded.

226

"Who was it — do you know? Who reported the — tragic situation at your flat to the police? Who gave them Pippa's name?"

"Trek," she said, quickly. "It was Trek."

"Trek?" It took a second for Dolly to remember who he even was. "Trek . . .? *How do you know?*"

Marina blinked. Shifted back in her seat. Looked at Dolly afresh, glanced at her cotton jacket as if seeing through it to the still-glowing mobile in her pocket.

There was breathing in Dolly's ear again. Breathing and the *drip, drip, drip* of a tap . . .

How could Marina have known who called the police, if — as she claimed — she didn't even know that Kaylin was dead until she, Rosie and the professor had informed her of it? It was inconceivable.

"You call someone?" Marina said. "Just now? You call your boyfriend in police?"

Dolly could see the girl's lips were moving, but she couldn't hear. "What's that, sweetheart?"

"You call your policeman. Show me your phone!"

"I can't hear you. What did you say?"

Marina was on her feet. She had pounced across the table and had her hand in Dolly's pocket. She pulled out the phone — it was ringing. Dolly couldn't hear it. Raff's name was flashing up on the screen.

Marina dropped the phone as if it had burned her.

Dolly stood up, upsetting the table, tipping the cards all over the floor. "Wait! Marina! Where are you going? Stop!"

But Marina didn't stop. Small and nimble, like a sylph on the wind, she slipped out of the broom cupboard door into the back garden and in two — three — graceful leaps had disappeared whence she came, over the wire fence, through the scrubland, to the bus station and the wide world beyond.

Dolly, having run as far as the back of the garden, could only watch in helpless amazement at the girl's athleticism. She could not begin to follow her. In her hand, her mobile was ringing again. Raff. Having dinner with his son, she remembered, and felt embarrassed for having interrupted him. She answered him.

"Raff," she said.

"Are you all right? I'm on my way over. I'm in the car with Sam."

"What? Nothing. I'm sorry — forget it. She's gone."

"Who's gone? We're about five minutes away, Dolly. Are you all right? Who's gone?"

"Marina. The Russian girl. She was here . . . I think she came for a reading, Raff. She wanted me to tell you — but God knows. She's just done a runner . . . Literally. She jumped over the garden fence. Anyway. She's gone again, Raff. Like an eel, she is. You think you've got her and then . . ." She heard Raff chuckling. She smiled into the phone. Perhaps she should start going to the gym — or yoga or something. Dammit. She was too young yet to be letting everything slide . . . Marina might be younger and more athletic — but this was the second time the girl had left her flailing. It was humiliating. "And by the way," Dolly added, "she is definitely hiding something."

"Which way did she go?"

"I don't know, Raff! She went towards the bus station. Have the police actually got *anyone* looking for her? I mean — it seems ridiculous. She's roaming around the place, in plain sight, in that stupid coat. Why on earth can't anyone catch her?"

"Fair point," he said.

But it didn't change much. Raff said he'd call the station and update them — and that Dolly should expect a call. He invited Dolly to join him and Sam for dinner; but she demurred. She apologised for interrupting their evening and insisted, which was true, that she had work to do.

She returned to her broom cupboard, where the table was still upturned and the cards were scattered all over the floor. She collected them up in silence. No breathing. No dripping water. Just a wretched sense of foreboding, and an itch that couldn't be scratched. *What was she missing?*

CHAPTER
TWENTY-EIGHT

Pippa didn't come home that night. She came back very early in the morning to pick up her laptop before heading into college, and found Dolly whey-faced, clasping a toothbrush, pacing their small sitting room in her pyjamas. She'd not slept. She'd got up and cooked herself pasta at four in the morning, and left it to burn on the hob. The ruined saucepan was still there, evidence of a rough night. The whole place smelled of burned onion, and Dolly was still no closer to the truth. The cards were no help. Each time she asked them to guide her, they came back with the same damn answer, the same damn cards.

Death and the Devil. And the King of Cups, reversed.

Water, water everywhere
Nor any drop to drink —

The King of Cups sits on his throne, alone on a raft, floating out to sea — too wise, or too tired, to fight against his fate any longer. Reversed, the card's melancholy tips into indulgence and abandon, self-pity and self-destruction.

Water, water everywhere . . .

So the explanation was waiting for her. She only had to see it.

"Mum?"

Dolly barely acknowledged her.

"Mum — what the —"

"I keep wondering . . ." said Dolly.

"What happened to the saucepan?"

"Pippa. Where the hell is Geordie?"

"What? Mum — are you all right? What's happened? What happened to the saucepan?"

"Darling. You're not listening to me. Where is Geordie?"

"I don't know! I have no idea where he is. And honestly, I don't care much, either."

"I think . . ." Dolly said. She was holding her toothbrush like a conductor's baton, waving it this way and that. She looked quite mad. "I think — I think — I think . . ."

"MUM! What's going on? Never mind what you think, the house stinks of onion. It looks like a bomb's hit it. What's going on? Is Raff here?"

"What? No. No, of course he's not. Darling, I think Geordie and Marina . . . I think . . . *The question is, how did she know it was Trek?* I have a bad feeling . . ."

Pippa sighed.

"I have a very bad feeling indeed . . . What are you doing now?"

"I'm washing a saucepan, Mum."

"I mean this morning? We need to get a move on."

"Mum! I have to go to college."

"She's been hanging around here. We saw her — I saw her, hanging around outside Eddison Grove. She was trying to get into the flat. *Why?*"

"Are you talking about Marina?"

"She was here last night again, Pippa."

"*Marina?*"

". . . I keep hearing that bloody bath running. We need to get over to Eddison Grove. But how are we going to get into the flat?"

"Mum! Pull yourself together! We've got no business in the flat." Pippa looked at her mother, and sighed. She left the saucepan in the sink and came over to give her a hug. But Dolly shook her off.

"Don't patronise me, darling. I'm going to the flat now. You can come with me or not. But there's something wrong. Something going on in that flat. And I'm going to find out what. Are you coming or aren't you?"

"I'm not coming, no. And nor should you. You can't barge into other people's property. It's against the law."

"Lots of things are against the law." Dolly waved it aside. She wasn't even bothering to get dressed. She was shoving her feet into the boots by the door, scrambling into her overcoat, and heading out. "Hurry up!" she said. "What are you waiting for?"

Dolly opened the front door, turned to her daughter. "Last chance. Are you coming?"

"No," said Pippa. "I'm calling Raff."

CHAPTER
TWENTY-NINE

That's how he found her. At nine in the morning, in pyjamas, boots and overcoat, standing on the street outside Kaylin and Marina's old flat, hands on hips, contemplating how best to get through the door. She had already knocked and received no reply.

Raff was on an early shift. He'd been working a couple of hours already when he received Pippa's call. And there was a moment, as the patrol car drew up beside her, sirens blaring, when he wondered if she was quite the woman he had thought she was. She looked fairly mad. Alluring — to his eye, at any rate — but really, quite mad.

Ollie, beside him, took one look at her and started laughing. Raff snarled at him to put a sock in it, and climbed out of the car. In his line of work he encountered figures such as the one Dolly cut this morning, several times every day. Most of them needed to be treated kindly, and escorted back to — well. Ollie's laughter said it all.

"All right, Dolly?" Raff said. He sounded casual, conversational, as he always did when approaching potentially difficult individuals. "What's up?"

Dolly glanced at him. "She called you, did she? Good. Raff, there's someone in there."

"You sure, Dolly? What makes you say that?"

"The bath is flooding."

He had the courtesy to pause, and listen. Ollie ambled up and stood beside him. "Hullo again," he said to Dolly. "How are you today?"

"Shh!" said Raff. "You hear that?" Sure enough: they were listening to the sound of pouring water. It was landing like a drum somewhere very close. Raff put his face to the letterbox. He couldn't see much. Only the stairs, and at the foot of the stairs a small space covered in worn brown carpet, with a large puddle in the middle. There was water raining through the light socket from the floor above.

"Looks like a pipe's burst," he said. "Have you tried knocking on the flat below? They may have keys."

"Of course I have. No one's in."

None of them knew about the twist-and-shove routine, or the chisel lying in the bush at their feet. Ollie and Raff tried to shoulder the door a couple of times and then Ollie ran back to the patrol car to fetch the metal enforcer. On the third lunge, the lock gave way.

"Stay back," said Raff to Dolly. She ignored him.

At the top of the stairs, a second door hung open, revealing another small, dark landing.

"Anyone here?" shouted Raff into the gloom. "Police! We are coming up."

No reply.

Ollie followed Raff up the stairs. He turned back, briefly, to Dolly (as expected): "Stay downstairs, please," he said. "You shouldn't be coming in here." She nodded (as expected) and continued to follow close behind.

The landing on the top of the stairs opened onto a corridor: thin and dark, with the same brown carpet as the hallway below. It smelled of damp and cannabis. To the left, an open door led to the sitting room: a stained, much used 1970s mustard Dralon sofa stood in the middle of the room and on either side, a couple of matching Easi-Chairs, no less grubby. In haphazard heaps along the walls, there lay great piles of junk; the tangled wires of old mobile chargers; an ancient answer machine; a fan heater; a couple of broken lamps; what looked like an old Amstrad computer; mountains of women's magazines; a bicycle wheel; a tobacco pouch; an empty Rizla pack; a rotten orange.

"Anyone in?" shouted Raff.

The sound of the water was coming from the far end of that drab corridor, back towards the front of the building. They moved towards it, past the bedroom, with unmade bed and discarded clothing strewn around it, before the kitchen — where dirty plates were still stacked high by the sink, and Marina's worthless Internet marriage certificate still lay abandoned on the toaster — to the only door in the flat that was closed. Water seeped from underneath it.

"Careful now," said Raff: "Floor may not be safe. Stand back . . ." He raised his voice one last time and shouted through the door: "Hello? Is anyone there? Police here. We are coming in."

He turned the handle. There was no lock. Slowly, carefully, he pushed back the door.

And there it was, all over again. The tangle of wires. The mobile phone submerged in the water. Only this time the deathly pale body lying limp in the spilling bathtub wasn't Kaylin, but Geordie.

His clothes were folded in a wet corner, and stuck to the mirror was a note: a familiar gathering of words.

My Darling,

Doubt thou the stars are fire; Doubt that the sun doth move; Doubt truth to be a liar. But never doubt I love.

You didn't believe me before. I hope this is proof enough.

I forgive you, my angel, for everything. Forgive me for this.

CHAPTER
THIRTY

Dolly had seen all she wanted to see. Horrified, she stepped back out of the room, and while Raff radioed for assistance, Ollie shepherded her through the flat and back onto the street. Dolly didn't resist. The sooner she got out of that place the better.

She should have seen it coming. All the warnings she'd been given. And now it was too late.

On the street again, Ollie hesitated — he wanted to leave her there to make her own way home, but the sight of her in her pyjamas made him think twice. He shouted up to Raff that he was going to drop her back at Tinderbox Lane, and Dolly put up only the most faint-hearted objection before thanking him and climbing into the passenger seat.

"Is he going to be all right?" she asked. It was a stupid question. "Is he dead?"

Ollie didn't reply. "What were you doing there anyway?" he asked, instead. "How did you know?"

"I didn't know," she answered. "How could I have known? If I'd *known* — it wouldn't have happened, would it?" She sounded angry — but it was hardly Ollie's fault. Not that it mattered, any more, whose fault it was. What mattered was that she was going to

237

have to break the news to Pippa. Somehow. This morning. *Now*. What would she say? What could she possibly say that would make it all right?

She didn't notice when the car came to a halt. Ollie had turned around to face her, engine still running. They were at the top of Tinderbox Lane. He was waiting for her to climb out.

"I need to get back there," he said, quite kindly. "Do you want me to take you to the door?"

"No." She didn't move. "Thank you."

"I'll get Raff to call you, shall I? Soon as there's information."

"That would be kind . . ." She sighed. Still didn't move. "You know, Ollie . . . There's something not quite right."

"There's a lot in this country not quite right, Dolly. Suicide's the biggest killer of males under forty-five in the UK. Did you know that?"

"I didn't," she said. "I'm sorry."

"Well." He shrugged. "There you go. You learn a new fact every day . . . Apologies, Dolly. But I'm going to have to ask you to jump out. You sure I can't take you to the door?"

"No." She shook herself. "I'm so sorry. I'm fine. Thank you. And please — if you would ask Raff to call me, soon as he can."

The builder-slaves were back at work inside Number Seven, but she passed them unnoticed. Inside Windy Ridge, Rosie was busy making waffles for the children's breakfast, and the professor, who didn't generally need to be at work before eleven o'clock, was enjoying a leisurely shower. She walked on by, grateful for the peace, and yet dragging her feet, dreading the moment when she would have to see Pippa: desperately hoping that Pippa would not still be at home.

She wasn't. She had left a note on the breakfast bar, weighted with Dolly's mobile, which Dolly had left behind, apologising for not being able to wait, and asking her mother to call her as soon as she was back. Even as Dolly read the note, her mobile began to ring. It was Pippa — her fourth missed call. But Dolly wasn't ready to talk to her. Not yet. She wasn't ready for anything; not even her cards.

She was remembering Geordie's diminished figure that last time he dropped by, and how inhospitable and harsh she had been to him — not just then, but always. She was thinking of the time she had read for him — how he had strutted into her broom cupboard as if nothing could touch him: how he had almost cried when she compared him to the sleeping beauty . . . She had been unprofessional. Worse than that, she had been unkind. When the cards had sent him that dire warning — and she had tried to tell him so, and he had taken such offence — she had simply disliked him too much to reiterate it. And perhaps, if she'd made that small effort, she might have prevented this tragic, wasteful end . . . Marina was unreadable, un-impressible; unwinnable, beautiful, hard — of course he had fallen for her: he was the boy who could charm his way into any girl's bed; with that big brain of his and those wonderful looks, he could run rings around most of the human race . . . When she read his cards she had known he was lonely; sensed his isolation, his longing for someone who wouldn't be dazzled by his cleverness and charm. In Marina, he had met his match — more than his match, his nemesis. And Dolly hadn't helped. She'd been so preoccupied, protecting her daughter — who was more than able to look after herself — she had left the boy to sink . . . A young man on the brink of adulthood, a young man so full of potential. And yet. And yet . . . Why wasn't her heart breaking?

Something wasn't right.

She fiddled with her phone — unwilling to call Pippa, and fighting the urge to call Raff. She didn't know what to do with herself. She had a couple of clients booked this afternoon, but this morning, she had nothing. Perhaps she should take Pippa's advice and print out some fliers? Or input some of the clients' feedback onto her website — if she could only remember how to do it . . .

But it was no good. The image of Geordie kept bouncing back at her, young and alive; his long legs sprawled out on her sofa; his lean body wrapped in her dressing gown; his limp body lying in that bathtub . . . She couldn't concentrate.

She would have a shower.

She would pay some bills.

She would ask the cards how to proceed.

She would . . . call her daughter. Or Raff. Or —

As she stood there, doing none of the above, she heard her computer ping. An email — any email — would provide a moment's distraction at least.

Even so, she almost didn't open it. At first glance it looked like something intended to give her computer a virus:

From: Suzy 132*f;

Re: Hi there Dolly!

. . . But then, even the possibility of giving her computer a virus seemed preferable to doing or thinking about anything else. So she opened it and found three files:

IncomingCal . . . 0124m4a

IncomingCal . . . 0203m4a

IncomingCal . . . 0208m4a

And below the files, a few lines of text:

Mrs Dolly

    This I am recording last night secret. Secret I record Joordy on my phone. I am sending you so you know truth. Joordy is dead now in Kaylin flat. Tell your boyfriend policeman. I am killing no one. As you will hear this recordings of Joordy telephone calls three. He explain in his words what wicked evil he commit and now you tell police. Thank you. Please listen. I am not animoor stay in this city. I go home now maybe.

    Goodbye from Marina

CHAPTER
THIRTY-ONE

A lot of noise. Heavy boots, and monotone voices. And a thumping head. And a taste on his dry lips, reminding him of Marina. Marina, Marina, Marina . . . Where the hell was he and why weren't his legs moving? His arms. Why couldn't he move his arms? What the fuck?

Panic.

Rising, fucking panic.

He breathed in. He breathed out. He swallowed.

What were those voices?

He swallowed again. Yes. And cleared his throat. Yes. Licked his lips again. Yes. Breathed in, breathed out. His fingers moved. His fingers were moving and he could feel his hands. Pins and needles. Fuck, holy fuck. Where was he? His body was crawling with ants. His whole fucking body . . . was being pierced with tiny pinpricks, fuck, fuck, fuck WHERE WAS HE?

He was . . . in a room. Is where he was. A remarkably familiar room — lying flat on a . . . stretcher? On a stretcher, maybe. Alone in a room. With a yellow sofa. Where had he seen that sofa?

Kaylin's sitting room. But Kaylin was dead . . . Holy fuck, was he in Hell? Was this where it all ended? And whose were those voices? Those monotone male voices

... talkie-walkies. No, walkie-talkies. Police radios. Where was Marina? WHERE WAS MARINA? She was supposed to come ...

Panic.

Panic.

Don't panic. Do Not Panic.

He was dreaming. He was in Hell. This was hell. This was HELL — yellow sofas, and pins and needles, and police radios ... Christ, he was cold! Was the door open? His chest was reflecting the light. How was that, then? Was he an angel, after all? Is this what it felt like?

Not dead. No. He was wrapped in a shiny silver blanket. And he was not alone in the room. No — a woman in a blue outfit ... matching blue shirt and trousers — too baggy; not attractive at all — she was doing something with his arm. Was she? Why? Where was Marina, anyway? She was supposed to come.

Marina never came — that was the crux of it. The crotch of it. He laughed. He must have done. Because Trouser looked up at him and said something. Probably. Her lips moved and noise came out, but God knows what she said. Marina didn't come. That was the thing about Marina. Molten rock. That's what it was like, having sex with Marina. Like fucking molten rock ... Something like that. She was the hardest, coldest, hottest woman he'd ever met ... cold as ice. And yet, so fucking hot. Was she a killer? That was the big question, wasn't it. Or was it Killer Kayle? She never said. She didn't need to. Kaylin could barely get off his arse to take a shit, let alone ... but he was always the one directing the traffic. *He told her to do it*. And she did it. That's why he knew they would be all right. Two killers together. No. That wasn't it. Two not-quite killers together. It wasn't their fault . . . Nothing was their fault. They adored each other. Or he adored her. Nobody had ever not loved him the way she didn't love him . . . Christ, she was hot. Why was he in this room, and why wasn't she here? She said she'd come. She was meant to come and rescue him. After everything he had done for her. Had she not seen the note?

Doubt thou the stars are fire; Doubt that the sun doth move; Doubt truth to be a liar . . .

It was beautiful, that. Beautiful. She was very angry with him. It was a problem. And, frankly, if this little stunt didn't turn things around, then nothing ever would. He would never be able to put it right.

Stupid Russian bitch.

No. That wasn't right. That was all wrong. He'd got it wrong.

Very wrong indeed. Misjudged her completely. She had led him to believe that the intensity was reciprocated.

But on the day that Kaylin died he realised how badly he had misjudged her. No — that wasn't quite right either.

Before then. He saw how unhappy she was after the Brazilian stripper called in — fucking amazing body — and Kaylin's lies had all unravelled — no flat, no marriage — nothing. A lazy bastard on a dirty yellow sofa. He knew how upset she was because they had met up immediately afterwards. He'd never felt jealousy before. Why would he? Always the cleverest, always the funniest, always the one the girls went for . . . But when Marina was sobbing into her crème de menthe she wasn't just sobbing about Kaylin's flat. Yes, she was fucking furious about it. But it seemed to Geordie that she was more upset about the crappy Internet marriage certificate business. Geordie had even said he would marry her — if it was marriage she was after. Geordie said that. He heard himself saying it. Marina hadn't even bothered to reply. It wasn't just marriage she wanted. She wanted to be married to that lazy, lying, junkie tosser Kaylin. Because for all her ambition, her hardness, her molten-rock hotness . . . (where was he going with this?) she loved Kaylin. The pathetic, darling girl loved Kaylin, because she didn't know any better.

He'd had to listen to that. And rub her shoulders, and try not to think about sex. Marina had left her passport behind, and the old lady's jewellery box — and she couldn't go back. She couldn't face Kaylin. She never wanted to see him again. But she needed her passport. And the jewellery box. The jewellery box was hers. She'd sent him back to the flat. Kaylin would be high by now. She said. Geordie knew how to let himself in — but what if Kaylin *wasn't* blitzed, Geordie asked her — and the smile on Marina's face as she answered; the weirdest, sweetest smile. The smile had not been for him. It was for Kaylin. "Of course he is high," she replied. "This is Kaylin. We know Kaylin. Anyway I make him tea with extra sweetie in." Geordie hadn't been satisfied: what was he to do if Kaylin wasn't blitzed? What if he hadn't drunk the tea with sweeties in? How was he supposed to get the passport — turn that filthy flat upside down and find the passport and the jewel box? How was he supposed to do that, if Kaylin was bouncing around, suggesting a trip to the pub? For example. Unlikely but —

She told him not to be stupid. She said he could spend an hour or so with Kaylin, and they could get blitzed together — Geordie could do what Marina did, and drop a few "sweeties" in his tea . . . She would meet up with him later. They had agreed on a pub; somewhere further afield, up towards Elephant and Castle, nearer the old crew. Geordie was going to crack a new place for them, and they were going to live together in a squat all of their own. Or maybe he would get a job. Go normal. Pay rent. Buy his little Russian bird a little ironing board and nice little diamond engagement ring, if that was what she really wanted . . . That was the plan. He was going to leave Trek and Gigi to their own drab bliss, leave Tinderbox Lane, and he and Marina were going to do the one thing he swore was impossible . . . That was the plan. His plan. Their plan. They were going to live happily ever after.

But when he called her afterwards — he said he'd left the flat in a rush . . . He said he didn't have the passport, or the jewellery box. He said there had been an accident, but he couldn't tell her what it was. He couldn't bring himself to tell her, not over the phone. Would she meet him anyway? She had left that long, long silence. Perhaps she hadn't heard him? She said nothing, in any case: and he realised then — that was when he realised, in an icy blast, that she wanted —

Not him. Not Geordie.

She wanted the fucking passport and the fucking jewellery box. And Kaylin.

He'd left her in the pub with her crème de menthe and her inexplicably broken heart and trotted off, like a good boy, to pick up the stuff she'd left behind in the flat . . . And on the walk he'd got to brooding . . . How did a lazy bastard like Kaylin persuade a woman like Marina to care for him. How? Even after she'd seen he was liar and a fraud? And a parasite . . . an ancient, corrupted, weak-willed, vain, filthy, licentious, misogynist, worthless fucking junkie — all the things, in fact, that Geordie so carefully was not. Geordie: the post-feminist heterosexual dream man. Handsome, young, virile, and fucking principled. Uninhibited, woman-loving, woman-appreciating, woman-supporting. A man who didn't enjoy pornography because it debased the other sex and by extension debased him, too. A man without a misogynist boner in his body haha. Not one. People didn't realise — women didn't realise what a rare thing that was. Marina should have been grateful. Instead she was sobbing into her crème de menthe over a waste of space like Kaylin.

Geordie had let himself in to Eddison Grove and found the sitting room empty, and Kaylin lolling in his bathtub, his scrawny chest bare, an undrunk cup of cold tea balanced in the soap holder between the hot and cold tap. Geordie sat on the broken toilet seat, trying not to look at Kaylin's pallid body, his shrivelled dick, distorted through the water. Kaylin was trying to roll a J, while in the bath, and he wouldn't stop talking

— complaining about pins and needles, about visits from terrifying landladies with amazing bodies and men with weirdly fat necks, about Marina having abandoned him in his hour of greatest need . . . Geordie listened as if he'd not heard it before. He watched Kaylin trying to roll the joint. His hands were shaking so much he could hardly hold the paper, so Geordie took it off him and rolled the joint himself: put it between Kaylin's lips and lit it.

He said he'd come to buy some grass. Kaylin told him to fetch it from the stashbox next door, and Geordie had gone into the sitting room to fetch it. He found the box lying open on the rug beside the sofa, with the stash inside — but no money.

"Put some cash in there, will you?" Kaylin had called out to him, with one of his wheezy, lazy giggles. "Put some cash in my honesty box. As you can see it needs replenishing. Ment. Replenishingment . . . Whatever." Kaylin's wheezy giggle turned into an extended coughing fit. "Stupid cow took all the money . . . She was seriously fucking pissed off, Geordie . . . Fuck me . . ." He sighed — a loud sigh, audible from the sitting room, full of self pity and surrender — and the sound of it enraged him. Killer Kaylin did not deserve her.

After that, everything Kaylin said set his teeth on edge. Made him angrier. He'd come for the passport and the bloody jewellery box — but Kaylin was as alert as Geordie had ever seen him. Geordie fumbled in the box, helped himself to some grass — and some Ketty, and some MD and a bit of cocaine, because why not, when it was there. And he took three tablets for Kaylin's tea. The idiot had been taking roofies for so long, he would need a fat dose to be sure of any effect.

". . . going to miss those tits, Geord," Kaylin was saying, "I tell you that for free . . ."

Geordie offered to make him some more tea.

And in the half-hour or so that followed, he had sat on the broken lavatory seat, trying not to look at the naked body, trying not to listen to Kaylin's maudlin ramblings about Marina, her tits, her this, her that — the stuff he liked to do to her and would probably never be able to do to her again; graphic, misogynist, repellent to Geordie . . . but he heard it all, every word of it — because he couldn't block it out. He said nothing. He only nodded and waited — and imagined Marina, beautiful, alone, thousands of miles from her home, having to put up with this monster —

Until, finally, splayed out in the bathtub, Kaylin nodded off. He passed out.

Geordie took his time after that. He had a pee while Kaylin lay comatose behind him. He thought, since he was there, and so were they, that he might help himself to a few more of the drugs lying unguarded in the open box next door. He stepped over the jungle of wires — the ancient multi plugs and tangle of extension leads between bathtub and toilet — and then what happened?

The woman in the baggy trouser/shirt thing was talking to someone at the door. She had her back to him . . . She was shaking her head. What was she saying?

Nose itching. He lifted his hand to scratch it. Couldn't do it. What the hell? He tried again. Nope.

The woman at the door turned around to look at him. She was saying something. He couldn't move his arm because — there was something attached to it — a bracelet attached to his wrist. Wrists. Both wrists. That's what it felt like — but there was the silver blanket covering his arms . . . Christ his head ached. His body was shaking with cold.

Extension leads — stashbox — he helped himself to more drugs. *Then* he took a pee. That was it. And he saw the mobile lying on the floor, recharging. Kaylin's mobile, obviously, because Marina had hers. He glanced at Kaylin's emaciated body distorted by the bathwater; imagined it still conscious, but barely conscious. With that mobile slowly slipping through its fingers, and Kaylin — too fucking out-of-it, too lazy to hold on tight . . . The world wouldn't miss him — it would barely blink. One less mouth to feed. One less fuckwit to milk the system. One less misogynist to degrade the sex — his sex, not hers. People like Kaylin degraded men, not women. Not Marina.

That was pretty much it. Jealousy. Justification. Opportunity. Geordie zipped up his flies. And turned to look at the bathtub. For a long moment, he simply gazed down at Kaylin: naked, weak . . . and then what happened? He picked up the phone, of course. Carefully — by the wire. He dangled it over the water. Swung it this way and that.

What if? What if? What if?

Kaylin hadn't smoked the joint alone.

Slowly — absently, almost — more absorbed by the ripple it made on the surface than by the lethal charge it was going to give, Geordie lowered the phone into the water, thinking:

Well — I wonder if this will kill him?

It might not have done, under normal circumstances. But it was an old iron bathtub. And God knows where they got that mobile charger. And the electrical wattage pumping through that crazy death-trap wire jungle could have been anyone's guess. The stupid bastard fried to death.

It was awful. Unreal. *Not his fault.*

So he panicked after that. Marina wouldn't see him, anyway, once he told her he didn't have the passport and so on. He didn't go back to Tinderbox Lane. He followed Gigi up to Elephant and Castle and — got off his face. What else was he supposed to do? He told Gigi to get Trek to stop off via Kaylin and bring whatever drugs Kaylin was willing to sell him . . . Which was clever of him. The Geordie of yesteryear. Who planned and plotted and kept himself out of trouble. Trek never made it up to Elephant. Obviously. He found Kaylin in the bathtub and went off the rails — calling the police: getting whatsername —

Whatsername

Whatsername

Whatsername?

Pippa. Getting Pippa involved. He shouldn't have done that. Fucking idiot, Trek.

Now his arms were handcuffed to the stretcher. And his nose was itching.

Why would he be handcuffed? Did they handcuff suicide victims? No. Something wasn't right. Someone was misunderstanding. The situation. Had they not read the note?

And where was Marina?

She promised she would come. She said she was on her way. How long ago was that then? He had no idea.

Before this . . .

. . . he ran himself a bath. He found the fuse box, and confirmed that the flat had no power. He was careful to do that. But he left the extension leads as they were, higgledy piggledy through the bathroom. And he took a single tablet. And he left the note. And he propped the envelope right beneath it: she was going to love that. Passport and crappy jewellery all inside. That would make her smile if nothing else did. And he called Marina. He told her he was in the flat. He told her he was in the flat, and he was going to kill himself, because of what he had done — for her. And because she would not forgive him.

No — that wasn't quite right. He'd got the order jumbled. The first time he called her, he hadn't taken the tablet yet. He had to be sure that it wouldn't be wasted — the lying in a bath, half comatose, waiting to be rescued. He had to be sure she was there, and would come, and that she knew what he was doing and why. So he called her the first time, and she was frosty. As she had been ever since — well, ever since ever, really. She said she couldn't talk. So he waited. Half an hour, and called her again. That was the second time.

That was when he told her he'd found the passport and the stupid bloody jewellery. They'd been shoved into a padded envelope. And then shoved inside the stuffing of Kaylin's yellow Dralon sofa. Because he was canny, old Kaylin. And lazy. He would never have hidden them too far away. He wouldn't, it transpired, have hidden them beyond his own reach. Plus, of course, most of the time, he would be lying on top of them . . . He didn't tell her that the jewels she was so concerned with looked about as authentic as her marriage certificate, still lying on the toaster in the kitchen. He didn't tell her that. Why would he? He wanted her to come — and he wanted to use everything he could to entice her.

The passport.

The jewels.

His love.

And of course — this: his penance for what he had done. He told her that. She said: "Penance for what, Geordie?" She'd made him say it. She made him say what he did. "Say the words," she insisted. "If you not say the words, how I believe you are sorry? How I forgive you if I not believe you are sorry?"

He said the words. Not the first time he called. Too canny. Not even the second. But the third time he called her — after he'd set it all up, and he'd taken the tablet, and he was about to climb into that bathtub, and he wanted to be sure, absolutely certain that she would come. He called her on the mobile, telling her to come — and his words were slightly slurred: *I am sorry I killed him. I'm sorry I killed your stupid boyfriend. I'm sorry I killed Kaylin . . . I'm sorry . . .* He may have been crying by then. *How shaming.* Yes, he may well have been. Well, he *was* sorry. And he wasn't sorry, because he loved her.

Anyway, she swore she was coming. She was on her way. She would be there in ten minutes.

So he'd waited, naked, on the edge of the bathtub — another five minutes — six — seven . . . but he had to be in the bath when she came, or it would be pointless. She wouldn't believe he meant it. He had to look like he meant it — he had to be unconscious when she found him. She had to believe that he was willing to die for her. Because what woman —

What woman could resist that?

Plenty of them, perhaps. But he was in love. He was in love. Geordie. Was in love. The impossible had occurred. The Earth had moved.

His nose was itching.

Where the fuck was Marina?

In the end, of course, he had thought better of putting his mobile into the bath. Not because it would have killed him. It wouldn't, with the electricity turned off. But — finally — there came the moment for immersion. A now-or-never moment, because he could feel the drug kicking in, and his grip slipping. He knew the phone would be wrecked. He knew he couldn't afford yet another one . . . He remembered, at the last moment, dropping his phone onto the floor instead. Perhaps, dramatically speaking, that had been an error?

Too late now, anyway. Marina hadn't even come.

He glanced at the woman in the bad trousers. She was standing at the door, with her arms folded, squinting at a broken nail.

"Vazzmll . . . Hnng . . . Shnfspb . . ." he said. He had meant to say: "Excuse me. Why am I here?" But his mouth wasn't working yet. In any case, she didn't seem to have heard him.

He must have fallen back to sleep after that. Was it possible? Yes. He remembered his nose itching. And when he woke up there were two police officers standing over him; one of whom looked vaguely familiar . . . Christ. That's right. What was his name? Whatsername's mum's boyfriend.

He was feeling better — clearer. And yet here he was, still lying on the stretcher beneath the shiny blanket, arms still cuffed to the frame.

They told him he was under arrest.

"For what, may I ask?" he said, ludicrous, under his blanket. "Is it illegal to be unhappy in this brave new world, now?"

"You what?" said the younger one.

The older one, who looked familiar, assured him he wasn't under arrest for being unhappy — he was under arrest for murder. Geordie objected — he wanted a lawyer; he wanted his clothes; he wanted his mobile phone.

Raff took pity. They released him from the stretcher, since he was clearly okay to sit up, and allowed him to put his clothes back on. He told Geordie a lawyer would be arranged for him as soon as they reached the station. But when Geordie asked, a second time, for his mobile phone to be returned to him, Raff couldn't help laughing.

"Your phone's dead, mate," he said. "Well. I imagine it is. Unless you can bring it back to life in a bowl of rice. That sometimes works . . . and I should think forensics'll be giving it a good try."

"I don't understand," said Geordie.

"It's what happens when you dump your mobile in the bath," Ollie told him.

"But I didn't," said Geordie. "I didn't do that. I didn't put my phone in the bath. I left it on the floor beside the bath . . ." Geordie looked from one to the other: what were they saying? Didn't they realise what they were saying? "Do you understand?"

Ollie wasn't listening. "Come on then, on your feet. Let's go."

They led him, handcuffed, out into the passageway. It was a squeeze. There were a lot of people shuffling around out there. They had to pause by the open door to the bathroom, where the "suicide note" was still in place above the mirror. And where, propped up beneath it — Geordie stood very still. He leaned against the wall, staring.

"You all right?" said Raff. "You sure you wouldn't prefer the stretcher?"

"The envelope that was there . . ." Geordie said, indicating the bathroom: "I left a big padded envelope — right there beneath the mirror. Beneath the note. Where is it?"

Ollie said: "Not sure I know what you're talking about, mate . . . Raff? Know anything about any envelope?"

"Envelope? Nope," said Raff. "Can't say I do."

"But — has someone taken it then? It must have been there when you came in. When whoever it was found me. I left it there specifically. On the shelf. Right there, beneath the mirror. I left it . . . It had her passport inside. And jewellery . . .”

“There was no envelope there when we came in. Was there, Raff?”

“No envelope,” agreed Raff. “Just the note.”

“Yes. The note. And *beneath* the note —”

“Nothing, mate,” said Ollie. “You’re probably still a bit confused.”

“I’m not confused. It was there. I put it there. So where is it now? It can’t have just disappeared. What happened to it?”

But Geordie already knew the answer. When he’d swallowed the pill and climbed into that bathtub, he’d believed Marina would come round and revive him; that the scene would be a fitting way for them to launch into their new life together. When he’d propped the envelope beneath the letter, they had only just said goodbye. And he’d believed in her. She’d assured him she was on her way. And so she was, of course. Marina had rushed round to the flat, all right. But not to save him.

CHAPTER
THIRTY-TWO

They dredged the pond, which was disagreeable not only for the good people of Barnes, who loved their pond, but for the ducks and swans and turtles who lived on it. It was especially disagreeable when a large refuse bag was pulled up with the remains of an old woman inside, her frail body neatly folded up; she must, indeed, have been tiny. The police said she'd probably been there for over a year. They found a scarf, wrapped around a small pillow wedged beneath the old woman's partially decomposed head, as if whoever dumped her there had had a sense of what they were doing — some little grain of remorse that made them, at least, want to make the dead woman comfortable. In any case, that little grain of remorse — that small and pointless act of kindness — proved to be Marina's undoing. She had left behind her DNA.

It wouldn't help Geordie's case, of course: he was in jail and awaiting trial for a different murder. But he was mighty gladdened to hear it when, a month later, his solicitor informed him that she had been identified loitering at the bar of a hotel on Park Lane, and arrested.

★ ★ ★

It was a beautiful, sunny afternoon on the day Raff called Dolly and Pippa with the news of Marina's arrest, three long months since Geordie had been behind bars, and for the most part Tinderbox Lane had reverted to its previous, more contented rhythm. Dolly had been thanked by the police for handing over her recordings of Marina's telephone-calls-three and Pippa, so robust and young, having learned the grisly truth about the man she almost fell in love with, had quite quickly recovered her balance. The boyfriend she had thought, briefly, that she loved, may have turned out to be a two-timing killer. But she was only twenty-two years old, and they'd hardly known each other long. One day it would be a story to tell her grandchildren. In the meantime she had a rosy future to attend to, and a barbecue to prepare. She and Dolly were actually in the middle of arranging a trestle table in the back garden.

"You see?" Dolly was saying. "I knew it would end badly for that girl. I told her so. The cards said it all along."

Pippa smiled: a smile tinged with sadness. "Maybe you could use the story in your publicity bumph, Mum," she said. "Remember that woman who was reading the cards for the murderer — and she had to call the police in the middle of the reading? It was all over the papers."

"I do," said Dolly. "The police thought she was a crackpot and took ages to get there."

"Right. Every Tarot reader needs a Raff on speed dial."

259

"Ha!"

"I bet she's been flooded with clients ever since."

"She probably doesn't get many murderers though. Murderers would stay away."

"But that's not such a bad thing."

"Oh, I don't know," said Dolly, mildly. "It keeps it interesting, doesn't it?" She looked at the table. The professor had called a Tinderbox Lane Residential Community Dinner, and since it was a beautiful evening and there was space for everyone in the garden, Dolly had insisted on having it at her house for once. After all, she pointed out, Tinderbox Lane Residential Community numbers were unlikely to be so low for long.

Isabelle Ferrari was gone. She'd packed her bags and left without saying goodbye to anyone, and nobody was sorry. Both her houses were up for sale — Number Three next door, she hadn't even bothered to refurbish, according to Rosie, and it was already Under Offer.

So only Derek, Rosie, the two kids, Raff and the dreaded Terry Whistle were expected tonight. And Pippa, of course. Pippa had finally signed a contract for the job in cardboard boxes only the day before and was in excellent spirits. And so was Dolly. She and Pippa had spent the morning handing out tinderboxtarot.com fliers at Barnes train station, and already there were several enquiries coming in. Added to which, she, Pippa and Raff had an announcement to make.

So.

They'd bought a paper tablecloth from Waitrose, but it didn't fit the table properly. And now there was a breeze kicking up, which meant, unless they weighed the thing down with some cutlery, it would soon be flying away altogether.

"Better lay the table," said Dolly.

"We can't," said Pippa. "Dishwasher's on. Everything's in the machine."

This information seemed, temporarily, to defeat them both. It was seven o'clock. People were invited for eight, but Rosie and the professor always arrived early . . . On the other hand, the non-barbecued supper elements were all done. And there was a bottle of cool Prosecco in the fridge.

"Shall we open it?" said Pippa. She didn't need to say what.

Dolly nodded. "Maybe I can text Raff to bring another bottle when he comes."

"Brilliant idea," said Pippa. Which was an overstate-ment, but as they popped the cork, it felt about right.

". . . To us!" declared Pippa.

"And the new job!" said Dolly

"And the cards!" said Pippa

"And . . . and . . . to us!" said Dolly.

"And to us again!"

They were pleasantly inebriated by the time the others arrived. The bottle was finished, as was the dishwasher, but Dolly and Pippa were so busy, lolling on the front door step toasting each other, they had forgotten what they were waiting for.

"I say!" said Derek. "Looks like the party started without us! Look at that, Rosie! And I thought we were the ones with something to celebrate! Is Raff here yet?"

He was carrying not one but two bottles of Champagne. "We've got a fabulous announcement, haven't we, Rosie?"

"We certainly have," she said. "You'll never guess!"

Dolly stood up and kissed them both. "You've got an announcement?" she said. "So have we. Haven't we, Pipps?"

"Yep. Well — Raff has, really. We should wait for him."

"Plus we've got Terry coming of course . . ." Dolly pulled a face, raised her voice, and added: "Which is *lovely* . . ."

"Oh," said Rosie. "I'm not sure if he *is* coming, actually. He sent me a text this afternoon saying he was feeling a bit poorly . . . I don't think he has your number, Dolly . . ."

"Well, but I only live next door. He could have poked his head out the window . . ." She sighed. "Never mind. More food for all of us. I hope he's okay? Do you think we should check on him?"

"*Nooo*," said Rosie. "I should think —" she dropped her voice to a whisper "— he's just feeling a bit *shy*. He may turn up later. If he's brave enough. What's your announcement, Dolly? I don't think I can wait until Raff arrives."

They killed the time talking about Marina's arrest. And when Raff arrived, also carrying a bottle, they shared the good news. Raff's clever son, Sam, who was moving to the US for a few years, having been offered an excellent job at Berkeley University, had joined financial forces with his father. Isabelle Ferrari would have put a stop to it if she'd known the buyers' identity — or at any rate, whacked up the price — but they had put in an offer for Number Three Tinderbox Lane, under Sam's name, and the offer had been accepted.

"My giddy aunt!" said the professor. "That's the best news I've heard in years! Strike that! It's the second-best news! Want to know what the best news is?"

"That I finally got offered a job?" suggested Pippa, "and that I'll be moving into Number Three, paying the rent, and Raff will be moving into Number Two with Mum?"

"Nope," said Derek. "That's excellent news — assuredly. Excellent news. Many congratulations to you, young lady, and I would like to know more in due course. But I can trump it."

Somebody's mobile was ringing.

Derek said: "Sounds like yours, Mrs B . . ."

Mrs B jumped, patted her pockets and pulled out the phone. "Ooh," she said. "Number blocked. Probably Terry . . ."

"Wait a mo," said the professor. "Let me just get the news out first . . . Mrs B and I, as you probably are aware . . ."

"I should probably answer it," said Rosie.

He held up a hand. "Wait a mo, Mrs B . . . The fact is — when Rosie and I first met each other not so long ago, we didn't think much of each other, did we, Rosie?"

"Derek —"

"But the more we got to know each other, the more we realised, didn't we, my sweet love, that we were, quite simply, made for each other. Personally speaking, I have never been happier in my entire life as I have been in these past few weeks, getting to know my Rosie . . ."

"*Derek* —"

The phone stopped.

"And when I say 'my' Rosie I say it because — well. Because I can."

Rosie and Derek looked at one another, as sweet and shiny and surprised and happy as two people can be who've found love, against the odds, in a lonely middle age. And then the phone struck up again.

"Derek. I really ought to answer this . . ."

"I think I must be the luckiest man in the world, when I say this. Rosie, your beauty, your grace under what must have been extreme and terrible pressure, your kindness, your exceptional cooking, your home-making skills, not to mention your extraordinary mothering skills. Whoever it was who coined that marvellous French phrase: *dans la cuisine, une ange, dans la chambre, une putain* —"

"Oh for heaven's sake, Derek," interrupted Rosie. "I have to answer this. Just tell them. We're getting married."

"— ah. Well. There you have it. We are getting married," said Derek. "As soon as we can finalise her divorce — which as you may imagine, presents one or two bureaucratic hurdles of its own . . ."

"Hello?" said Rosie, with face semi-scrunched and a finger in one ear. "Hello, who is that?" I can't hear you . . . *Who is it?* Terry? You sound miles away."

". . . but as soon as all that's sorted, it will be my honour, my *greatest* honour, to make this beautiful lady my most treasured wife!"

"*Pardon? 'who's Terry'?*" She was silent, trying to listen. Her face fell. All the happiness, all the colour — gone. She looked like a startled rabbit. With botox. And no fur on its face. ". . . where are you?" she mumbled, and fell silent, listening. She pulled the telephone away from her ear, stared at it, and then, without another word, cut the line.

Derek, Raff, Pippa, Dolly waited, but she didn't speak.

"It's your bloody husband, isn't it?" Dolly said. "He's back."

Acknowledgements

With many thanks to Krystyna Green and all the fine team at Constable; also to my friend "Squatter X" (who preferred to remain nameless) and to my good-natured godson, Xavier Buxton, who put us together.

Above all thank you to my family, Peter, Zebedee, Bashie — and to Panda, without whose warm encouragement and sharp advice I might have given up long ago.

Other titles published by Ulverscroft:

THE PRIME OF
MS DOLLY GREENE

E. V. Harte

In the heart of southwest London, just a short stroll from the Thames, lies an enclosed and overgrown bike path and a single row of cottages. Foremost among Tinderbox Lane's hotchpotch of loyal residents is professional Tarot reader Dolly Greene. When, one stiflingly hot summer's day, Dolly reads the cards for the hedonistic Nikki, her usually professional patter is interrupted by a sudden vision — a flash of Nikki's face, covered in blood and bruises. A few days later, when the body of a battered woman is washed up by Chiswick Bridge, Dolly is haunted by the belief that Nikki's time may have come . . . but can she be sure? How far is Dolly prepared to go to act on her intuition?

THE COLOURS OF ALL THE CATTLE

Alexander McCall Smith

When Mma Potokwani suggests to Mma Ramotswe that she run for a seat on the city council, Mma Ramotswe is at first unsure. But once she learns about the proposed construction of the flashy Big Fun Hotel next to a graveyard, she allows herself to be persuaded. Her opponent is none other than Violet Sephotho, who is in the pocket of the hotel developers. Although Violet is intent on using every trick in the book to secure her election, Mma Ramotswe refuses to promise anything beyond what she can deliver, hence her slogan: "I can't promise anything — but I shall do my best." Through it all, Mma Ramotswe uses her good humour and generosity of spirit to help the community navigate divisive issues, and proves that honesty and compassion will always carry the day.

RUSSIAN ROULETTE

Sara Sheridan

Brighton, 1956: When Mirabelle's on-off boyfriend, Superintendent Alan McGregor, is taken off a gruesome murder case, she steps in to unravel the tangle of poisoned gin, prostitutes and high-stakes gambling that surrounds the death. It isn't long before McGregor's integrity is called into question, and Mirabelle finds herself doubting him. So when a wartime hero's body turns up on the Sussex Downs, she is glad that he is caught up in a mystery of his own as Brighton's establishment close ranks. Mirabelle is in a dangerous situation, though, and she doesn't have McGregor watching her back on this one. And when the dead man on the Downs turns out to have been a member of a deadly thrill-seekers club, related to the earlier murder, Mirabelle is determined to uncover the truth . . .

DEATH KNOCKS TWICE

Robert Thorogood

Reluctantly stationed on the sweltering Caribbean island of Saint-Marie, Detective Inspector Richard Poole dreams of cold winds, drizzly rain and a pint in his local pub. Just as he is feeling as fed up as can be, a mysterious vagrant is found dead at the historic Beaumont Plantation. Immediately assumed to be suicide, DI Poole is not so convinced, determined to prove otherwise. Never mind that the only fingerprints on the murder weapon belong to the victim. Or that the room was locked from the inside. Before long, death knocks twice and a second body turns up. The hunt is on to solve the case — despite the best efforts of the enigmatic Beaumont family . . .